JO CROW

THE
FOUND
CHILD

BLURB

One mother's life will change in the blink of an eye—and there's no going back.

Elaine's worst fears become reality when her beloved son Jakob is diagnosed with cancer. She needs to find a bone marrow donor, and time is running out. But while awaiting test results to see if she's a possible match, Elaine learns a shocking truth about her son; a truth that threatens to send her back to the pills that almost destroyed her life once before; a truth that pushes her already fragile mental state to the breaking point.

Even as the family faces this new crisis, a ghost from Elaine's past emerges to jeopardize everything she's built. But is the threat real, or is it all in her mind?

Elaine needs to stay strong for her son, but as her whole reality continues to unravel, she can't trust anyone—not even herself.

CONTENTS

PROLOGUE

Telling parents that the search for their missing infant had gone cold was a job that no one wanted. And honestly, Detective Aaronson had tried to pass it off to someone else—to his partner, Miller, and then to a uniform. Ultimately, though, the chief had put his boot down and pushed it back on Aaronson. He was the point man. He and Miller had worked the case together for a month before the leads dried up, but it had been Aaronson who had sat with the parents, talked to them on the phone, and kept them updated.

He'd been the one to give them hope, so it followed that he should be the one to take it away... right?

They had agreed to meet him at the station. That seemed to be the best choice. No one wanted to get this kind of news in their own home—it would put a stain on the place that would never wash out. No, it was more professional to have the talk here in one of the small conference rooms. No decorations, no distractions, nothing to make the moment seem too casual. Only gray brick, white linoleum and a wooden table and chairs that were plain and utilitarian. Unemotional.

Now he sat across from them, steeling himself and trying to work up some moisture in his mouth. There was water, but they hadn't poured a glass so he wasn't about to. Both of them had dark circles under their bloodshot eyes, and a waxy pallor to their skin. They hadn't slept in a month, he figured. He'd have put money on it. Hell, he could barely sleep when his teenager stayed out late with her friends on a weekend. And their child had been gone for more than a month. As a parent, he understood part of their pain. Just part of it. That's what made this so damn difficult.

"We're not closing the case," he said, his tone as flat as he could manage. "But as of now, the leads—"

"You're not looking anymore?" the mother asked. Fury filled her eyes, and loss. One of those was for him.

"It's only been a month," the father said. "You can't stop now. Please, our son is out there somewhere—we know it."

"I can feel him," she said. "You have to believe me, I can feel him here." She clutched at her chest, at the threadbare, peach-colored sweater she wore.

You have to keep it short, the chief had said. *Keep it direct and then refer them to the counselor. That's your job.*

Aaronson wondered if the chief had ever done this before. He imagined he had, but to make it seem so simple... Of course, there were regulations. He couldn't be the counselor and the detective, and there were good reasons for that. "We will keep the case open," he told them. "If any new leads come in, we'll follow up on them."

He meant it, too. But the truth that he knew, and that these two knew even if they didn't want to believe it, was that after seventy-two hours, most of these cases were never solved. Every day after that windows closed, the likelihood of finding a child like theirs dropped exponentially until it plummeted to a fraction of a percent which itself really only represented the handful of miracle cases that had been resolved sometimes decades after a disappearance.

"Please don't do this," the father begged. He took his wife's hand, and they leaned into one another. "One more month. There was that woman—"

"At the moment, Andrea Williams has been cleared as a suspect," Aaronson said. That poor woman's life had been all but destroyed already. "We've been over her life with a fine-toothed comb. If new evidence emerges, we'll look into it again, but I'm telling you that she's not who we want."

"So, what do we do now?" the mother asked. "What do we do now that you've abandoned our boy? Abandoned us?"

Aaronson was so close to breaking. He stood from the table. "I swear to you both," he said, the words bitter on his tongue, "that we will pursue any and every lead that comes across my desk. We're not abandoning anyone. Alright?" And while it may have been technically true, it sure felt like a lie.

Nothing but contempt came from them, and he didn't blame them at all. And he hated himself for what he had to say next. "There's a counselor here. Doctor Amari. She's a grief counselor, and it's free to see her. I can send her in, but I have to leave you now. I'm sorry. Really, I am."

They turned their faces from him.

As he left, he closed the door gently even though he wanted to slam it hard enough to shatter the glass. He wasn't even sure who to be angry with. Himself, mostly, he guessed, or the whole damn department. And Andrea-fucking-Williams, who had wasted their time from the beginning by lying to protect herself instead of telling them the truth about her record so that they could have moved on.

He took only two steps before the mother wailed loudly behind him. The entire department went quiet. That sound was one they all knew. It was the sound of a woman who had lost the last shred of hope she'd had. The shred that he'd taken away from her.

That was the sound of a mother whose child had died. And, at this point, Aaronson had nothing to suggest it wasn't true.

He'd failed them.

1

Alert from Morgan Heights Correctional Facility: There has been a change in status for an inmate you are tracking. Inmate #33614 Hank B. Turner's status has been updated to Paroled. You are receiving this message because you are subscribed to…

I read the email three times, hoping that I had misread it; that the words would rearrange themselves and say something different. They didn't, of course. The man who had abducted my son eight years ago was walking free. All the air left the room, leaving me alone with the sound of my own heart pounding in my ears, drowning out everything but the panic as memories I had struggled to put behind me came surging back to the present as clear as the day they'd been inflicted.

"Elaine, are you listening?"

I blinked away the burn of impending tears. Seven other parents watched me from the edges of a large round table in one of the classrooms of Greenway Heights Preparatory Academy. Everything from concern to outright judgment was present and accounted for. I forced words out of my throat. "My husband's company can donate laptops," I said. "I'm sure he can provide software, as well; we just need to tell them what we want."

Linda Keeler put a hand on my knee under the table. Her southern drawl drew at least as much enmity from the other parents as my brief lapse of attention; I wasn't totally alone here, at least. "That would be just fantastic, Elaine," she said. "I think that covers the robotics club, then. Anything left?"

The rest of the members of the Parents' Board of Extracurricular Activities seemed satisfied enough, and so began the process of wrapping up the meeting. While they did that, I found myself watching the windows that looked out over the school's perfectly landscaped central courtyard. I needed to see Jake, to remind myself that he was there with me. I knew he was, of course, and that he was safe, but my body refused to believe it until I could put my hands on him and hold him.

"The next meeting is Tuesday, March 12th at 4 p.m. All agreed?" Jessi Wyndam gave me a pointed look as if I was the only parent to get bored with these meetings or who sometimes had to reschedule.

"I'm sure I can manage," I said. Not that it mattered; the decision had clearly been made.

As the other parents left the table, Linda leaned toward me. "I think Jessi's just pissed that you one-upped her. I wouldn't pay her any mind, hon."

"I don't," I said. "And I didn't, did I?"

"You really must have been out of it," Linda said. She snorted. "She offered to bake some kind of gluten-free, vegan, alternative sweetener garbage for the Junior Developers' club for their big showcase day." She opened her mouth and poked one of her pink-manicured fingers toward the back of her throat. "I bet her kids binge on Skittles and Mountain Dew when she's not looking. I know for a fact that her husband stops by Burger King every day after work before he goes home."

I wanted to muster the good humor to give Linda a genuine laugh, but all that came out was a weak chuckle.

Linda wasn't buying it either. "Are you okay, sugar?" She looked into my eyes, her brow knitting as she searched for something there. Nothing got past Linda, but this time there was nothing to find.

"I'm a little tired," I said. "I should go get Jake. And call Nathan about those laptops."

"He'd better make sure they're top-notch or you know Jessi'll complain at the next meeting about 'commitment to excellence' or some other passive aggressive nonsense."

Linda and I both stood from the table and gathered our purses.

They were almost a match though that wasn't intentional. At least, I hadn't intended it.

Filling my part of the conversation as well as hers, Linda offered, "I'll walk with you. Jake and Ty are probably still at Robotics Club. Can you believe what kids get up to these days? When I was eight, I don't think I knew what a damn 'robot' was."

I wasn't much good for any conversation on our way through the trophy-laden halls of the school. The place was a maze that I hadn't quite memorized, so I relied on Linda to guide us toward the classroom where our two sons' club took place after class hours. Consequently, I also had to match her ambling pace while she delivered all the gossip she could think of. Most of it, I didn't even hear. My stomach was tied in knots and my hand ached from gripping the strap of my bag too tightly. From the classroom where the PBEx met, it was the first left, the second right, and then the first left, wasn't it?

Linda took a turn that I didn't expect, proving it was a good thing I hadn't left her behind. The sounds of chattering kids met us at the corner and I sped up to follow the noise toward the door of the technology lab. I drank in the relief of arriving like it was oxygen.

That is, until I looked into the classroom to find Jake. The kids were all putting away their projects on the shelves at one end of the room, but Jake wasn't with them. His coat was still hanging by the door. "Jake?"

Mr. Edmond, the teacher who ran the club, looked up from a conversation with one of the students and blinked at me through his Coke-bottle glasses. "Mrs. Jennson," he said as he approached me, "there you are. Is Jake not with you?"

"With me?" I asked, incredulous. "No, of course he's not, he's supposed to be here. Why isn't he?"

Mr. Edmond shook his head, his hands spread. "I'm so sorry, he said he wasn't feeling well. He told me you were here for a meeting, and he was going to find you. You saw him after class, I believe?"

"He never made it to me," I snapped. "When did he leave? You didn't go with him?"

Linda cleared her throat from behind me. "I bet he's visiting the restroom. Why don't we go check?"

My face had grown hot. I didn't need Linda to manage me and almost told her that... but she had a point.

"He left here about half an hour ago," Mr. Edmond said. He pointed to my left down the hallway. "The nearest restrooms are over there, but I'll phone administration and have them call for him over the PA just in case. I'm sure there's nothing to worry about, Mrs. Jennson. He's a very smart boy, so I'm sure he hasn't gone far."

I didn't wait for more assurances or excuses. While Linda retrieved Tyler, I stormed down the hallway to the restrooms and checked both the boys' and girls' rooms. Jake wasn't there.

It took an effort for me not to scream aloud for him as dark futures played out in my panicked imagination. It wasn't difficult math. The man who claimed Jake was his son was out of prison, and now my son was missing. Again.

And what kind of mother did that make me? I'd lost my son for the second time.

2

True to his word, Mr. Edmond called administration and, by the time I made it back to the tech lab's door, they were calling for Jake over the speakers. *"Jakob Jennson, please come to administration. Jakob Jennson, please come to administration for pickup, your mother is here."*

"You should go," Linda said. "I'll catch up with you."

I wanted to run to the office, but there were still parents and their children milling around the halls and the last thing I wanted was further scrutiny. The last year had been better, but in the four years we'd been here I had generated plenty of gossip. These people weren't friends. Not like Linda. They were all born to privilege and they wore it easily. I avoided eye contact as I made my way to admin; they'd all heard the announcement. *There she goes,* I imagined them thinking,

Elaine Jennson, poor thing, can't even keep track of her one kid.

On the way to the office, I passed the school clinic and almost ran into the door as it opened. Before I could curse at the woman who'd opened it, Jake came through it and looked up at me in sheepish embarrassment.

I practically leapt to his side. "There you are, baby." I breathed and pulled him close to me as I sank to my knees. "God, I was so worried. Are you okay?"

Jake indulged me for only a second before he struggled to extricate himself, glancing at the other children peppering the hallway, "Mo-om, don't."

"Jakob was feeling a little sick," the nurse said. "He's running a bit of a fever."

I stood. "And you didn't think to call me?"

The nurse regarded me with a flat expression. "Jakob informed me you were here. I took his temperature and gave him a Children's Tylenol for the fever. We were about to come find you when we heard the announcement."

"Oh, you found him," Linda said. She and Tyler came up the hallway and stopped near us. "There, see? No need to worry."

The nurse gave Linda a brief, unenthused smile and then gestured for me to follow her into the clinic. "If I could have a moment of your time, Mrs. Jennson."

Her tone was alarming. I didn't care for confrontation most of the time, and after a scare like I'd just had all I wanted was to take Jake home.

"I can look after him," Linda said. "No problem. We'll meet you out front?"

The nurse wore an impatient, serious look.

"Sure," I said finally, "I'll see you there. You be good for Linda, don't run off." I ruffled Jake's hair.

"I didn't run off," Jake muttered as he fixed his hair back.

They slip away by inches, children. Only a year ago, Jake and I were inseparable. As he left with Linda and Tyler, I wondered briefly if that stage had really ended, or if he was simply grumpy over my making a fuss.

"If you please, Mrs. Jennson," the nurse said. I followed her. "I don't believe we've met before. I'm Amanda Wiltshire, I run the school clinic."

She didn't extend a hand.

"A pleasure to meet you," I said. "What's this about?"

"As I said, Jakob has a fever." She turned and picked up a clipboard with some kind of chart, along with a pen. "It's not serious, only a 100.4. However, I do have a few questions."

I didn't really have the time for this. Nathan would be home at six, it was already five, and the PBEx meeting had eaten up most of my time to make dinner. It was looking more and more like a pizza night. "Alright," I said. "What?"

The nurse quirked an eyebrow and glanced at her clipboard. "Are you aware that Jakob has a bruise under his right scapula?"

I blinked. "Excuse me?"

"His right shoulder blade—"

"I know what a scapula is," I said, measuring my tone carefully as irritation quickly escalated to outright anger. "I meant what exactly do you mean by asking me."

"Has Jakob fallen down recently or had any accidents that might have caused it?" she asked, her pen hovering over the clipboard.

"If you have an accusation to make," I said, "then by all means, come out and make it."

Nurse Wiltshire regarded me for a moment. "It's my job to look after the well-being of the students here." She made a note on the clipboard.

My fingers itched to snatch it out of her hands and see what it said. *Mother abusing son,* maybe.

"I'm aware that you've had previous difficulties around prescription medications," she went on. "I'm required by the state and by our school policies to follow-up on any possible cases of—"

"Let me stop you right there." I took a step toward her. "I am not violent with my son. What I've had to deal with is frankly none of your business, *Nurse* Wiltshire, and I would appreciate you keeping your inquiries limited to my son's health as and when they arise in school. If you want to make some report, then you go right ahead because I have nothing to hide. I assure you that my husband and son will corroborate that testimony right before my husband's company pulls every penny of our not insignificant support of this institution and we take our son to Chapel Prep where they will be more than happy to cash our check."

God, that felt good. I quashed the bit of guilt that tried to worm its way out of my stomach to make an apology. Sometimes, you have to vent.

She narrowed her eyelids at me. "I'm sure it's benign, but your son insists that he hasn't had any falls or injuries recently," she said coolly. "So I recommend that you take him to a pediatrician to have it looked at. It could be a sign of anemia, which might be the result of a lack of proper nutrition—as an example. But I'm sure you would know better than I do what his diet is like."

"You're damn straight I do." I looked her over, head-to-toe, for good measure. "Are we done here?"

She only held a hand out toward the door, inviting me to leave.

I didn't need her invitation, but I took it. I left the door open on my way out; if I'd closed it, I would have smashed the glass in the window.

I took me until I met Linda and the kids for the red to bleed out of my vision entirely. It was also enough time for me to consider the potential consequences of tangling with the school nurse over an accusation of child abuse. Of course, I didn't beat my son—but that wouldn't make a visit from Child Protective Services any less terrifying and it certainly wouldn't assuage the curiosity of neighbors who already had plenty to whisper about.

"What was that all about?" Linda asked as I reached them. "Are you okay?"

Apparently I didn't look it. I swept stray hair behind my ears and put on a smile. "Just some paperwork and recommendations. Nothing major. Thanks for looking after Jake." I reached for Jake to give me his hand. "You ready, buddy? I think it's a pizza night."

He stuffed his hands into his pockets. "Okay."

Linda offered me the kind of sympathetic look shared between two moms whose sons were growing up too fast. "See you around."

Probably before the end of the night. Linda was my next-door neighbor. "Tell Malcolm I said hi," I said. "We should have dinner soon."

"It's a date," Linda said.

We left in search of our car. I found myself examining Jake. Did he seem a little pale? I didn't particularly care for the school nurse, but maybe she wasn't entirely off base. I'd been anemic when I was pregnant with him; maybe it was a condition you could inherit. As we got into the car, I called Jake's pediatrician and made an appointment for him. Better safe than sorry.

And it certainly beat a visit from CPS. The last thing any of us needed was someone digging into our lives. Especially now.

3

J ake's prep school was fed primarily by the sprawling suburban maze that was Avila Grove. The brochure for our place had used words like "elegant" and "pristine." A gated community, it had its own park in the center that was dyed green year-round, and even a small shopping center with no less than three organic, locally sourced smoothie shops. It was the insular nature of the place that had really sold it to us; truly a paradise on earth.

We had been catapulted right out of the lower middle-class and into, well, *this*, when Nathan's company, Lighthouse Soft-works, had been handed some lucrative development contracts. I was careful to keep my preference for smoothies filled with delicious things like real sugar and chocolate quiet so I'd fit in.

By the time we made it home, Jake was rubbing his eyes and

yawning. He seemed sluggish as he poured himself out of the back seat and trundled into the house. I looked up at the small, tinted blister camera over our porch, one of seven around the house, to check that the red indicator light was on. It didn't eliminate all of my worries, but it did help.

"Come sit," I told Jake when we were inside. I pulled out one of the stools next to the white granite-topped kitchen island and patted the seat. "Let's take your temperature."

Jake did so without complaint and yawned again as I fished the thermometer out of the medicine drawer. "I'm sleepy."

"Open wide," I said and placed the thermometer under his tongue. He clamped down. "You can nap if you like, but Dad should be home pretty soon. Think you can stay up for him? Plus, you don't want to miss pizza, do you?"

He shrugged and then shook his head.

What I didn't want was my eight-year-old waking up at three in the morning.

The thermometer beeped, and I took it back to read the number. What had the nurse said? A hundred point four? "One hundred point eight," I muttered. I put the back of my hand to his forehead. "You're pretty hot, kiddo. I think maybe you should stay home from school tomorrow. What do you think?"

"Do I have to?" His big brown eyes, almost mine and almost Nathan's but not quite a match for either of us, widened with pleading. "I have a science test tomorrow."

I fought a grin. What kind of kid begged not to have to stay home from school? I was pretty sure he didn't get that from either of us. "I'll write you a note so you can make it up. Come on, let's order pizza. You can call."

That perked him up a bit. I wrote down our order, after negotiating for more vegetables, and dialed the number for him—and then monitored the exchange to make sure he didn't renege on our deal. As he spoke to the restaurant employee, I spotted Linda's car as it passed our driveway to get to hers.

Another car caught my eye, too. A shiny, classic-looking black town car I hadn't seen around before. Something from a *Godfather* movie, I thought. Nathan would love that—he loved those movies and had wanted one of those wide, long Chryslers for ages, with white paint and red seats. I had, thankfully, convinced him that the gas mileage alone was a hard 'no.'

This one was parked on the curb across the street, between two driveways that had no cars in them. Was there someone in the driver's seat?

"Also, brownie bites," Jake whispered. Not so quiet that I didn't hear him.

"Hey," I said, "that wasn't part of the deal."

Jake grimaced, caught in the act, and held the phone out toward me.

"Your dad likes cinnamon sticks," I said, winking at him.

"And you only get two brownie bites. Last time they gave you a tummy ache."

He ordered the cinnamon sticks, and when I looked back at the town car, it was pulling away. Perhaps someone had stopped to look up directions.

The pizza delivery girl did beat Nathan home. Six o'clock came and went. Jake held out as long as he could, but when he began to nod off at the table, I let him go upstairs to rest.

It wasn't until almost seven that Nathan finally made it home. He came in through the garage door, shucked his coat and hung it up. When he finally looked at me, it was with an apology on his lips. "Sorry," he said. "I know, I should have called. Roger and I were caught up settling some last-minute business."

"It's okay," I told him. There was no sense in getting upset about it.

He came to me, arms open, and pulled me to him. I couldn't resist smiling at his warm expression. Maybe he didn't always call when he should, but he was always there when I needed to be held and right now I desperately needed a hug. I clung to him as he put his arms around me, and I rested my cheek against the soft layer of fatherhood that now covered his muscular chest.

"Hey, everything alright?" he asked. His breath was warm against my hair.

"No," I said. My instinct was to keep it from him, but after the things we'd been through together, honesty was important.

He let me go but held my hand, searching my face for an explanation. "What happened? You're not...?"

"God, no," I said quickly. "No, no. Nothing like that. It's been a good year, I'm not about to ruin it. No, it's ah…"

He waited, wordless and patient while I put my thoughts together so that I didn't become a blubbering mess.

I let it out in a slow telling. The email, Jake's brief disappearance. My run in with Nurse Wiltshire, I gave a slightly edited version of it so I didn't come off quite so badly. "So for all I know," I finished, "we're about to get a call from Child Protective Services. That woman looked like she had it in for me."

"That lady sounds like a bitch. Kids get bruises, hell, I was covered in them as a boy." He sighed. "I'm sorry, babe. It sounds like it was a rough day."

He squeezed me again and then let me go and rubbed the back of his neck. "So, you're still following Hank Turner?"

"I can't help it," I said. "I unsubscribe, and then I get anxious and go back to the website to check. Honestly, knowing that he and his wife are still locked up has helped."

"I thought we'd talked about this, Ellie. That we were through with it." He rubbed his forehead as he carefully considered what he was about to say. He wouldn't want to set me off. "Listen to me. Hank Turner is 400 miles away. Even if he is now out on parole, he doesn't know where we live, and he's going to be on a leash for years to come. We're safe here, okay? *Jake* is safe here. This house is a fortress."

"Of course," I breathed. I leaned against his hand, hoping I could soak in some of his confidence. "I know that. But it's like my body doesn't, I can't convince it to stop panicking. The constant anxiety is exhausting."

"Maybe you should go and see Dr. Werner," he suggested. "Your next visit is coming up, isn't it? Bring it forward."

"I'll be okay until then, it's only a few weeks away." Dr. Werner was my psychiatrist. I liked him just fine but seeing him often reminded me of things I had tried very hard to forget. "Really, I will. Having you here is enough for now."

"Whatever you need, beautiful, you let me know. Okay?" Nathan kissed me, a distant echo of a younger, more passionate us. "We're doing good; we can keep going. You have to stay with me here, in the present. Let the past be the past."

I pressed my forehead to his shoulder and nodded a weak promise to try while he stroked my hair and held me close.

I did want to live in the present. I wanted to move on, and to love this new life we had built. Somehow, I had to forget that

Hank and Millie Turner even existed. I could do that, couldn't I?

Whatever my mind was ready to do, my body wasn't getting the message, I still had a sick feeling in my stomach and my heart was racing. We ate a quiet, lukewarm pizza dinner and went about our routine as if like finely tuned clockwork people—Netflix, showers, tooth brushing at our respective sinks, and bed all choreographed to music neither of us actually heard.

Nathan was able to fall asleep easily as he did every night, snoring softly and sprawled over his side of the bed—and part of mine. But I lay awake for hours before I finally got up and went down to the kitchen to have a glass of water and take an aspirin. I didn't have a headache, but it soothed my desire for something stronger. As I sipped my water, I checked the locks on the doors and windows, reassuring myself that we were secure.

At the window by the sink, something shiny outside caught my eye, the pale light of the streetlamps reflected off glass.

It was that same black town car from before, parked on the other side of the street now and in a different direction. As I watched, a puff of smoke, illuminated by the lamplight, curled out of the tinted driver's side window and drifted over the top of the car.

I closed the blinds and took several slow breaths with my eyes closed. *It's only a car,* I told myself, *just someone waiting for something that has nothing to do with me.*

I kept repeating that in my head as I returned to bed. It was like Nathan said: we were doing good. I wasn't about to ruin it by coming unglued again. Not when we'd gotten so far.

4

J ake was still asleep when I awoke to Nathan rummaging in our walk-in for a tie. I could hear his alarm clock from down the hall outside our opened bedroom door. *"Avengers assemble! Ultron is at it again!"*

"How long has that been going off?" I asked.

Nathan glanced over to me and grinned. "Morning, gorgeous. I guess I didn't notice."

I got out of bed, but Nathan was at the door before I'd got my slippers on.

"I'll check on him, you take it slow." He was gone before I could respond.

Of course Nathan loved every moment he spent with Jake, but I knew there was more concern than marital altruism in it. I worried him. Not without reason; there were *plenty* of reasons. But I hated knowing that it was getting to him.

Once I was fit to be wandering the house, I left our bedroom and stopped by the door to Jake's. Nathan was sitting on the edge of the bed, the alarm clock silenced, talking softly with Jake.

"You want to stay home today, kiddo?" he asked. "You're still pretty hot. I bet your mom would love to have you home for a day."

"I have Robots Club with Tyler after school," Jake said. "And a science test. I don't want to miss it."

Nathan chuckled. "You definitely get that from your mom. Tyler can catch you up, but if you don't take some time to get better, you'll end up missing more school. Plus, I think maybe Mom needs a little extra love today, you know? Could you do that for me, be extra good for her?"

"Is Mom okay?"

The distress in Jake's voice struck me in the chest, and I didn't stay to hear Nathan's answer. I padded away from the door and down the stairs to the kitchen where a pot of coffee was already brewed. I made a cup and sipped it pensively as I worked out my strategy for the day. I was determined to give Jake no reason to worry about me. It was bad enough knowing Nathan was concerned. The anxiety had lessened a little overnight. Though, I still couldn't quite bring myself to look at my emails.

Nathan came down the stairs smiling. "Would you believe our kid doesn't want to miss school? How did we raise a kid to love education? It's not down to me."

"Thank God for that," I said. "I can't imagine Jake putting me through what you put Catherine through."

"I don't know what you're talking about." His grin was impish as he tugged his coat on and came to kiss me goodbye for the day. "I was a saint."

"I'll tell her you said that the next time we talk about your high school days," I said.

He chuckled and headed for the door but paused before he left. "Oh, I almost forgot; I may bring Roger back here after work."

Roger was a longtime friend and Nathan's business partner. I had known him as long as I'd known my husband. I kept my expression neutral. "Okay. I'll make extra?"

"Pretty sure Roger lives on gin and tonic," he said, "but if it's not too much trouble. We may have good news."

"God, that would be nice," I said. "Is Roger bringing… Ronda, or… Rita…"

He rolled his eyes. "Riley," Nathan said. "And no. They broke up."

"Can you break up with a stripper?" I wondered. "Or do you just stop paying her?"

"She was a glamour *model*, not a stripper. Anyway, he'll come alone." He watched me a moment longer with the look of someone about to say something but not quite ready.

"I'm fine," I said, and waved him off. "Go. I love you."

"I love you, too," he said, and then more seriously, "I need you, baby. You and Jake. Our family. More than you can possibly know."

My chest tightened. I didn't know what to say so I simply nodded then blew him a kiss and watched him leave for the day. For a little while I stayed seated, finishing my coffee and giving my phone wary looks until finally I picked it up and pointedly ignored the email from Morgan Heights.

I didn't delete it, but I managed not to read it again. Instead, another message caught my eye. Finally, some good news. *Elaine,* it read, *I'm Christine Orrey with West End Publishing. I love your resume and your references had only good things to say about you. I'd like to schedule an interview when you're available…*

It was a rush of a much kinder variety than the day before. Eight years was long enough to be without a job. Mothering had been my full-time occupation for five years, and one that I did plenty to complicate, but now that Jake was in school most days it seemed like it was time to go back to work.

I looked at the time and regretted that Nathan had let me sleep in. "Jake, honey!" I called upstairs. "You need to get dressed, we've got an appointment with Dr. Mindy coming up. We'll get breakfast on the way."

"McDonald's?" he called back, hopeful.

I could hear Nurse Wiltshire in the back of my head, criticizing Jake's nutrition. "We'll see," I said. "Just hurry up, please."

I finished my coffee and went to change as well. Jeans, a t-shirt sporting an old-school Batman logo, a pair of flats, and my hair tied back in a ponytail. I declared to myself that it would be a casual day of chicken soup and cartoons with my son. When I found Jake downstairs on the couch, he'd put on his Superman shirt.

"Practically the Justice League," I said. I half expected Jake to go change.

Instead, he hopped off the couch and gave me a fist-bump. I needed it. Today would be a good day, and I would be a good mother, and Jake would remember that he was still my little boy.

We donned baseball caps and left the house. Outside, the black town car was gone, and I kicked myself mentally for even thinking to look for it.

5

J ake liked Dr. Mindy, for the most part. She was a squat, fifty-something woman with tattoos and multi-colored hair. Her office was decorated with movie posters and comic book paraphernalia, rather than the usual boring land-scapes that I must admit made even me reluctant to sit in a waiting room for more than a few minutes, much less an eight-year-old boy. Getting Jake to the doctor was rarely the challenge.

"Alright, take a deep breath for me Jake," Dr. Mindy said, her stethoscope pressed to his ribs beneath his shirt. "Hold, hold… how long can you hold it?"

Jake gave her a thumbs up and held his breath.

"I'm kidding, now breathe out nice and slow for me… good, good." She winked at me as if we were in on some joke together. When we first started seeing her, when Jake was four years old, I was impressed by her bedside manner. Four years later, it didn't seem wink worthy anymore, but I returned it anyway. All the moms in Avila Grove came to Dr. Mindy, and they all loved her.

Same lawns, same houses… same doctor.

"Well," Dr. Mindy said as she stood, "I don't think it's the flu, he's got no congestion. A bit of a fever could mean he's fighting something off. As for the bruising, well—you could be right, he might have gotten your anemia. He's a little young for a growth spurt just yet but these days you never know. That could trigger some imbalances."

"So, do we wait it out?" I asked. Jake busied himself with the array of tools mounted on the wall by the exam table.

"Not necessarily," Dr. Mindy said. She picked up her clipboard and ticked a few boxes before she scribbled something. "Tell you what, though; what I would like to do is draw a teensy, weensy bit of blood, Jake-a-roo, and put it under my mi-cro-scope and take a gander. You think that would be okay?"

Jake's ears perked at that like a dog who'd heard a burglar. He rubbed one arm where he'd gotten his last set of shots. "Needles?"

"I'm sorry, you want to run a blood test?" I rubbed Jake's back, trying to be reassuring, even though the need for blood tests alarmed me as much as having to have it drawn alarmed him. "For what?"

"For starters," she said, "we can look at his iron levels and tell for sure whether or not that's the problem. While we're at it, I can look at his aminos, blood sugar, insulin—"

"What, like he could be diabetic?"

Jake looked up at me with wide eyes. "What's diabetic?"

Mindy put her hands up. "It's just to take a look. This is a good age to see what's going on. In any case, he's about due for a yearly check-up." She cuffed Jake on the shoulder. "It's the fastest way to cover all our bases, and it'll take two seconds."

"If you think it's best," I said. She wrote it up and left, and Jake and I waited nervously for the tech. He hated needles, and when the tech finally arrived I had to hold his hand tight and let him bury his head in my chest while the man very efficiently got what he needed. Afterwards, Jake got a Superman bandage to match his shirt and a sucker for his trouble, and the trauma of being poked seemed to dissolve quickly enough.

We left the pediatric complex and started negotiating what Jake had earned by being well-behaved at the appointment and for enduring military grade torture at the hands of the phlebotomist.

"Can we go to Spark?" Jake asked. "They have this dinosaur robot that you can build and it can stand up and make sounds and Tyler got a stegosaurus and I want the T. rex so they can fight. Can we please?"

I relented without much of a fight. "If we do," I said, "I don't want to hear about you and Ty fighting over breaking each other's robots." I eyed him in the rearview as he got in. "Deal?"

It was worth the promise of a ridiculously overpriced STEM toy to see him do his victory dance in the back seat. Spark was on the way home, so it wasn't a major detour. It was practically deserted while all the other kids were at school. While Jake hunted for his dino-bot and ogled the other treasures on display, I worked up the nerve to respond to the email I'd gotten from West End. I kept it short and simple, a professional "thank you" and a few times I'd be available for an interview. If Jake was sick for much longer, Linda could take him for a few hours during the day.

I looked up after I hit the send button, feeling somehow guilty for having sent it. What would happen at home if I got the job? Who would do the laundry, or make sure dinner was cooked? What if Jake was sick again? Would I be able to get off work soon enough to be home when Jake finished school? Would he think I loved him less if I wasn't? The potential for Jake's vast criminal future unfolded before me.

They were mostly legitimate concerns but countless mothers worked once their kids were in school and the world wasn't overrun with unloved hoodlum children. And I was ready for this. I needed the distraction, for one thing.

I put my phone away and worked on being happy for having made the choice. And besides, there was no guarantee I would even be offered the job. I wondered how many of the women walking past the store's windows were working mothers on their way to business lunches or presentations. When was the last time I wore a pantsuit?

As I watched, I spotted a man across the street, smoking a cigarette as he looked in my direction. My blood froze, and for a moment all I could do was stare at him in abject horror. That khaki jacket, those deep-set eyes, and that head of white hair. Those wide set shoulders. I would have recognized them anywhere.

I hadn't been crazy. There was someone watching us in that car.

It was him—Hank Turner. He was here, and he wanted my son.

6

_____

"Nine-one-one, what's your emergency?" the operator said. I heard her voice before I even realized I had called.

"The man who kidnapped my son is here," I said. "He's outside the store, watching us, I need you to send the police."

"I hear you, ma'am," the operator said, "I need you to give me more detail. Where are you right now?"

"I'm at the Spark store, the toy store, on Cortland Avenue. It's in the shopping center there."

The click of keys on a keyboard stuttered on the other end. "Are you alone? Are there people nearby?"

"I'm in the store," I said. "He's outside. There are other people around. It's lunchtime, I guess. I don't know anyone here though."

"What's your name?"

"Elaine Jennson," I said.

There was a tug at my elbow. Jake had found his dino-bot. I pulled him close with my free hand.

"Mom, gross," he complained.

"Ma'am?" the operator asked.

I froze briefly. I didn't want to let Jake out of my sight, but he didn't know about Hank and if I had anything to do with it he never would.

"Are you there, ma'am?"

"Just a moment," I said. "Baby, go to the register, okay? Wait for me there. You can pick something else out if you want." He'd be where I could see him, but hopefully Hank wouldn't be able to. I had the horrible thought that if Hank saw my son that would be the end.

"Is that your son?" the operator asked.

"Yes, Jakob Jennson. The man's name is Hank B. Turner. I don't know what the B stands for. Did you send the police?"

There was a brief pause. "Has he shown any aggression, any clear intent to make contact?" she asked.

"He's staring right at me," I said. "He's waiting for us to come out. I think he's been following me. He drives a black town car, the old boxy looking kind, either a Lincoln or a Chrysler. He's on parole, he shouldn't even be here. You need to send the police to arrest him."

"Ma'am," she said, too slowly and too calmly, "I need you to remain calm and stay on the line with me. Can you do that?"

"How am I supposed to stay calm?" I glanced over my shoulder. The kid at the register, college-aged, was staring at me. He looked away, to my son, and leaned over the counter to talk to him. "Send the police, now, please. God, he's leaving. He can see me on the phone he must know that I'm calling. Is there a car nearby?"

"Ma'am, do you have an active restraining order against Mr. Turner?"

Mr. Turner, she'd called him. I wanted to reach through the phone and slap her. "I don't—he was in prison until only a few days ago, how could I have a restraining order on him?" I had my face practically pressed to the glass watching him turn a corner. "Please send a car and check him out, that's all I'm asking."

"I did send a car, ma'am," she said. "They should be very close, but it's my job to get the details, alright? Can you still see him?"

"He went around a corner," I said. "He's in a khaki jacket, he's fifty, maybe fifty-five years old or a bit older, white hair, he was smoking and he had cargo pants on. I think they were white or maybe cream colored, and tennis shoes. He's tall, and pretty heavyset. Should I follow him?"

"No, ma'am," the operator said quickly, "you should absolutely not follow him. I've taken his description down; the car should be there any moment. Stay right where you are."

It was agony to stand there and watch the street outside, waiting for the evidence that she'd really sent someone. I wanted to throw up.

"Is everything okay?" the kid at the register asked.

I looked back to see Jake standing sullenly at the counter. "Christ, I'm so sorry," I muttered, and made my way over to him. I left the call long enough to pull up my digi-pay and wave it over the machine's sensor. "I'll be a minute longer, I promise."

He printed the receipt and handed it to me. I started to put it away, along with the pen, before I realized he wanted me to sign it. I did so with a frantic scribble and then hauled Jake with me back to the front of the store.

There were police lights flashing from around the corner. The operator had come through. I hung up and took Jake to where we'd parked on the curb. "Get inside, honey, and I'll be right back. Keep the doors locked, please, don't open them for anyone, okay?"

He crawled into the car, his face pinched with anxiety. "What's wrong?"

"Nothing," I said. "Everything is fine, just hang tight for me." I closed the door and hit the key fob to lock the car, and then made my way across the street and toward the corner. I needed to see him, to see the police arrest him and send him straight back to jail where he belonged. That son of a bitch had hunted us down as soon as he was free and I had *known* he would—I marched to the corner, vindicated that my instincts had been right and swearing that I would never doubt them again.

I came around the corner to see Hank with two police officers. Not in handcuffs, no guns drawn. They weren't even taking notes. Hank's back was to me. When I approached, one of the officers stepped past him and held a hand up.

"If you wouldn't mind, ma'am, let me have you cross on the other side, please," he said. He was polite about it; he didn't realize I had made the call.

"I'm Elaine Jennson," I said. I pointed at Hank. "I'm the one who called the police. That man is stalking me, he's on parole and is across state lines. I want him arrested. He was convicted of child abduction, look him up."

The officer frowned and looked over his shoulder as Hank turned around.

I froze.

"I'm very sorry, but I don't know you, miss," the man said.

And he didn't.

Because it wasn't Hank.

7

The gentleman who introduced himself as August, was far more forgiving than the police. They kept me for five minutes to lecture me on the dangers of calling in false reports as if the whole thing had been a prank. I endured it red-faced, my eyes glued to the sidewalk, and left with a stone around my neck that got heavier as the day went on.

Jake seemed to bear some weight of it, too. He barely talked the rest of the day, absorbed with building his new toy. The hours slipped away from me as I relived the moment I had seen August like a skipping CD I couldn't turn off. I had been so sure it was Hank. The image of him was burned in high definition into my mind. I watched the clock, waiting for Nathan to return so I could unload on him, have him tell me everything was okay.

When Nathan finally came home, he brought Roger with him.

Jake alerted me when he leapt off the couch and went running to the door. "Uncle Rog, Uncle Rog!"

Nathan laughed as Jake ran right past him and engaged in some complicated hand game that ended with a fist-bump that exploded into waggling fingers. Once they'd finished, Nathan hoisted Jake up and squeezed him, whispering in his ear.

Roger saw me and smiled, his green eyes glittering and handsome. "Hey, Ellie."

I let him kiss me on the cheek. "Rog, I didn't realize you were coming over, I would have made dinner."

Nathan cleared his throat and gave me a kiss. He leaned in a bit, his voice lowered. "I told you this morning, remember? That we might have good news? Is everything okay?"

Of course, he had. How had I forgotten? "Why wouldn't it be?" I said. "I think that was before I had my coffee, is all. I should have written it down or something."

He held up a bottle of wine. "We can order in again," he said, grinning. "Turns out there is good news."

I eyed the bottle dubiously. "Wow, okay. It must be. Is that a good idea?"

"Only a couple of glasses," Nathan said as he straightened. He lowered his voice again. "I think if you can go through a bottle of aspirin a week, I can handle a couple of glasses of wine. Don't you want to hear the news?"

"Sorry," I said. "Of course, I do. I'll get some glasses."

Nathan had quit drinking years before I'd got off the pills. Once we'd got Jakob back, it was bad for a few years. We almost hadn't made it. Sometimes, I think the only reason we did was because of what we'd been through together. Still, a couple of glasses surely couldn't hurt. It wasn't hard liquor.

We poured the wine, and a glass of orange juice for Jake, and Roger ordered dinner. He offered an extra fifty for the delivery driver and the cook if they rushed it. Once that was done, Nathan finally broke the suspense.

He raised his glass. "Baby, kiddo, everything is about to change. Today, Roger and I finalized the deal of our lives."

Roger raised his glass and clinked it to Nathan's. "You are looking," he said, "at the new development partners for Legion Financial's groundbreaking investment A.I. and portfolio management platform."

"Legion?" I cheered with them, trying to recall where I knew the name. "Do they have commercials with a centurion? They offer identity protection, don't they?"

"Among other things," Roger said. "That's them."

"Honey," Nathan said, his lips quivering into a smile as his eyes brimmed. He reached out to take my hand. "It's a five-*million*-dollar deal. An exclusive development and support contract for the next fifteen years that'll pay out god-knows how much more. We finally made it, baby."

"We're gonna be filthy-fucking-rich," Roger announced. He winced at me when I shot him a warning look and downed his glass in one go. "Here's to the good life."

By the time we finished the bottle and the five-star delivery meal that Roger refused to let us help pay for, Jake was slumped on the couch dozing and I knew more about financial planning software than I ever cared to. Nathan and Roger were both as excited for the challenge as for the money, and apparently their connection to Legion was expected to get them introductions to a slew of companies in related industries. It wasn't just the deal with Legion—it was everything that came with it.

I should have been more enthusiastic. This was the next leap, out of the middle class entirely and into rich and famous territory. Almost, anyway. Certainly, it was enough that we'd never have to worry about money again and would eventually be able to enjoy an actual retirement. To say nothing of being able to send Jake to college without him needing to saddle himself with fifty years of debt. It was a very good thing.

"I should put the boy to bed," Nathan said, waving his empty glass toward Jake's sleeping form. "He'll wake up with a pinch in his neck."

"I can do it," I said. "You hang out, I don't mind."

But Nathan stood before I did. "I want to. It'll only take a minute."

He gathered Jake from the couch and crept upstairs while Jake mumbled at him.

"He's a good father," Roger said. "Talks about Jake all the time, you know."

I pushed my chair away from the table and cleaned up. "I know he is."

Roger gathered the remaining glasses and followed me to the kitchen. "Did you hear from West End? I heard they liked your resume."

"Yes, we've been emailing to fix an interview date." I glanced at the stairway. "Thank you, again, for making a call. I appreciate it. And I think I really need this. Lately…"

Roger raised an eyebrow. "Nathan mentioned something about the Turners."

"Let's just say, I could use something different to focus on," I said. I took the glasses from him and started loading the dishwasher.

"Nathan must be glad to hear it," Roger said. "It seems like a good sign, right? He must be proud."

I dropped a fork. "I haven't quite found the best moment to tell him. If you wouldn't mind, I'd appreciate it if you didn't say anything either."

"If that's what you want," he said. He stooped where the fork had bounced to a stop and picked it up to hand it to me. "But I'm guessing he'll catch on. Why not tell him?"

"Honestly? Sometimes I think he'd rather me stay a house-wife." I took the fork back and put it in the caddy. "I think he means well. He's just worried about me getting too stressed, having a relapse. But really, it's not healthy for me. I need something to focus on, something that's mine, you know?"

"You never were one to stand still," Roger said. "Always liked that about you."

I wasn't sure what to say to that. I opened my mouth to come up with anything, but before I did, Nathan came back down the stairs. Roger took a step away from me.

"Like a sack of potatoes," Nathan said. "Did the doctor say what she thought was wrong? I haven't seen him this exhausted since he was a toddler."

"She didn't," I said, and busied myself with putting soap in the dishwasher before I closed it. "She took a blood test, thinks it could be iron, like the school nurse said, or some other nutritional thing. We should know soon."

"I hope he starts feeling better soon," Roger said. "I should get myself home. Ellie, it was good to see you." He kissed me lightly on the cheek again and then took Nathan into a bear hug. "I guess I'll see you tomorrow. Walk me out?"

"Are you okay to drive?" Nathan asked as they headed for the door.

Roger waved his concern away. "Please."

They were out the door after that, and I finished cleaning the table while they finished up whatever last-minute talk they had. There was always something. I waited a few minutes before I went to rescue Nathan from whatever story Roger was telling. I paused at the cracked garage door when I heard them talking. It wasn't some bar story.

"...really need to make sure she can keep it together right now," Roger was saying. "She needs something to keep her grounded, maybe."

"It's only been a year since she got off the pills," Nathan said. "She's doing better, you can see that. This thing with Hank Turner has her on edge but she'll get over it."

"She doesn't need to worry about that," Roger said. "Look, after everything I had to do to get this deal with Legion, we can't afford to screw it up. We need all hands on deck. We do this, and we're free."

They were both quiet a moment before Nathan said, "You don't think I know that? We're fine, alright? I appreciate you being concerned about us, but frankly, my marriage is none of your business, Rog."

"I guess it isn't anymore, right?" Roger asked. "Look, just do whatever you need to. She's a good woman. But this is bigger than us. This is what your kid will have when you're gone. When I'm gone."

"You've had too much to drink," Nathan said. "Time to go home, I'll see you tomorrow. Let me worry about Elaine, it's my job. Not yours."

"Tomorrow, early," Roger said.

Shoes scraped over rough concrete and then tapped across the smoother floor of the garage. I backed away from the door and scurried to the couch where I sank into it and looked up when Nathan came through and closed the door behind him. "Roger's on his way?"

"Yeah," Nathan said. "He wanted to strategize for tomorrow. We have to hire some more people, organize interviews with the recruiter, things like that." He sighed and plopped onto the couch next to me.

I wanted to dig into him but resisted the urge. What exactly was Roger so concerned about?

"You were quiet tonight," Nathan said. He leaned over and pulled me to him. "This is okay, right? This deal? It's what we wanted. And once it's underway, I'll have more time to be home. We can finally hire project managers, delegate more. Take vacations. That would be nice, wouldn't it?"

"Of course it would," I said. I snuggled against him and tried to let the tension in my body go. "I'm excited. It would be great to have you home more, to travel. I'm proud of you, baby."

"Good," Nathan said. He kissed the top of my head, inhaled deeply and then sighed into my hair. "Did something happen today? You seem… tense. More so than yesterday. You're not still worried about Hank, are you?"

"No," I said. "No, I'm not worried. Nothing happened. It was a long day that's all."

Nathan grunted quietly. "If you say so. Come on, let's go to bed. Gonna be an early day tomorrow."

We got up and made our way to bed, dancing to that nightly cadence with thoughtless ease even though I was twisted up inside. Honesty had always been important to us. Critical, even; they tell you that in rehab. Some huge percentage of married addicts get divorced within a few years of getting out.

But there's a time and place for the little lies, right? No one tells their spouse everything.

8

I got the call from Dr. Mindy just after lunch the next day. Jakob had been a little feverish that morning and slept like the dead until almost ten, so I'd kept him home from school again. The only thing he seemed interested in was finishing his new dino-bot. I watched him puzzle over the instructions that came with it as I answered my phone.

"So, we've got some results back on Jakob's blood test," Mindy said once pleasantries were exchanged. "Now I don't want you to panic when I tell you this, but I'd like you to meet me today so that I can introduce you to another doctor, Arnold Saito. He's a specialist."

Anyone who tells you not to panic is, in my experience, delivering news that would make any rational person panic. "I'm sorry, I don't understand," I said. "Is he a nutritionist? We

50

were only testing for iron and aminos or something, weren't we? What kind of specialist is this Dr. Saito?"

"He's in pediatric medicine," Dr. Mindy said, her tone the kind of careful, gentle handling that made me want to reach through the phone and shake her until she told me what was wrong with my son. "Can you and your husband meet us at about four this afternoon at Saint Monica's?"

My stomach clenched. "The pediatric hospital? Why? Can't we meet at your office? What exactly did you find?"

"It would really be better if we met in person," Dr. Mindy said. "Can we meet you then?"

"I… sure," I said. "I'll have to call Nathan home from work. Does he need to be there?"

"That would be best, I think."

Was it about the bruise? Were we walking into some kind of judgment over how I raised my son? Maybe the blood test results were being used as an excuse to get us in. I shook all of that away. "Four o'clock," I agreed. "We can be there."

"You may want to see if someone can watch Jakob," she said. "If not, Saint Monica's has a childcare facility."

"Okay…" I hung up and went to Jake's side. "How's it coming, Iron Man? Does that thing shoot lasers yet?"

"Mom, no, it's a dino-bot, it doesn't have lasers," he said. He pointed to parts that were all just springs and paperclips to me.

"These are the legs, and this is the motor, and these springs go like this… and then when you turn it on it moves."

"How cool. Listen," I said, and kept my voice steady, "I have an appointment that I need to go to in a little bit, so would you be okay to hang out with Linda until Tyler comes home? I'll only be gone a short while."

I hardly had to ask. "Okay! Can I take my dino-bot?"

"Of course," I said. "Please don't lose any pieces."

"I won't!"

I texted Nathan and only got pushback until I told him that it was an emergency. He and I would meet there so that he could go back to work afterward.

Linda was thrilled to be asked to help. "Well, of course Jake can hang out for a while," she crowed when we showed up on her door to ask. "Come on in, sugar, Ty should be home in about an hour. Has he had lunch yet?"

"He ate, but I'm sure he can snack," I said. "Um… not too much sugar for him." Maybe his test results had turned up diabetes? That didn't seem to warrant a visit to a hospital, but there was a history of it in my side of the family though it was a few generations back, on my grandmother's side.

"Oh, of course," Linda said. "I make all my cookies and brownies with stevia these days. It is so much better for you; you can substitute all your sugar with it. I'm thinking about

52

trying out agave next. Have to keep up with Jessi or they'll stop inviting me to the bake sales."

I blinked to keep from staring blankly at her. "Great. Ah, so, we should be back around…" How long did it take to deliver a diagnosis that required both parents and dropping your kid off at a babysitter's? "Six-ish."

Linda practically herded me to the door. "Don't you worry your head about it, Mama, I'll take good care of him. If it runs much later, he can always spend the night. You know I don't mind and Ty will be thrilled. They can play Playstation all night or build a transformer or something."

"Thanks, Linda," I said. "Bye, Jake, be good for Linda, okay?"

"I will," Jake called plaintively from inside Linda's house.

I managed to get away without another of Linda's spiels. Once in the car, I found that actually turning the ignition took an effort. When it rains, it pours. That's been true my entire life. I knew that whatever I was going to find out, it was going to be bad. It would have to be, wouldn't it?

At least Nathan would be there with me.

I pulled out of the driveway and headed to Saint Monica's to find out how bad it was going to be.

I arrived at the hospital before Nathan. I didn't want to face Dr. Mindy and her "specialist" alone, so I waited in the car for him to arrive.

A *specialist*, she had said. What kind of specialist? There were a lot of them, it turned out. As soon as I parked, I found myself on my phone, combing the Internet for clues—connections between blood tests and *specialists*. It didn't help, of course; the list was too long, and all the problems were dire, bordering on terminal. A lot of the time, they *were* terminal.

I started to plug "Doctor Saito" into Google, but a text popped up. Roger. *Everything okay? Nathan's worried, wouldn't talk, just said he's going to the hospital.*

I wasn't sure what to say or whether to say anything. But I couldn't leave Roger to worry. *Will tell you later. Some meeting with a specialist about Jake. We don't know what about yet.*

It was a long wait before another text came in. *Stay strong. I'm sure everything will be okay. Let me know if you need me.*

There was no response that I trusted myself to give, so I put my phone away. If I needed Roger? I had needed him once before, and he had been there in his way. But that was before Nathan and I saved our relationship. I didn't *need* Roger anymore.

The problem was, I liked that he made the offer. *Stupid, stupid girl.*

Nathan's BMW pulled into the lot for patient parking, and I got out to meet him at the entrance. Saint Monica's was a relatively new hospital, all concrete and glass. The entrance was massive, with an arched overhang that made it look like the mouth of some giant sea creature, opening wide to swallow its prey whole. I hate hospitals.

"What's this about?" Nathan asked, as if I'd somehow failed to give him critical information when we'd texted before. "Did Mindy say anything else on the phone?"

"Of course she didn't," I said. "If she did, I would have told you."

"I know," he said. He opened the door for me, and I didn't want to be the first to go in but I did anyway. "It's going to be okay, though, right? Whatever it is, we can handle it."

"You don't know that." I headed to the reception desk ahead of him. Better to get this started than argue with him over how bad it could be.

We didn't have long to hang around, and we waited in somber silence as I imagined all the various things they might tell us. Twice, I watched an orderly push a child with a bald head in a wheelchair through a massive set of sliding glass doors that led to some kind of garden courtyard. One of them had an oxygen tank. The sight of it nearly broke me as I imagined Jake in that chair.

It only got worse from there. I imagined him in a hospital bed, and then in a child-sized coffin, and my heart ached so deeply that I wondered if it was possible to die from this kind of hurt.

I wouldn't say that Dr. Mindy saved me, exactly, but she interrupted my preemptive wallowing at least, and gave me something concrete to focus on. "Nathan, Elaine, thank you for coming," she said. "I'm sorry we couldn't talk more on the phone, but it would have been against ethics protocols. If you'll follow me, please, I'll take you to Dr. Saito."

We did as asked. Hospitals are already stressful places, and maybe they would be more stressful if they were stark white and utterly devoid of personality. Certainly, there's no reason to make them bleaker than they already are. But Saint Monica's was utterly cheerful inside, the hallways all painted with bright colors and decorated with pictures of children playing and of mothers holding newborns, interspersed with wildlife scenes to break up the monotony of smiling children. All of it seemed wrong to me. This wasn't a place children came to have fun.

We passed several more children in varying states of illness that all looked vaguely terminal before we went into Dr. Saito's office. There was a sign at the beginning of the hallway leading there that froze my blood. *"Pediatric Oncology,"* it proclaimed. I was reminded of the gates to hell from Dante's *Inferno.*

Abandon all hope, ye who enter here.

Saito was a man about my height, white-haired but not really old yet. His hands were cool and soft when we shook. As Nathan and I sat down, I took his hand and held it tight.

"Mr. and Mrs. Jennson," he said, "my name is Arnold Saito. I was apprised of your son, Jakob's, test results and asked to take over his treatment. Of course, you are free to use any doctor you prefer after our consultation. No one is forcing you onto me, just so that we are clear."

I squeezed Nathan's hand, and my eyes already burned with tears that were building up behind them. *Get to the fucking point*, I wanted to scream.

"Elaine, Nathan," Dr. Mindy said, her voice too gentle to have any good news, "Dr. Saito is a… he's a pediatric oncologist."

"Oncologist," I repeated, quietly. I knew what the word meant. Of course I did. I had seen it on the sign, too. But in that moment, it may as well have been in a different language, some alien word that could have meant "dirt" or "cloud." It wouldn't congeal in my brain into something that made sense.

"Specifically," Dr. Saito said, "I specialize in the treatment of a particular variety of childhood cancer, acute myelogenous leukemia. My success rate in treatment is very high, over eighty-seven percent."

Loss has a sound. I had heard it before, eight years ago almost, when someone else said words that tore my world in half. *Mrs. Jennson, we understand your son has been reported missing.*

It's not a tearing sound. Not like it should be. It's the single beat of a drum, bigger than the world, that hits you like a train. That sound is the first beat of your heart when your whole world turns upside down and tries to shake you into the sky.

"Leukemia," Nathan said. His voice was strong. As if he could somehow handle it. I kept my lips sealed tight. "Are you certain, one-hundred percent, about what it is and... what kind?"

"I wasn't," Dr. Mindy said, "which is why I consulted with Dr. Saito."

Dr. Saito nodded once. "The diagnosis is not in doubt," he said. "I have dealt with this condition many, many times. It is not common in children, but it is treatable. More so now than it was ten years ago, or even five."

"Okay," Nathan said. He took a deep breath and spared me a pained glance. "Okay. So, what can we do? What happens next?"

"The first thing," Dr. Saito said, "is that we will need to collect blood samples from you and your wife. Jake is O positive, so you're both a potential donor. I understand Jakob has no siblings?"

Was Jakob O positive? I tried to remember the last time I'd seen his blood type but couldn't be sure. How could I forget something like that? "No," I said, weakly, I didn't want to sit there mute while they talked around me. "No, there are no siblings. Why do you need blood samples from us if it's Jakob that's sick?"

"We will run tests to see if either of you is a potential bone marrow donor," Dr. Saito explained. He gestured toward the two of us. "Unfortunately, it is statistically unlikely, but a donor doesn't need to be a relation. Jake's blood type is the most common in the U.S., however, so our chances of finding a suitable donor are high if it turns out you're not compatible. While we are testing, we will also consult a donor database that has an international reach, starting close to home and working our way out. In the meantime, we'll take a bone marrow sample from Jakob, and begin chemotherapy right away."

"And… you're looking for a genetic match?" I asked. I hated the sudden panic that cut through the sadness and pressed against my veins. "From either one of us? Is that necessary? I don't want us to waste any time."

Nathan's body stiffened. Instantly, shame replaced my panic. But Saito might need to know. If he was going to be running tests, comparing genes…

"Yes," Dr. Saito confirmed. "If enough matching markers are present, we'll then take a bone marrow sample. But that will take time to process and it will be faster to start with a basic comparison. Our lab is state-of-the-art. And, as I said, we will be consulting the donor database immediately as well. All of this takes place concurrently, I assure you. We were lucky to have caught this early, but we still need to work as quickly as possible before it advances any further."

From that moment on, I kept my mouth shut. Nathan and I

gave our blood samples and scheduled Jake's biopsy and intake. My mind raced with a million questions and worries until I felt physically hot from the friction of them. And Nathan…

As we left, I couldn't look at him.

"I'll be home later," he said. He started to leave without kissing me goodbye, or even saying it, but stopped. When he spoke, he didn't look at me. "The donor doesn't have to be related, right? We should ask around the neighborhood, see if we can get more people to join the donor program. I'm sure Linda could help."

"Yeah," I said. "I'm sure she can."

"That's good," he said. And he left.

I got into the car. My eyes clouded, and every muscle in my body seemed to curl into itself until the first sob burst from me and opened the gates wide until the steering wheel was soaked with tears and I couldn't breathe through my nose or swallow.

In two days, we would bring Jake to the hospital. I had two days to figure out how to tell my son that he had cancer.

And how to tell Nathan that he might not be Jake's father.

9

A fter my meltdown, I drove around town trying to figure out how I was going to explain leukemia to Jake. When I did finally make it back home it was dinnertime, and I could see Linda, Malcolm, their two kids and Jake at the table eating. He looked happy.

There was no time to waste, and at least four people I knew were potential donors. But I didn't want to have that conversation in front of Jake. Still in my car, I steeled myself and dialed. The phone rang four times. I thought it might go to voicemail—it was what I deserved, after all, and I couldn't remember the last time I had answered her phone call.

But the fifth ring stopped, and a confused voice answered. "Hello?"

Deep breaths, Elaine. "Diana," I said quietly. "It's me."

Silence.

"Elaine." Not a question or a greeting, really, just a pronouncement that she recognized the voice of her sister.

"It's been a while," I said. "How are you? How are the kids?"

"Seriously?" The line on her end became muffled, and I barely heard her speaking. "One moment, please."

I waited. Last time we had spoken was when Jake had gone missing. Actually, no; it had been a few months after we'd gotten him back. When it was time to unpack everything we hadn't talked about. Except, I hadn't wanted to unpack it.

Her voice was flat when she spoke again. "Did something happen? What do you want?"

If I could just spit it out, she would help. But her tone—judgmental instead of sympathetic—compelled me to hold back. "We haven't spoken in a while," I said. "Can I not check in? How is Lawrence? The girls?"

"You want to check in?" Diana said. "After seven years, you decided to call and see how we are?"

"Can't I do that?" I asked. I squirmed in my seat, pulled one knee to my chest. She didn't have to be in the car to make me feel like a petulant teen.

She scoffed, and I heard the flick of a lighter.

"You're still smoking? Thought you were going to quit."

"I did." A long pause, and then a rough exhale. "Lawrence is working at a bank. Loan officer. He tried to get back into tech for a while, before he gave up."

I winced. Nathan had been sure he would bounce back. I guessed he was wrong about that. "Well, I'm glad he's working." Entirely the wrong thing to say. I should have gotten to the point already and been done.

"Fuck you," Diana muttered.

I deserved that, maybe. Lawrence had brought the FBI down on Nathan and Roger's company, claiming they were in bed with the mob. They had come through it and made sure Lawrence was blacklisted. Temporarily, had been the idea. That was between them, of course—but I hadn't fought Nathan on it.

"The girls are fine," Diana said resignedly. "Arianne is in college. Bria recently graduated high school, thank God. With honors. She's been a nightmare. Rose is twelve now, she's in ballet. She's good."

I smiled, remembering briefly how Diana and I had fought over Mom's old ballet slippers, the last pair she'd worn before she had Diana. "Takes after Mom."

"What do you want, Elaine?" Diana demanded. "Do you finally want to talk about Mom? Why you abandoned us? 'Cause I have plenty to say about it."

My hands shook. I had to press the phone more firmly against my ear to keep the tremors from driving me crazy. For a moment I was frozen, the last expression I saw on Mom's face burned forever into the back of my eyelids. She'd been long gone, hadn't known who I was. One day we would have to talk about it. But not tonight. "No, I didn't."

"No," Diana sighed. "Of course not." She took another drag, rasped it out. "So what do you want?"

I cleared my throat of the knot in it, mostly, and wiped my eyes. "What blood type are you?"

"What? Why?" Whatever was between us, she seemed to set it aside at the moment. "Jesus, Ellie, what's going on? Are you okay? Is Jake?"

"I need to know if you're O positive," I said. "You or Lawrence, or the kids."

"I'm not," she said. "I'm A negative, Lawrence is B positive. The girls all got AB positive. Ari can donate to O positive recipients, though, so can Lawrence. Is that what this is about?"

My sister the nurse. "No, it's not like that."

"So?" She asked. "What is it? Talk to me."

I realized then that I hadn't said it out loud. They had told me, but I hadn't repeated it. The words stuck behind my teeth, refused to let me open my mouth without a struggle. I thought I might swallow my tongue instead. "It's Jake." My voice came out a croaking whisper. "He's been diagnosed. With cancer. Leukemia."

"Fuck." She took another drag. "Fuck. Ellie, I'm so sorry."

It hit me wrong. Like she was sorry he had died. "Don't say that," I snapped. "He's going to be fine, I don't need your pity, they just told us we had to…" The words choked off, my eyes burning again worse than before.

"You're looking for donors," she finished for me, gently, despite my outburst. Ever the mature older sister. "They're testing you and Nate?"

"Yeah." I wiped my eyes again. "He's going to Saint Monica's, they say it's state-of-the-art."

"I've heard of them," Diana said. "They are. Very high success rate, a lot of good research comes out of their labs. Jake is in good hands."

We sat in the quiet for a time. I could hear Diana puffing her smoke on the other end while I stared into the darkness of the garage on mine. Diana broke first.

"They'll be running a lot of DNA tests," she said. "That's what Saint Monica's is known for, the latest genetic medicine. If they're testing for compatibility, they're going to see. They may not say anything, but Nate will have access. They can't hide it from him, legally."

"I know," I said.

"Did you ever…?"

"No," I said. "I never had the tests run. It… it could go either way."

"If it isn't Nathan," she asked, "do you know for sure it's Roger?"

My stomach turned. "God, Di, what do you think I was up to? Screwing every guy in sight? Roger was the only one, okay?"

"All I'm saying is that if he's the only other possible father, then you should talk to him, too," Diana said. "What am I supposed to think? You barely talked about it and we hadn't spoken in four years, I barely knew who you were. I still don't."

"That's pretty fucking obvious."

"I don't want to fight right now," she said. The fight was out of her voice, too. "Look… keep me updated, okay? And if you need me—"

"I don't," I said quickly. "You stay with your family."

The garage door was still open. In the driveway, I saw Linda peeking around the corner from her mailbox, curious. "I have to go," I said. "Tell everyone I said hi."

"It's better if I don't," Diana said. "We're going to have to talk, Ellie. Eventually."

Lights brightened the tree standing between our house and Linda's and then turned into the driveway. Nathan was home.

"Sure," I said. "Eventually. I really have to go, Nathan's home."

"Okay," she said. "Go take care of your family. I, ah…"

"Me, too," I said. "Night."

We hung up, and I wiped my eyes again before I got out of the car. Nathan turned his lights off, and before they faded from my eyes, his door closed. I went to stand next to him. "Jake's at Linda's," I said. "I should go get him."

"Yeah," Nathan said. But as I went to leave, he put a hand on my arm and held me fast. "I'm sorry about before. I was in shock, I shouldn't have left like that."

"It's okay," I said. "I haven't done this before either."

"We'll talk," he said. "After Jake's in bed. I don't want to, but we have to."

I nodded, and he let me go. I put on the best smile I could and waved to Linda. "You ready to send that kid home?"

Linda's expression was pensive for a second longer as she looked from me to Nathan and back, slowly, trying to work out what the deal was and whether it was something she should know or not. But it switched to her usual jovial self in a flash, and she waved my deprecation off. "I'd keep him if you'd let me," she said, loudly. When I was closer, she lowered her voice. "Everything okay?"

"It was a rough meeting," I said. "But no big deal. Want to get Jake for me? I don't want to intrude."

"You're never intruding, hon," she said. "I'll have him right out."

She left, and I watched Nathan as he leaned against his car and stared at something a thousand miles away. From where I was, I could see into the car, into the passenger seat. It was dark, and I couldn't be sure, but I thought that I saw the edge of a paper bag.

10

J ake went down quickly, but not before he, Nathan, and I
got some quality snuggle time in on the couch together. I
needed that moment to pretend everything was fine. Just
one more day for us to be a normal family, with a healthy son
and two loving parents. Maybe Nathan needed it as well. He
offered to let Jake stay up late, which he did—by about five
minutes.

Once Nathan and I had tucked him in, we returned somberly
to the living room and sat on opposite ends of the couch with
the television off, only a weak illumination spilling in from the
kitchen where the counter lights were on.

"Have you thought about how we tell him?" Nathan asked.

"I tried," I said. I pulled my knees to my chest and drew the soft throw blanket that was draped over the back of the couch to me. "Maybe Dr. Saito can help."

"It should be us," he said. "I don't want him hearing it from a stranger."

"We can figure it out." I reached for him and after a moment he came closer and intertwined his fingers with mine.

"You were still in the garage when I got home," he said. "Where did you go after you left the hospital?"

"Nowhere," I said. "I needed some time to process the news. Jake was having fun at Linda's."

It was hard to read his face with the only light coming from behind him, but he could see my face clearly. I could feel him searching it. "We can do this," he said. "But only if we stay strong together."

"Can we?" I wondered. "How do you know?"

"There's a risk our son will be taken from us again," Nathan said. "We got him back before; this time we won't let him be taken away. Not by that bastard Turner, and not by cancer. He's ours."

It came out of my mouth before I could stop it. "Was there a... a paper bag in your car?"

He let my hand go. "Excuse me?"

"In your car, outside," I said. "I thought I saw a paper bag. The kind you get at a liquor store."

He leaned back and shook his head slowly. "Seriously, Elaine? You think I'm going to crawl into a bottle at a time like this?" He looked toward the stairs. "What about you? Should I be going through your car looking for pills?"

"Of course not," I said. I rubbed my eyes, they were puffy and sore and still burned with leftover salt. "I'm sorry, I didn't mean to suggest you were drinking."

"Yes, you did." He let his head fall back and studied the ceiling. "Not that I haven't thought about having a drink. The bag contains new business cards. I picked them up from the printers on my way home. Roger didn't want to wait for them to ship. You're welcome to go check."

I moved closer and snuggled into him, my head on his shoulder. "I don't need to check, I trust you," I said. "But I'm rather off balance right now, I'm worried about everything. And, I need to tell you…"

"Hm?" He let one arm drape over me and with his other hand he tipped my face up toward his. "Tell me what?"

Blood rushed in my ears. Now was the time to tell him my concerns about Jake's paternity, I had to say something, Nathan deserved to know, and he deserved to hear it from me. But what if I was wrong? There was a chance Jake was his and I would hurt him unnecessarily. "I saw Hank," I rasped.

Nathan panicked immediately. "Jesus, what? When? Tonight?"

I sat up straight, cursing myself for chickening out of telling

Nathan, and for blurting out what had happened yesterday the wrong way. "I mean, I didn't see him," I said, "but I saw someone I thought was him. I called the police and they stopped the guy but it... wasn't Hank."

"Christ," Nathan breathed. "You should have led with that."

"I know," I said. "I just mean that... I'm worried that I'm seeing things."

He drew me to him again, put his arms around me and held me fast. We fell asleep that way.

The next day was rough for Jake. He slept late, and when he woke, he had a new bruise. It was angry purple and crescent-shaped, cutting around his waist and angling up toward his back. His fever was higher, a hundred-and-one, and after a tiny breakfast he lay on the couch watching cartoons and floating in and out of sleep. I sat with him, chewing the nail on my forefinger down to the quick.

I tried to do some research, to learn more about his diagnosis, but couldn't stay calm enough to read very much. The photographs were the worst, and twice I looked over at my sleeping son and found myself assailed by visions of him bald, wasting away, reaching out to me for help that I couldn't give. Ultimately, I threw my phone to the carpet and resolved not to look at it again until all of this was over.

I managed to get some chicken soup into him at lunchtime and he fell asleep again. Moments later someone knocked at the door.

I didn't answer right away. If it was Linda, I wasn't in the mood for company. And I had this irrational fear that if I were apart from Jake for too long when I returned I would find him more than just sleeping. I knew it didn't work that way, of course, but there was an invisible tether connecting us. If I wandered too far, it pulled at my heart and maybe at his as well. I had to stay close to keep him alive.

But the knock came again, more urgent this time. I brushed Jake's damp hair to one side, kissed his forehead, and went to find out what couldn't wait.

The woman on the other side of the door was middle-aged, with brown hair pulled into an immaculate bun sporting a pair of number-two pencils. She was dressed for business and held one of those metal clipboards with a compartment for files.

"I'm not interested," I said as politely as I could. "Sorry."

"Mrs. Jennson?" the woman asked before I could close the door.

I opened it the rest of the way. "If I'm on some list, I'd like to be taken off, please."

"I'm afraid that's not how this list works," she said. She held a hand out. "My name is Gertrude Olman. You can call me Gert if you like. I'm with Child Protective Services."

Shock gave way to anger pretty quickly. That horrible nurse, Amber or… Amy or whatever her name was—that bitch had called CPS after all. I had to unclench my jaw to respond, without shaking the woman's hand. "I see. Look, there has been a misunderstanding—"

"I don't doubt that there has been, Mrs. Jennson." She peered past me, a pleasant, placid expression on her face as if she weren't spying into my house to see if my son was maybe lying on the floor with a broken arm, or maybe to check if our place was infested with swarms of roaches. "Unfortunately, I still have to visit, to clear everything up. May I come in?"

"Jake is sleeping," I said, "I'd rather we talk outside."

Gertrude's brow pinched in a mockery of sympathetic concern. "I wish that were an option," she said, "but I'm afraid the law requires that I enter the household to complete my visit. I could come back with a warrant, but that will complicate this whole matter needlessly. I'm sure you don't want that. I promise, I'll be brief."

I will have that nurse's job. "You'll have to be," I said as I stepped aside. "I have a lot to do today."

She looked around as she picked her way through the foyer and into the living room where she peeked over the couch to see Jake. She looked back at me and whispered, "He is just darling. Poor thing, is he still sick?"

"Can we talk in the kitchen?" I asked. I left the living room without waiting for her answer.

She followed in her own time, taking note of everything as she did. The house wasn't a mess by any means, but dishes from breakfast and lunch were still on the counter, and the door to the laundry room was open to show the growing pile of clothes I hadn't gotten around to washing yet. Were those signs of a household full of abuse? I wished I knew what she was looking for.

I led her to the kitchen island where she set down her clipboard and drew a pen from her breast pocket. She pulled an ID card from the board and passed it to me. "My identification, in case there was any doubt," she said.

I looked it over and handed it back to her. If it had been fake, I wasn't sure how I'd know, but I doubted that it was. "As I told you," I said, "there's been a huge misunderstanding. I know who reported me, and she has no idea what she's talking about."

"I'll be completely up front with you, Mrs. Jennson," Gertrude said, "We have to take every report seriously. I only have a few questions, and then I can be on my way. I will, of course, need to speak with Jake as well."

"Please," I said, "slow down a little. If you could wait right here for a moment, I'll get something from my car in the garage."

She nodded, and I checked that Jake was still sleeping before I went to retrieve the papers that Dr. Saito had given us. Just handling them made me nauseous, and when I came back inside, I thrust them at Gertrude.

She raised an eyebrow, and took the papers from me, unfolded them, and began reading.

"Bruising is one of the early symptoms," I said quietly. "I'm not abusive, neither is my husband. So I'd appreciate it if you could close this case and leave us in peace while we deal with much bigger concerns."

Gertrude continued reading until she laid the papers down on the counter. "I'm very sorry."

There it was again, that *condolence* tone.

"Do you need anything else from me?" I asked. "Or can we be done now, please."

She gave me that false sympathy again. "To complete the visit, I'm afraid I still have to speak with Jake. Can we wake him? It won't take very long."

"What do you want to talk to him about?" I asked. I waved at the papers. "It's all right there. There's nothing going on here, the nurse that reported us was mistaken, we have his diagnosis. His treatment starts tomorrow."

She sucked in a breath over her teeth. "I'm afraid my interview questions are confidential. It's procedure. We can schedule another visit if you like."

"Well, it will have to be at the hospital then," I said, louder than I meant to. I counted silently to ten. "I'm sorry. As you can imagine, I'm under a lot of pressure at the moment."

She tapped her pen several times on her board and then made a note on the form there. "Now clearly isn't a good time. When in the next forty-eight hours would be appropriate? I can make a hospital visit."

That would be just great. Gert from CPS walking onto the oncology ward to interview my son just as his cancer treatment started. Saint Monica's had been teeming with parents when I was there yesterday. What would they think? Would Dr. Saito judge me, along with Dr. Mindy and the nursing staff? The last thing I wanted was for any of them to watch over Nathan and me when we were there with Jake. God, we were going to be living there for who knew how long. In a hospital, again, day in and day out.

The reality of that settled on me, and I put a hand to my stomach.

"Mrs. Jennson?" Gertrude asked, intruding on that whole new shower of fears.

"Please leave," I said. "I'll have to speak with my husband, and with the hospital,"—I spat the word at her—"to see when an appropriate time would be. Visiting hours, I would imagine."

She tapped her pen twice more, then clicked it and put it away.

She produced a card and placed it on the counter. "I need to see Jake within the next forty-eight hours. You can either bring him down to the office or I can come and meet you. I'll be discreet, I assure you."

This was a woman simply trying to do her job. She hadn't been cruel, or particularly condemnatory. I took the card from the counter and slipped it into my back pocket. It wasn't something I wanted either Jake or Nathan to see by accident before I had a chance to explain her visit. "I will call you as soon as I can confirm a time. Thank you for... understanding. I apologize for being so abrasive."

"In my line of work," Gertrude said, "I've seen far worse. Please don't forget to call me. I do have to file non-compliance if you don't."

She looked toward Jake and then back at me and put her hand on my arm to give a gentle squeeze. "Leukemia is something I've had the misfortune of encountering before," she said. "We do more than what most people realize. If you need someone to talk to, our services are freely available to the public. This district has some very capable counselors."

"Maybe I'll take you up on that," I said. "Let me show you out."

I led her to the door, and we exchanged final pleasantries before I closed it behind her. I took several deep breaths to calm myself. This would all be cleared up. Meeting at the hospital could even be the better idea—at least there she could speak with the doctor himself, maybe, or one of Jake's nurses. That would put an end to this nonsense.

"Mom?" Jake asked from behind me. I turned to see him sitting up, confusion on his face. "What's loo... lookeema?"

11

We sat in the lobby of Saint Monica's, waiting to be admitted while Jake picked at the upholstery of one of the hospital's hard-seated chairs and watched sick children come and go from the back hallways. I wished we could have waited somewhere else.

"Why are we here?" Jake asked when I gently brushed his hand from the tubing that lined the arm of his chair. "I'm bored."

Nathan and I shared a look. We'd been doing it for the last twenty-four hours, trying to signal the other that it was time to tell our son the truth but neither of us willing to be the one to start.

"Just hang tight for me, sweetie," I said. I handed him my phone. "You can watch some videos if you want."

He took it, but it would only occupy his attention for a little while.

"Is that Roger?" Nathan asked.

I turned to see Roger coming through the main entrance, dressed impeccably but absent was his usual charming smile. "I called him," I said.

Nathan sighed. "Why did you do that?"

"Uncle Rog is here?" Jake perked up and grinned when he saw Roger.

"That's why," I said. "Hi, Rog. Thanks for coming."

Roger endured half a tackle from Jake, wrestled carefully with him for a moment, and then brought him into the semicircle of chairs and ottomans that we'd more or less claimed for our own. "Of course," he said. "Anything you two need. Nate, I approved two of the senior engineer resumes, and they're in your inbox when you get a chance. Not now, of course."

"I'll take a look," Nathan said. He shook Roger's hand and glanced at me before he sat down again. "Glad you're here."

"Me too," Jake said. "This is the most boring place ever. There's a snack machine in the hallway. You want to get a candy?"

Roger glanced at me, one eyebrow raised. "Mom?"

Nathan stood before I answered. "Sure, buddy. Come on, I'll take you."

"Better go with your dad, little guy," Roger said. He took a step back as Nathan passed between them to lead Jake toward the hallway.

"He's just on edge," I said. "I am too."

"Of course you are," Roger said. He looked around and picked the chair on the other side of mine to sit down in, leaning on his knees to peer at me. "Any idea when he gets admitted?"

"Supposed to be soon," I said. "Then time's up."

"Time's up?"

I nodded. "We haven't told him why he's here yet. And they want to do the bone marrow biopsy today, so…"

Roger leaned back in his chair. "Jesus, Elaine. Seriously?"

I glanced toward the hallway where Nathan and Jake had disappeared. "Look, I asked you to come because I want to know if you'll consider getting tested as a donor for Jake. For bone marrow."

He pursed his lips, hands spread. "Sure, of course. Why wouldn't I? I could ask everyone at the office to get checked as well. I can't make it mandatory, of course, but—"

"That's not the only reason," I said. "Can you stay for a little bit? We're supposed to be assigned a room and then meet with the doctor. I'd like it if you could be here afterward. Nathan would too, I'm sure, and you know Jake loves having you around."

Roger watched me as I shifted my legs to find a more comfortable position to sit in. These stupid chairs. If they were going to make people wait this long, you'd have thought they'd provide more cozy seating. "What's this about, Elaine?" he asked.

"You're our friend," I said. "Since before Jake was born, you're practically family. Does it need to be about something else?"

He shook his head and looked at something behind me. "No," he said. "Of course not. What'd you get, kiddo?"

"Gummy bears," Jake said as he came around my chair and wandered toward his own with a small package in hand. He popped a red gummy bear into his mouth.

I eyed Nathan as he took his seat again. He caught my look and shrugged. "It's fine."

"It's pure sugar," I said.

"It's what he wanted," Nathan said. "Now doesn't seem like the right time for a boundary check."

Someone with a file came toward us from the doorway we'd followed Dr. Mindy through the last time we were here. A blonde-headed woman with a bright smile, wearing some jewel-toned lipstick that didn't belong in a children's hospital. "Hi, are you all the Jennson family?"

"We are," Nathan said, gesturing at himself, Jake and I—not Roger. "Are you ready for us?"

"We're all set," she said. "Come on back."

"I'll wait here," Roger said. When I looked over my shoulder from the corner of the hallway to the children's ward, he had a grim look on his face.

The nurse led us to a room that didn't match the hallways. Out there it was all optimism and platitudes about perseverance and hope. This room was white, top to bottom, except for the powder blue hospital blanket on the bed.

"My name is Signey," she said as she led us inside. "I'm here for the first shift Monday through Wednesday, and double on Thursday and Friday, first and second; that's seven to eleven. I know the room doesn't look like much yet, but we keep it like this so it can be decorated. We'll bring in someone from the children's—"

"Can we have a moment?" I asked. "To have a talk with our son?"

Signey looked from me to Jake, and then to Nathan. Her demeanor cracked, and she looked away momentarily before she tucked the clipboard to her chest. "Absolutely. If you need anything, you can have them page me at the nurses' station." She smiled at Jake as she made her way out, but paused near me, and touched my upper arm, her eyes full of understanding.

She must've seen this a hundred times. A thousand, even. I waited until she was gone to close the door.

Jake looked around the room, concern etched on his cherubic face. "Am I in trouble?"

"Oh, God no, baby," I said. I sank onto the edge of the hospital bed and patted the space beside me. "Come here, have a seat."

Nathan joined us, leaning onto the bed on the other side of Jake. "Listen, buddy," he said, "we need to tell you something. And it's gonna be hard to understand but you have to stay strong and know that we both love you and that you are perfectly safe, okay?"

Jake shifted on the edge of the bed, his eyes glued to the ground. "I guess. Okay."

"Jake," I said, "remember when we went to see Dr. Mindy? And she took your blood?"

Jake nodded weakly. "Uh huh."

"Well... Dr. Mindy found some, ah..." Jesus, how does any parent have that conversation? "You know in school, in science class, when Mr. Garvey talked about red blood cells and white blood cells and platelets? And you did a science project about them, remember? You and Dad cut the pool noodle in half and glued the different colored puffs inside?"

He shrugged. "I remember."

"Look at me, Iron Man," I told him. He did, and I swallowed the lump in my throat. I could do this, I told myself. "You're going to be okay. But your bones—where your blood comes from—they're making red and white blood cells that are...

shaped wrong. And when that happens, there's not enough room for the other, healthier cells. And that makes you sick. That's why you've been feeling so bad lately. And we're here because the doctors are going to make you all better. Does that make sense?"

Nathan watched me, not Jake. There was a look in his eyes that I wasn't sure I'd actually seen before. Well... maybe, once. When I gave birth, I think he had that look on his face. Like he was really and truly *proud* of me. It gave me the bit of strength I needed to face Jake.

"Am I"—I knew what he was going to ask, and it broke my heart—"going to die?" Jake's eyes were wet. His face was ruddy, blushing pink the way it did before he had a real, genuine cry. The kind of cry he had when his hamster died. The kind he was too young for back then and too young for now.

"No," Nathan said. Jake sniffled as Nathan held his face in both of his hands. "You are not going to die. It's going to be a little rough getting better. You're not going to feel very good sometimes. But your mom and me, we're going to be here with you all the time. We're not going to leave you alone even for a minute and I promise you that you are going to be okay."

I didn't know how he could make a promise like that but I didn't know how he *couldn't*, either. He held Jake close, and the two of them reached for me. I huddled in, and we held tight as if we could physically hold our family together if we clustered up close enough and didn't let go.

Jake waited outside, hanging out with an orderly who had superhero tattoos, while we met with Dr. Saito to go over the details of his treatment. Tattoos weren't something I wanted Jake to get in his head, but if he could get through this and be healthy again, I'd let him ink his body head to toe if that was the toll to get across this bridge.

Dr. Saito smiled in a professional, pleasant kind of way. He was optimistic or trying to look it. *Eighty-seven percent success rate.* I wanted to believe those were good odds, that he dealt with leukemia with the frequency other doctors treated the flu. He sat down behind his desk and opened a file. He picked up a pair of reading glasses and leaned over it. *Here is where he says that I'm a match,* I thought. *Here is where he makes everything better.* This was the part where I could finally breathe again.

"I'm afraid that none of the markers we found in your samples indicate a possible bone marrow match," he said. My heart sank. "I only have Jakob's medical records from the last few years so far, since you moved to the area, I assume, so I didn't have a complete picture and for that I apologize. The truth is, the most likely donor would be a sibling. I know it may be a sensitive subject, but I must ask if you are in contact with Jakob's birth parents."

It was like he'd asked if we knew aliens from Mars that we could call up.

"We're not, I'm afraid," Nathan said. "It was a… closed adoption, so…"

I froze, paralyzed. The world began to spin past me, whatever glue keeping me attached to it somehow eroded away by what was happening. I was dreaming, I decided. I was having one of those horrible stress dreams again, and my mind was somehow rejecting the cancer, definitely not Jake. That was it. I was going to wake up. I always woke up at the worst part.

It all kept unfolding around me.

"I understand," Dr. Saito said. "That is unfortunate, but we have already identified five potential donor matches. None of them are nearby, I'm afraid, which means we will have to reach out to them, collect samples, do further rigorous testing. However, now that Jakob has been admitted, we will begin chemotherapy immediately. There is also another course of therapy that has recently been approved by the FDA, it's a gene therapy. Very advanced, and the results look very promising. With your permission, I'd like to try it as well, as an alternative in case the donors don't work out. It takes some time to prepare, but we will start the lab work now. I'm very confident about this approach, but we can conduct our initial trials there before Jakob undergoes any treatment."

I wanted to tell the doctor that he was wrong about the test results. Surely there had been a mix-up? But my throat wouldn't allow the words out. How could Nathan lie to the doctor like that? *Adoption?*

The rest of the conversation passed me by. I came out of my daze when Dr. Saito offered his hand and I took it on pure reflex. I couldn't even feel his hand in mine.

"I have the utmost confidence and optimism that we can successfully treat your son's condition," he said. "He's in very good hands here at Saint Monica's, I give you my word."

"Thank you," I muttered, and Nathan led me out. He took me into the hallway where we retrieved Jake. We went back to Jake's room, where he suggested that Jake lay down and try to get a little rest. Once the TV was on, he tugged me gently into the hallway, and then to a waiting area. I hardly registered the chair beneath me as I sat.

I looked up at Nathan, trying to make sense of the world.

"Elaine," he said, softly. He knelt in front of me, took my hands in his and held them tight when I didn't answer. "*Elaine.*"

I shook my head slowly, trying to wake myself up.

"Nathan," I rasped, my whole body wracked with pain, "where is our *son?* Where is Jakob?"

12

"We have to tell the police," I said. "We have to tell them we have someone else's child, I—Jesus, Nathan, what if the Turners were *innocent?* That woman was adamant that Jake was her son."

"No," Nathan said, his voice hard. He regretted his tone immediately, I could see it in his eyes. "I'm sorry. If he really was theirs, the Turners would have allowed the DNA test instead of clinging to a Bible to get around it on religious grounds."

"It doesn't change the fact that—"

Nathan's hands squeezed mine almost painfully, and he pulled me to him. I tried to push him away, but the strength left my arms and I let him hold me for a long moment. Finally, he spoke quietly into my ear. "Think about what you're saying," he said. "He's about to start treatment. We will do everything we can to find out where Jake—the original, I mean, *biological* Jake—is, but this is the boy we raised, Elaine. I love him. You love him. We can't abandon him."

I shrugged his arms off of me and leaned back as he stood. "I'm not saying we should," I breathed. "Of course, I love him; I'm his mother in every way that counts, I know that. But..."

A pair of nurses walked past the waiting area. I lowered my voice once they were gone. "Think about his parents. Somewhere in the world there's a mother and father who never got their son back. Maybe the Turners, or maybe someone else— that doesn't even matter, does it? And our son is—" A sob wracked me, sneaking up and attacking, choking off what I was trying to say. I had to bury my face in my hands to keep from screaming.

Nathan placed his hand on my back and let me cry. There was nothing cathartic about my tears; I was drowning, and this was the excess pouring out of me—the pain that would otherwise kill me.

For years there had been a piece of me missing. Some panicked corner of my soul must have known the truth. Every mother knows the scent of her own child, doesn't she? On some unconscious level that had to be true. And only mothers who were entirely disconnected from their children could mistake someone else's baby for their own. But that wasn't me —I loved Jake, I was utterly, hopelessly devoted to him. I was a good mother.

Wasn't I?

"We can't do this now," Nathan said. "I know that this is painful. It's killing me, too. We have to—"

"Is it?" I asked. I looked up at him and could no longer stand to sit. I got up and paced the waiting area. "You didn't seem at all surprised when the doctor assumed he was adopted."

Nathan blinked and folded his arms. An expression of hurt flashed across his face and faded as quickly. "I was thinking of our son," he hissed. "I had to say something, didn't I? If they'd registered our shock, we would all be in an enormous amount of trouble. They would take him from us, Elaine, and he'd end up in some state hospital as second priority under some rich kids which, by the way, he *is* right now. I don't care who I have to lie to or what I have to do, even if it means I end up in prison, so long as he gets the care he needs. What about you?"

I turned my face toward the wall as more people passed by. Crying or bickering parents couldn't possibly be that uncommon in a children's cancer ward, but the last thing I wanted was for any of them to stop and ask if everything was okay. There was no telling what I might have said.

"I'll do whatever needs to be done," I said. "But I'm not going to forget. I can't, Nathan—it will kill me. Do you get that? If I ignore this, it will kill me, I can feel it."

He came to me and pried my hands away from my arms where I'd been hugging myself. He held them in two vice grips, pulling me back down to Earth. "I'm not saying you have to ignore it or forget," he said. "Just… for now, keep quiet about it especially around Jake, and the nurses and doctors and pretty much everyone else. We can't tell anyone about this, not even Roger. Especially not Roger."

"Why?" I asked. "Why especially him?"

Nathan shook his head. "The timing of all of this is bad enough, with the new contract and everything. Roger loves Jake, and he's a good friend, but…"

I searched his face for the rest of it.

He sighed. "Please trust me."

Did I? I couldn't be sure. I wanted to—I wanted to believe in that moment that everything would turn out okay, and that he knew best. He was stronger than I was, I thought, but he could also hide what he was feeling. I've never been good at that.

"Trust me, baby," he said. "Please."

"Okay."

He leaned in and kissed me. If there was a spark still alive there, I couldn't feel it. There's only so much a person can take before they shut down. I wasn't quite there, but the numbness was beginning to creep in. It was a familiar feeling and one that terrified me. That's the feeling you get right before the seams start to come apart. I remembered it too well.

"This bench can be lifted to pull out a cot," Signey said, demonstrating how the bench cushion could be raised to reveal a small bed beneath. "I can get you blankets, pillows, anything you need. Most parents bring their own in and that's fine, but we'll need to clean them in our facilities before they enter the room."

She handed me a slip of paper. "Here's a list of some other items that parents bring; you'd be surprised what you might forget in times like these. Oh, the recliner is pretty comfortable and we can fit another in here if you need it. And there are also sleeping rooms down the hall if you need them."

"We'll be staying here with Jake," I said.

"Of course." Signey smiled at us. "On that sheet there is also the number for one of our in-house organizations, Dream a Little Dream. They collect decorations, bed sheets… you just tell them what Jake likes and they'll come in and spruce his room up. We make it a surprise, and it doesn't cost anything."

"We don't need charity," I said.

Nathan cleared his throat. "Elaine…"

Signey was unfazed and waved Nathan off. "It's okay, Mr. Jennson." She gave me a compassionate smile. "I can't imagine what you're going through, Mrs. Jennson. I don't have children of my own but I've seen parents in this situation more times than I can count. So I know that it's terribly painful, you don't have to be careful around me. There will be many times when you'll feel like you have to keep your feelings in check, but you and me, along with your husband, and Jake and the other nurses—we're a team now. We're like family, and none of us expects you to minimize what you're feeling."

I wiped my eyes. "Thank you," I whispered. "You can call me Elaine, please."

She tapped the paper in my hand. "Don't think of it as charity, think of it as a gift. They do a really great job, and I promise it'll make Jake smile. That's what we try to do here; keep the kids smiling."

"Thank you," Nathan said.

Signey left us alone and for a few minutes all I could do was watch Jake sleeping and wonder which of the two wounds inside me was going to be the one to take me down.

"I'll go home and pack a suitcase," Nathan said. "There are some arrangements I'll have to make at the office as well. I can set up a remote workstation, but there are meetings I have to be present for over the next couple of months."

I heard him, of course, but I couldn't think of what to say.

"When I'm back," he went on, "you should go home, get a bit of rest and bring a suitcase as well. Maybe let Linda know what the visiting hours are, what room Jake's in. I'm sure he'd like to be able to see Tyler."

"I know we can't talk about our discovery here," I said, "but we do have to at some point."

"Alright," Nathan said. "But not in the hospital."

He kissed Jake's forehead lightly, careful not to wake him, and then came to me and did the same. "Roger's still downstairs," he said. "We'll head out together, so I can leave you the car."

Roger. I'd forgotten he was down there, waiting. He would want to know why I asked him to come. I supposed it could wait now. If Jake wasn't even my biological son, he certainly wasn't Roger's. "Sure. Make sure he knows to come and give a blood sample."

He left, and I sat down in the recliner to keep vigil for when Jake woke up. The television quickly got on my nerves, though, so I stood to switch it off. Silence descended, and through it I could barely make out Nathan's voice. I went to the door and looked outside to see him with Signey.

"...don't think that she'd go that far," he was telling her, "but in the past, she was triggered by stressful situations. I'm only telling you to make sure she doesn't have access to the pharmacy or wherever you keep your medications and to make sure no one gives her anything."

"We don't just hand out medication, Mr. Jennson," Signey said, "and our pharmacy is locked with key card entry; she can't get in there. But I'll take it under advisement."

She glanced past him, spotted me, but made no indication that she had. I slipped back into the room, my face hot with embarrassment. Easy enough for Nathan to ask me to trust him, but apparently trusting me was too much to expect.

My anger towards him simmered, but I wasn't sure whether it was entirely out of line. I didn't trust myself one hundred percent right now. My mind kept going back to the moment that I had gotten Jake back after he'd been taken. Or, the moment I thought I had gotten him back.

I had been in treatment at the time. That whole six-month period that Jake was gone I was an "in-patient," which, as far as I was concerned, was just a polite way of saying I had been committed. Day in, day out I had lived a nightmare, broken into a hundred jagged pieces that no longer fit together. That was until Nathan had come to me with our baby, recovered at last and healthy. Mine again. My son.

I held Jake in my arms and snuggled close to him and it was like all those pieces picked themselves up and fitted together neatly again. The cracks were still there, but they were glued in place with something stronger.

How could I have mistaken that infant for my own son? Had I wanted it so badly that I couldn't see the differences? Had Nathan?

The memory of Mildred Turner's red face and bloodshot eyes assaulted me, wet with real tears, the snot and spittle over her lips almost a froth, inside the courtroom the day she was sentenced along with her husband. She had raged and screamed at me as the bailiff took them away. *"You took my son, you monster, you bitch! God will never forgive you. You're going straight to hell!"*

Her shrieking may as well have happened seconds ago. My stomach turned.

Was it possible? Was there any way that she could have been right?

Had I stolen that poor woman's son from her?

13

In the hours after Nathan left, the only reprieve I got from the pit I was slowly digging for myself was hardly an escape at all. Signey came in to take Jake for his bone marrow biopsy. The time had gone by quickly while I stewed. When she knocked, I was startled out of my brooding.

"Sorry," she said. "I didn't mean to surprise you. We're all ready for him. Would you like to wake him up or...?"

"I'll do it," I said. I stood and went to Jake's bedside, but hesitated. "I've heard that it's painful."

Signey shook her head. "His records show that he's been under anesthesia before without any reaction when he had a tooth pulled," she said. "So the plan is to put him under for it. He'll be sore for a couple days afterward, but it won't be bad."

That didn't make me feel any better. As my hand wavered over Jake's form I had the most ludicrous thought.

This was the first time I would touch my son after learning that he wasn't the child I had lost. It seemed wrong, almost, to wake him up—as if I no longer had the right. His biological mother should be the one to do it.

I pushed through the guilt and woke him, and for the next hour as he changed into a hospital gown for the first time and then lay on the table, I was distracted by Jake's vulnerability. He hated the needle, but the tattooed orderly who had entertained him before was present. Mark was his name, it turned out—I hadn't caught it before, or hadn't remembered.

Instead of having Jake count backwards from one hundred as they gave him the shot to put him under, Mark had him list every Avenger he could think of.

"Captain America," Jake said, "Iron Man, Thor... um... Hulk..."

The corners of his lips turned up slightly as his eyes closed. Horror gripped me as I saw his eyes roll up just as his eyelids shut. I held one of his feet, searching for some sign of a pulse.

Of course, the machine monitoring his heart made a regular, if slower, beeping.

The bone marrow aspiration was fast, and I forced myself to watch it from start to finish even as they drove a needle that could have been an ice pick into his hip.

Although they woke him up afterward, Jake promptly fell back to sleep. Mark and Signey helped move him back to his room, where I took up my post once more and waited there in the dark and the quiet of the hospital room until Nathan returned.

By then my eyes were burning and I was exhausted, but I couldn't imagine sleeping. The only time I left the room was to retrieve coffee, and when he arrived, the cold cup beside the recliner was either number four or five.

"How is he?" Nathan asked as he put his suitcase down—as if his condition could have changed in the time since he'd left.

"They took some bone marrow," I said. "For the donor comparison and I guess also for the gene therapy. I don't know, I barely looked at the papers."

"You signed something without looking at it?" he asked. "Elaine, you have to—"

"It's Saint Monica's, Nathan," I said. "Not the *Island of Doctor Moreau*."

He stood by Jake's bed, watching him. "You need some rest," he said. "Why don't you head home? I had Roger drop me off at the house and came back in your car. It's in patient parking, lot C, all the way to the back."

"I could have Linda bring a suitcase," I said. "She wouldn't mind."

Nathan pressed his lips together and busied himself pulling

Jake's blanket over his shoulders. "Even so, some rest would do you good. Help you clear your mind."

"My mind is perfectly clear," I lied. It was nothing of the sort. That was the problem—sleeping wasn't going to fix that but being alone might well make it worse. "And we have things to talk about."

He shook his head. "Not right now we don't," he said. "Not when you're…"

"When I'm what?" I rubbed my forehead and reached for the coffee. It was cold and bitter and swallowing a gulp made me want to throw it up.

Nathan took the cup from me as I leaned to put it back down and held his hand out. "Come on, at the very least you need to go and get your things. We're going to be pretty much living here for weeks."

Living here. I hated the way that sounded. No one 'lived' in a hospital.

Nathan had implied I was in a bad state of mind and he wasn't wrong. This wasn't me—I wasn't an angry person, I wasn't combative with my husband. But nothing sounded more dangerous than sleep and all the horrible things my unconscious was likely to start unpacking the moment my guard was down.

"I'll go get a suitcase," I said, ignoring his hand and standing on my own. "When are we going to talk?"

He ran his fingers through his hair and rubbed the back of his neck, his jaw muscles trembling. "Goddamn it, Elaine—I don't know, alright? Maybe you can handle dealing with both of these things at the same time but I'm under a ton of pressure here and at work. This isn't easy."

I was close enough to catch a whiff of something on his breath. Alcohol.

Roger, that son of a bitch.

"Have you been drinking?" I asked.

Nathan took a step away from me like I'd hit him, but his eyes sank and anchored to the floor. "It was just one drink. Roger insisted, and I accepted because I'm frightened out of my mind. It's fine."

It would have been a convenient moment to lay into him, and there was a part of me that felt a sudden justification coming on that was dangerous in the extreme. I quashed both of those impulses. For one, I didn't want to wake Jake with our fighting. For another, well—bad enough he was worried about me losing my mind or falling off my own wagon, I didn't need to make it worse by losing my temper in public.

"I'll be back tonight," I said.

He didn't argue, just watched me as I left.

I found the car where he said it was and made my way carefully out of the hospital parking deck. No amount of coffee could make me as alert as I needed to be after a day like this one. I was exhausted but determined to make it home and back.

When I did finally pull into our driveway, having driven there on autopilot, unable to remember almost any of the drive itself, I turned the car off but left the lights on.

Our garage door was open as was the door to the kitchen inside.

14

I dialed 911 but ended the call before it connected. The kitchen light was on, casting light into the garage through the door, but the rest of the house was dark. My last encounter with the police had left me feeling like I was seeing things, and I wanted to be sure there was something tangible to report before I called them this time.

For a few minutes I closely watched the light through the door, looking for a sign of some shadow, someone moving around inside. Hank came to mind immediately. Had he come here looking for us? Had he come hoping to get his son back? And if he had, could I possibly turn him away?

A knock on my passenger side window scared me badly, and I gave a short bark of fright before I realized who it was.

Linda's concerned face peered at me through the window. She motioned for me to unlock the door, and I did.

"You scared me to death," I muttered as she got into the car and closed the door behind her. She had her purse with her and settled it on her lap.

"I saw you sitting out here and wondered what was up," she said. "I tried to get news from Nathan a couple of hours ago when he came by, but—"

I shook my head. "A couple of hours? I just came from the hospital. I left right after he came in."

Linda frowned as she caught sight of my open door. "Well, he didn't leave your door open. I'd have noticed and closed it."

Who needed a guard dog when I had Linda Keeler for a neighbor? "Did you see anyone coming in?"

"Not since Nathan left, but I've been putting the kids to bed," she said. "Maybe you should call the police?"

"Not yet." I opened the door to get out.

"Where are you going, hon?" Linda asked, but she opened her door as well. "You can't go in there, what if someone's still there?"

"If someone's broken in the alarm would have gone off," I said. "There would be police here already. Look." I pointed to the eave above the garage door where a tiny red light indicated the cameras were still working.

"Alright," Linda said, "well, I'll go in with you at least."

The thought of going in alone wasn't appealing, so I didn't argue. We crept through the garage to the open door, and I hovered in front of it trying to get as thorough a look as I could before going in. What I could see was still the way I'd left it, though it looked like Nathan had changed shoes and left his other pair sitting out of place by the shoe rack inside the door.

"See anything?" Linda asked.

"Nothing out of the ordinary," I whispered. The door creaked a bit as I pushed it further open. Linda followed me into the kitchen, and from there we crept into the darkened living room. There was no light coming from upstairs. Could it have simply been Nathan leaving in a hurry? I tried to see through the darkness of the downstairs hallway. A faint glow came from the office. "The office door is open."

I heard a distinct sound of a gun being cocked behind me. I stiffened as I sucked in a breath, but a gentle hand pulled my attention around. Linda had a *handgun*.

"What is that?" I asked sharply. "Put it away, Linda, I can't believe you brought *a gun* with you."

She brandished the weapon. I didn't recognize the type, I don't know a thing about guns, but it looked modern; the sort you see on television in cop shows, gunmetal black and dangerous even if it was pointed at the ceiling. "I have a permit," she said as if that excused it.

"Be careful," I breathed. "Don't *shoot* anyone."

"The safety's on," Linda said. "Don't be so jumpy. This is exactly the reason I have it in the first place. Stay behind me."

I let her go ahead and we made our way to the office. The glow inside came from the computers, a small collection of them that Nathan had set up to both store footage from the cameras and to use on the occasions he worked from home. The light they emitted was weak, but since there were a dozen or so, the room was cast in a pallor that was a step above pitch black. Satisfied there was no one there, I switched the light on.

"Anything missing?" Linda asked.

"No," I said, though I'd only glanced around. If someone had come in to rob us, there was plenty to take.

For good measure, Linda insisted on taking a look at the rest of the house. There was nothing to find. No intruders that Linda could fill with bullets, and when that became clear, Linda put her gun away in her oversized purse. "Well, I don't know," she said. "Maybe Nathan did leave the door open. I could have sworn that he didn't but maybe I wasn't paying enough attention."

A thought occurred to me, which I hoped wouldn't make Linda think I was crazy. "You didn't happen to see a car outside, did you? A black town car? The fancy looking kind?"

Linda shook her head slowly. "I don't think so... why?"

As much as I appreciated her, Linda was decidedly not the

person to tell that whole story to. "No reason. I guess I'm on edge with everything going on. It's been a day like you can't imagine."

"If you say so," she said. "Do you want to talk about it?"

The idea of being home alone did make me a bit nervous though the specter of Linda's firearm did as well. I waved the offer off with a weary smile. "There's a lot to say but… not right now. I need to pack my things. We're going to be taking up residence in Jake's room for the next few weeks. Actually, if you wouldn't mind bringing in our mail from time to time? I can leave you a key, I'd appreciate it."

She practically lit up with the joy of being asked. "Well of course I can, sweetie. You know I'm happy to help you with anything. Ask and I'm there."

We made our way to the kitchen as Linda insisted that I detail any other chores she might need to do. Most of them she supplied herself—watering the flowers in front of the porch, mowing our lawn, basically anything she could think of. How she found the hours in the day was a mystery to me, but I didn't deny her anything. She made it sound like I was chartering a vacation to somewhere tropical and should be thanking me for letting her help.

"And I'll bring Tyler by to hang out a couple of times a week after school," she said when I had finally herded her to the door.

"Jake would like that," I said. "And so would I. Visiting hours are nine to eight, I think. He's on the second floor, room 52. You can ask for him at the front desk."

"I'll do that," she said. She hugged me and then wagged a finger at the inside of the house. "If you see or hear anything funny, you call me and I'll be over faster than you can say 'license to carry.' Okay?"

"Good night, Linda," I said, and let her leave so that I could close the door and breathe a sigh of relief. A lingering thread of nervousness hummed in my spine and in my stomach, but we had checked the house thoroughly. Surely, it had only been a mistake.

To be sure, though, after I started a pot of coffee I went back to the office and sat down in front of the computer desk to examine the camera footage. If Nathan had left home two hours before he'd arrived at the hospital, where had he been? Maybe drinking with Roger, though almost an hour and a half seemed enough time for more than a single drink. I'd have to have a talk with Roger about that.

I opened the files where the cameras dropped ten minute videos and scrolled through what should have been the most recent ones.

There weren't any. Not from any of the cameras. All the footage from that day was gone.

15

Nathan answered the third time I called him, just as I was about to give up. "What is it?" he asked, his voice low. "Everything alright?"

"Why didn't you answer before?"

Nathan breathed heavily into the receiver. "It's late, and I didn't want to wake our son. Are you on your way back?"

"All the camera footage from today is deleted," I said. "At the house, I checked the cameras and today is blank. Did you clear it out?"

"Did I delete the footage? Why were you looking? Did something happen?"

"It doesn't matter why I was looking, Nathan," I said. "Did you delete it or not?"

"Yeah," he said. "I cleared it to make some space since we're going to be away."

I scrolled through the videos. They went back two weeks. Everything older than that was deleted automatically. "And you only cleared today?"

"Elaine, what's this about?" His voice was louder now, with the slight echo of a larger space. He must have left Jake's room. "Why does it matter?"

"When I came home the door was open," I said. "And the cameras were on but they haven't gotten any footage since you left the house. There should be at least six or seven videos by now."

"I turned them off," he said. "The door was open? Is anything missing?"

I stood and paced the room, disbelieving what I'd heard. "Nothing is missing—you turned the cameras *off*? Why would you do that?"

"The only reason they're even there is to make you feel safer, Elaine," Nathan breathed. "No one is going to break into our house, we live in Avila Grove—the crime rate is zero. I must've left the door open when I took off. I was in a hurry."

Not so much of a hurry that he came straight to the hospital. What was going on here? What was my husband hiding? "When did you leave?"

"The house?"

"Yes, Nathan, when did you leave the house?"

He didn't answer immediately. "I guess... about seven or so."

A little shy of three hours; it was ten now. It fit with what Linda said. "Where did you go before you came to the hospital?"

"Do you really have to ask?"

I opened my mouth to tell him that yes, I really did have to—but closed it when I recalled the smell of whiskey on his breath. So, he had left, and gone with Roger to have a drink. And maybe he really had left the door open.

But the cameras? They were active now, watching, but they hadn't deposited any recordings. Maybe it was overkill to even have them but that didn't really warrant switching off the recordings. "I guess I don't," I said. "I'll be back soon. I made some coffee—real coffee—so I'll pack a bag and maybe shower. It'll be late."

"You should stay at home," Nathan said. "Get some sleep. I think you need it, and it's going to be a long day tomorrow. I can stay here until about seven, maybe eight, so come over in the morning."

"I can't sleep here," I said. "Not with Jake over there."

I clicked through the camera controls and turned the record feature back on. There was some way to have the videos uploaded to a cloud service in there somewhere, but I couldn't find it.

"One night," Nathan said. "For me, Elaine, please. I need you to get some real rest."

I leaned back in the office chair and closed my eyes. They almost didn't open again. "Maybe," I said. "I'll call you when I'm on my way."

"Alright," he said. "Try not to worry so much. I love you."

The words I should have said never made it to my lips. I hung up, and laid the phone down on the desk, staring at it like it might scold me for being a bad partner. Especially right now. Nathan was hurting, I could see that, could feel it in my own heart. But at the moment the words "I love you" seemed hollow.

I could barely breathe knowing that my son was missing. Nathan somehow was managing to carry on. How could we possibly mean the same thing when we said those words? When I said them, I meant *us*—our family, our home, our lives together. What did he mean when he said it?

I drummed my fingers on the desk, watching the camera feeds on the computer monitor, or at least looking through them. There had to be something that I could do. Some place I could look, or someone I could talk to. I could hire a private investigator, maybe. But there was no way to do that without using our mutual accounts, and Nathan seemed insistent on doing nothing for the moment. Of course, there was the interview coming up soon…

It had entirely slipped my mind. When was that? A few days

away. I should have rescheduled or even cancelled it. Who was going to hire me at a time like this? *I'd be thrilled to work here, but so we're clear, I can't actually come in for any length of time and I have no idea how long that will last because my kid has—my kid is* sick *and might be for months to come. Would you mind waiting?* Fat chance.

It occurred to me, though, that there might be someone I could speak with. For that matter, someone who deserved to hear from me now. Someone who was bound to know the truth whether she cared to give it to me or not after what I'd done.

In the back corner of the office there were a set of filing cabinets. In the bottom drawer of the older cabinet was a thick file that I typically tried to forget was there. I took it from the drawer now and paged through it, looking for the papers I had put in here after the Turners were sentenced. The court filings were there as well as the transcripts… but not all of them. I paged back through the documents, looking at the dates. November 10th, 17th, 21st… and then the day before the jury returned their guilty verdict a month later. The summary of the sentencing was missing, along with a month's worth of transcripts.

I looked through the papers again, pulled them out and laid them on the desk one at a time. They were all in order, and by the time the file was empty I was sure—I hadn't misplaced the papers, they were gone.

This wasn't right. It had been years since I looked at these documents, but I was certain I had kept all of them. Had

Nathan gone through them and thrown out portions? If he had, why not throw the entire file away?

My phone rang. Roger. Must be calling to find out what I hadn't told him at the hospital. I let it ring while I weighed whether to answer. In the end, before it went to voicemail, I did.

"Roger," I said. "Nathan tells me you two had a drink before he came back to the hospital. Care to explain?"

"Elaine, I didn't know if you'd answer," he said. "Ah... yeah, about that. Nate seemed like he was a little stressed. It was only one, I promise. He didn't even push for a second one, you've got nothing to worry about. How are you holding up?"

"Don't change the subject," I said. I picked the documents from the trial up and stuffed them back into the folder and left the office.

"Alright," he said. "I apologize. It was my idea. The poor guy looked like he'd been wrung out. I'm sure you're no better off."

"That's an understatement." Once I was in the kitchen, I got myself a mug and filled it with coffee. I barely tasted it. "Please don't do it again. Now of all times, I need him to stay sober. I need *me* to stay sober."

"Understood," Roger said. "Listen, are you at the house yet? Nathan said you'd gone home."

"I'm there now," I told him.

"Oh," he said. "Well, it's probably too late now, but I came by after Nathan left and dropped some papers off in his office. I got a call from work while I was there, one of our servers crashed and I had to run and... well, I think I may have left your door open."

Linda hadn't mentioned anyone else coming by... but she had said she was busy with the kids. Surely Roger wouldn't have a reason to lie to me, and how would he have known otherwise? Unless Nathan called him. Hadn't Nathan also said he left the house in a hurry? Maybe it was just to placate me, calm me down. Was it possible they were somehow working together to cover up something as minor as leaving a door open?

"Elaine?" Roger asked. "You still there?"

I put the coffee down. "Yeah, I am," I said. "I'm spent, exhausted." And maybe the lack of sleep really was beginning to take its toll. Conspiracies over open doors? Insomnia, paranoia... all concerning words. "Don't worry about it. My neighbor was on lookout."

"Was she?" Roger asked. "She must have freaked out when she saw me, then. I'm surprised she didn't call the police."

"She must have missed you," I said. "She didn't see anyone. Thanks for calling, though, I was a little freaked out myself."

"I'm sorry, Ellie, didn't mean to cause you any more stress." He was quiet a moment. "So, at the hospital, you'd said you wanted me there for something other than the donor registry. Care to talk?"

"It was nothing urgent," I said quickly. I couldn't possibly tell him the truth at this point, that I had worried he might be Jake's father. I scrambled for some other reason. "It had to do with Jake. I've got that interview coming up so I'll need to take some time away. I wanted to see if you'd mind staying with him from time to time. Just a few hours, and I can ask Linda as well, so…"

"Oh, okay," he said. "Sure, of course. Anything you need, Ellie, call me."

"Great," I said. "Thanks, Rog."

"Well, if that's all," he said, "I should let you get some rest. Maybe I'll see you sometime tomorrow, I'll check in. I should order you two some delivery for lunch. Hospital food is the worst."

I chuckled and tried to make it sound genuine. "That'd be nice. Good night, Rog."

"Good night, Ellie. Sleep tight."

We hung up, and I leaned against the counter while I tried to slow my mind down. Mania—that was another word that fit right in with the other two. *You're making too much out of nothing,* I told myself. Me, Nathan, Roger; we were all stressed and running around in a hurry, focused on everything but the details.

Still, there were the missing pages from the case.

I poured the rest of the coffee out. Nathan was right. I needed sleep. The least I could do was try. I went upstairs, packed a suitcase with clothes that seemed comfortable enough to spend potentially weeks in the hospital, and stuffed a couple of extra blankets and pillows into a trash bag to take in as well. I didn't think Nathan had taken any with him.

Once that was done, I lay down with no real expectation of falling asleep. Unfortunately, I was wrong.

16

I dreamed.

I was back in our old apartment in the city, getting Jake ready for a bath. His face was a blur, but that didn't seem unusual to me. I took him from the kitchen to the bathroom where a bathtub the size of a pool was quickly filling with water that was too hot. In the middle was the bathing carrier that Jake fit into even though he wasn't really infant-sized.

Then Nathan was there, in the doorway to the bathroom. Yelling at me. *"What kind of mother are you? Who would leave their child alone in the bath?"*

"He's not alone," I shouted back, "I'm right here, I'm with him."

But I wasn't. Something was raining from above me like hail.

I caught the ice in my hands, but the ice was pills. Blue and orange and white. They melted just like hail pellets on my palms and sank into my skin. I fell backward, onto a hospital bed. I was screaming for them to let me go, but the hollow-eyed people standing over me didn't seem to hear me, or they didn't react. I clawed at them to no effect.

"He's gone, Elaine. Jake is gone."

I awoke, gasping for air, and immediately curled into myself to sob into my pillow. The alarm was going off and I let it blare at me while I cried until I was spent.

I hadn't had that dream for years. It had plagued me for months after I got Jake back—or, after I thought I had gotten him back. With it came the jagged guilt that filled my stomach like broken glass and made it hard to breathe or move.

After I turned the alarm off, I lay in bed staring at the ceiling. I had decisions to make.

I knew I had to do something. I had to look and find some-thing, anything, that could tell me where my son was. A part of me that sounded very much like Nathan scolded me for even thinking like that. I knew where my son was, didn't I? He was in a hospital bed, about to undergo a trial that I couldn't even fully comprehend. At the same time, though, he wasn't. I considered calling the police, the detective who had handled the case. Detective Perlman. But, if I did, there was the problem of my sick son and what would happen to him.

At length I pushed myself out of bed and dragged myself to the shower. *One more step,* I told myself at each turn. *One more step is all you have to take and then you can stop.* As long as I kept telling myself that each time I finished one small task, I could keep going.

I took those steps, one at a time, from the bathroom to the kitchen, and then to the office to collect the file so that I could look through it again, until finally I was getting into the car to leave. As I pulled out, a brown and tan station wagon down the street, some artifact of the seventies, pulled away from the curb. I watched warily as it followed me first down my own street, and then down the main road toward the exit from Avila Grove. By the time I turned onto the road toward town and saw it pull out and follow close behind me my heart was starting to speed up.

At the first light, though, the driver took a left while I went straight through.

Yeah, I was starting to come apart.

I got to the hospital just after six thirty, and Jake was awake, playing on his tablet while Nathan sat nearby looking at his phone with a familiar look of concentration and frustration. They both glanced up when I came in.

"Mom!" Jake waved me over and held his tablet up. "Dad got me a game, wanna see?"

Nathan smiled, but it was weak and didn't reach his eyes. "Did you sleep?"

"A little," I said. I put my suitcase in the corner and went to sit down next to Jake. "What have you got?"

"It's a sima… a simyoo…"

"A factory simulator," Nathan said. "Some of the guys at work play it. I thought he'd like it."

"You have to make these guys here," Jake said, pointing to the little robot icons in one corner of the screen, "and they make these little robots, and you have to make sure these things connect them all. And then you get points when these things get over to the blue box here."

It made no sense to me, but I grinned anyway and put my arm around Jake's shoulders. "Looks complicated. You're so smart, kiddo."

"I should get going," Nathan said as he stood. He tucked his phone into his jacket and ruffled Jake's hair to get his attention. Jake opened his arms, and the two had a long bear hug. "You be good today, don't burn the place down while I'm gone, okay?"

Jake giggled. "Okay, Dad."

Nathan came around the hospital bed and gave me a kiss on the way out. "You're going to be alright here?"

"Of course," I muttered. "We'll watch a movie or two, hang out."

He nodded slowly. "I may be a little late tonight. Not too late, I hope."

The unspoken question between us remained unasked and unanswered, but I could see in his eyes a suggestion that whatever the time to discuss it was going to be, it wasn't now and maybe not soon. "I'll see you tonight, then."

Nathan left, and I leaned back on the bed with Jake to watch him play. He stopped playing a few seconds after his dad left and looked up at me. "You and Dad didn't say I love you," he said. "I thought you were always s'posed to say I love you when you leave."

I had to catch the lump in my throat before it got out and kissed him on the head. "You're right. I guess we forgot this time, baby," I said. "I'll have to make it up to him when he gets back."

It was easy to forget that he was getting older, wiser, paying more attention. Some part of me wondered as well if he knew, deep down, what the truth was—if on some level he wasn't even aware of—he missed his real parents. *One day,* I thought, *he'll find out the truth. The truth always comes out. When it does, will he hate me?*

The chemotherapy drugs they started Jake on didn't show any particular side effects at first but within a few hours of their administration that morning, he drifted off. He was restless when he was awake and only ate a little at lunch. Jake was in and out of sleep most of the day. He was only twenty minutes into *How to Train your Dragon*, which I'd downloaded because it was one of his favorites.

Roger, true to his word, ordered Chinese food. Sweet and sour chicken for Jake—it was his favorite and had been since he was three—and Mongolian beef for me. It was a nice surprise even if he'd said he would do it. Signey warned me that Jake may not be able to keep it down depending on how fast he responded to the drugs, but it seemed to stay down.

I was busying myself looking for where Millie Turner had been sent when an unfamiliar number rang my phone. It was a local number, so I answered thinking it might be West End calling about my upcoming interview.

It wasn't. "Mrs. Jennson, hello. I hope you're doing well," the woman said. "This is Gert Olman, from Child Protective Services. Is now a good time to talk about our next visit?"

With everything else occupying my attention, I'd forgotten to call and schedule it. There was no telling how bad that looked. Jake was back to sleep, but I got up and left the room just in case he woke up. "Miss Olman, of course," I said. "I'm so sorry, I meant to call you back but with checking into the hospital and Jake starting chemo it slipped my mind."

"Oh," she said, "of course, of course. I'm terribly sorry you have to go through all of that. Well, I suspect that our visit will be short. What would be a good time to arrange it? The sooner we can get this all done and over with the better."

I wondered if she believed me. She'd seen the paperwork, of course, but who would arrange a visit like that to a hospital? I had to remind myself the woman was only doing her job. And she was right—the sooner it was over, the better. "Why don't you come by today? I've practically moved in. Though, if you want to speak with my husband as well, he won't be here until tonight."

"The main thing I need to do is to speak with Jake," she said. "And if there are any follow-up interviews needed, we can always arrange them afterwards."

In other words, if Jake said something to make her think we were somehow abusive or neglectful. I held my tongue for a couple of seconds. "Visiting hours are over at eight pm, so any time before then would be fine. You may have to wait for Jake to wake up, so I'd say block out a couple of hours to be safe. The drugs make him sleepy, you see, and it's important we let him rest when he needs to."

"I completely understand," she said with a tone that was just a little stiff. If she was dead set on this, I intended to make it as inconvenient as possible so she got the full experience. "Then, how about four this afternoon? And if I need to wait for Jake to wake up, then I don't mind at all."

I was sure she did mind. I considered waking Jake up around two to make sure he would sleep the afternoon away. Maybe it seemed cruel, taking my frustrations out on bureaucrats with no control over what job they had to do, but it beggared belief that she honestly thought there was anything here to investigate. "Four o'clock sounds... fine," I said. "I'll see if I can make sure he's awake before you get here, but I can't promise."

"I know it seems like I'm the enemy, Mrs. Jennson," Gert said. "No one likes dealing with Child Protective Services, and there are plenty of cases that get misreported or are misunderstandings. I'm just looking out for Jake's best interests. I hope you understand that."

"I'll see you at four, Miss Olman," I said quietly. "Thank you for calling."

I mashed the end-call button. Maybe she did mean well, but it felt more like an excuse for piling more stress on my shoulders.

Jake was still asleep when I returned to the room. I checked that his blankets were high enough and gently wiped some cold sweat from his forehead. Did he look like Millie Turner? Or Hank? My memory of their faces wasn't clear; I could only recall their eyes.

I took the court file out of my suitcase and sat down with it in the recliner, paging through it for the third time as if it would yield something new.

In a way, it did. I hadn't noticed before but near the end of the file was a sheet of paper where I had scrawled notes. This had been… maybe a month after the end of the trial. That's right— I had begun obsessing over the Turners. That was the first time I looked Hank Turner up and subscribed to the prison system's notifications. I had claimed to be a family member and expected to get denied, but apparently no one at the prison bothered to check.

Scribbled next to Hank's prisoner number was another one. I hadn't labeled it but it was Millie's prisoner number. I hadn't followed her because it was Hank that I had always been more worried about. Hank, the quiet one. Hank, who had watched me from the stand while he gave his testimony with a flat voice and empty eyes.

It was the quiet ones you had to watch, I had always heard. So, I watched Hank.

I went to the website and looked up Millie Turner's prisoner number. She'd been moved, apparently several years ago, from the Onida Women's Correction Facility to—

My breath caught and I had to close my eyes as horrible memories came rushing forward like a swarm of chattering bees all begging for attention. The off-white walls and slate gray tile. The uncomfortable bed that I had spent more than one or two nights cuffed to with no knowledge of what I had done. The doctors who smiled patiently, nodded understand- ingly, and then condemned me to "another couple of weeks" of "observation."

They'd moved Millie to Northgate Psychiatric Hospital.

The same hospital I was taken to the day after I tried to kill myself.

17

My hand shook as I put my phone down and closed the file. Mildred Turner was in the place that I had come to think of as my own personal hell. A place that I had buried so deep in my memory that there were even times when I could forget that I was ever there.

It wasn't that Northgate was a terrible place. As far as psychiatric facilities went, it was toward the high end. They had a criminal psychiatric wing on the opposite side of the complex from where I had stayed. Me and the other middle-class people who could afford to be there while we underwent treatment for everything from eating disorders to nervous breakdowns and, yes, failed suicide attempts.

Like plucking the silk of a spider's web, being reminded of that place triggered so many other memories I'd wanted to put away forever. The night I had made a mistake—one terrible mistake—and it had broken me. The deep, hollow pit of depression I had fallen into after Jake was born and all the self-loathing I had piled on myself. What kind of mother wasn't instantly, deeply, madly in love with her infant the moment she laid eyes on him? What kind of mother couldn't even do something as basic and human as produce breast milk for her hungry baby? Why was it that I struggled so hard to even get up in the morning when millions, no, *billions* upon billions, of mothers throughout human history had managed to power through the sleepless nights to raise the next generation?

I hugged myself as I watched Jake's chest rise and fall in the bed. What kind of mother didn't recognize that she was raising *someone else's child?*

I left the hospital room and headed for the café. I was so absorbed in my thoughts that as I turned the corner I nearly ran into a tall, heavyset gentleman in a suit. He smelled of cigarettes, maybe just coming back from a smoke. I muttered an apology and looked up into a stony face that gave me an inadvertent chill before I looked away.

"Perfectly alright," he said, his voice deep. "Don't worry about it."

We went around one another and I marched to the elevator and took it up to the third floor where the better cafeteria was. There was one on the main floor where we were, but it was more for the general populace of the hospital. The one upstairs had fewer people, something I'd learned the first day there.

"Medium dark roast," I told the girl behind the counter where the coffee was. "With a shot of espresso, please. No room."

"Sure thing," she said. A petite thing, with bright red hair, the same girl who had been there the day before. "It was Elaine, wasn't it?"

I looked at her, embarrassed. "Yes, that's right. I'm sorry I... don't think I caught your name before."

"I'm Lucy," she said, her smile genuine and bright.

"Hi, Lucy," I said. "I suppose we'll be getting to know one another, huh?"

Lucy plucked a medium cup from a stack of them and went about getting my espresso shot into it. "You've got someone staying here?"

"My son." I dug in my pocket for cash, came up short, and realized then that I had left my purse and my cards in the room. "Oh, damn—wait a moment on that, Lucy, I left my money in the room."

She flipped the switch, and the machine began to burble out espresso. "Whoops." She winked at me. "I guess I'll have to remember for next time. Don't worry about it."

Mortified, I made a note to myself not to forget. "Thank you."

While she went about her work, I examined the other people here, wondering who had heard the exchange. The last thing I wanted was to be the local charity case. In one corner, away from the entrance to the café, I saw the man I'd run into in the hallway. He was looking at his phone with nothing on his little bistro table.

I tore my eyes away. It was a public space, anyone was allowed to be here. For all I knew, he was in the same boat as me, staying with a son or daughter and praying this wouldn't be the last place he spent time with them. In fact, we'd probably be seeing a lot of one another if that was the case. I considered introducing myself after our previous run-in. It might be nice to have a friend after all.

"Here you go," Lucy said.

I turned to take the coffee from her. "Thank you so much, Lucy. I promise, I'll pay for it next time. Don't let me forget, okay?"

Lucy waved a hand. "The doctors get free coffee here all the time," she said. "I won't tell if you won't."

I thanked her again and headed toward the door. The necessary nerve to introduce myself to the stranger didn't quite congeal. I had never been particularly social even when I was at my best. Instead I left the café and returned to the pediatric oncology ward. Signey intercepted me before I reached Jake's room.

"I've got some news," she said. "Dr. Saito should come and tell you himself pretty soon. He's ordered a series of comparison tests. It's a panel we have to do, it means they've got a short list of possible donors. It's good news!"

A bit of relief swept through me, taking the edge off of everything else. "That's great," I said. "God, I needed some good news. If that's the case, when will it start? How long does it last? Does it mean we're almost done?"

She deflated slightly. "Well... not exactly. There's still the chemo to finish first. But now we've found these potential donors, it may mean Jakob will only need one round of chemotherapy."

That was disappointing, but I supposed it was still a positive development. I imagined there were people who waited for a donor and never found one. "Thanks for letting me know."

Signey accompanied me into Jake's room, took down his vitals and checked all the machines and fluids. As she was leaving, I saw the man again, passing by the room. Maybe on his way to the nurses' station.

"That man," I asked, "the big guy in the suit, do you know his name? I ran into him earlier. He must have a child in the ward, right?"

She peered out the door and then looked back and shook her head. "No, I don't think so. I'm familiar with all the patients here, and their parents. He could be visiting someone though."

I went to the door to lean out. He was sitting on a chair at the end of the hallway. After a second he looked up, saw the two of us watching him, and then reached into his pocket and pulled out his phone. He stood and left.

"Have you seen him before?" I asked.

He had smelled like cigarettes. Maybe I was crazy, but hadn't the driver of the black car been smoking that night?

"I… can't say that I have, but it's visiting hours," Signey said. "Is everything okay?"

"Could you keep an eye on Jake for me?" I asked. "Just for a little bit."

She nodded, confused, but I didn't care to explain. I trotted down the hallway and turned the corner. There was no sign of him right away, but the elevator door was closing and there was a sliver of black suit sleeve visible through the brief opening. The arrow above the door pointed up. That was four floors… but one of them led to the parking deck.

I entered the door to the staircase and then raced up the stairs two at a time. When I arrived at the fourth floor, I was winded but determined to confront the man, I had to find out why he was watching me. Maybe Hank was smarter than I'd given him credit for and had hired a private investigator. Maybe someone was still looking for Jake, his real parents if it wasn't the Turners, and this man thought he'd found him. Whatever it was, I had to know.

When I came through the door to the fourth-floor hallway, the elevator light was already pointing down. I took a left and jogged down the hallway toward the bridge to the parking deck, scanning every corner as I did. I couldn't miss him, he was a big guy and there weren't that many people here in black suits.

I made it to the sliding doors that led to the bridge without spotting him. Had I been wrong? He could have gone back to the café, maybe forgotten something. Or he was staying out of sight.

The doors opened and I went through them to check the parking deck, just in case. It was relatively quiet. I didn't hear any doors opening or closing, or any engines running. My lack of fitness caught up with me, and I had to lean against the concrete pillar that marked one side of the entrance to the deck to catch my breath.

I'd lost him. And what was worse, I wasn't even sure that he was up to no good. Oh, hell—what would I *do* if he was? I didn't have a gun, unlike Linda. It wasn't like I had any kind of training or any other means of defending myself. What was I thinking chasing this man?

I suddenly felt very exposed and turned to head back into the hospital. As I did, I heard a car's engine. Half out of reflex and half out of curiosity I looked over my shoulder.

A black town car came down the ramp from the upper level of

the deck, drove past the bridge, and continued toward the lower level.

I realized I was pressed against the wall of the bridge, holding my breath.

It was *him*. That was the car, and the man I'd seen in the hospital was the man inside it. I *wasn't* crazy.

18

I chewed my lip and what was left of the nail on my right middle finger as I rode the elevator back down and hurried to Jake's room. Now that I was certain someone was following me, I scoured my memory for every instance I'd seen that car. There had been more than a few times, I was sure of it. I chided myself for not having thought to try and get the tag number.

"Mrs. Jennson," Signey said as I came close to the room. She'd stayed, God bless her.

"Signey," I said, "I'm so sorry, that man from before... I thought... well, I'm not sure what I thought. You're going to think I'm crazy, I know, but if you see him here again would you mind introducing yourself, maybe asking if he knows someone here?"

"Sure, Mrs. Jennson," Signey said, "I don't mind at all but—"

"I realize how it sounds," I cut in when she looked distressed about the prospect. "It's likely to be nothing at all but it would be one small favor that I would really, really appreciate."

She put a hand on my shoulder, her eyebrows pinched. "It's no trouble at all, Elaine, but there's someone here to see Jake. She says she's from, ah… from Child Protective Services."

"What?" I looked past her, down the hallway, and then into Jake's room. "Where is she? What time is it?"

"Ten till four," Signey said. "I took her to the waiting area. She said she was early. It's none of my business, and I haven't said anything to anyone. But you should see her. We've had social workers come in with warrants when parents denied them access…"

I stiffened. "There would be nothing to say, I was expecting her visit. There was a whole misunderstanding at Jake's school, it's no big deal. Could you show me to her?"

"Of course," she said. "She's down in the waiting area by the nurses' station."

I stopped her as she turned to lead me in that direction. "Ah, this is silly, but… how do I look?"

Signey's sighed and smiled sympathetically. "Like you've been living in a hospital for the past two days and been worried out of your mind. Anyone would understand, and

139

every parent here looks the same. If you need me, page me from the room, okay?"

She led me down the hall to where, indeed, Gertrude Olman waited in a chair, her back straight, a small briefcase over her knees. She was in the kind of plain brown pencil skirt and jacket that made her look like a disappointed schoolmarm. When she spotted me, she stood quickly and plastered on a professional smile.

"Mrs. Jennson, it's good to see you," she said. "I'm a little early, my last visit wrapped up quickly. Is Jake up?"

I hadn't looked in on him before I left the room. "Possibly," I said. "He's been in and out. Please, he's this way."

She followed me to Jake's room. He wasn't up, but he'd been asleep for some time, so I gave him a gentle nudge and brushed sweaty hair from his feverish face. "Hi there, sleepy head."

"Hi," he mumbled. He looked around. "Is Dad here?"

"No, sweetie." I hid my disappointment at not being enough for him. I doubt he meant it that way, but I wanted to be the one he looked for when he woke up. Selfish, I know. "Listen, this lady is Mrs. Olman. She's from... well, she wants to ask you a few questions. How are you feeling?"

He eyed her warily. "What kind of questions?"

Gert took a step further into the room and waved. "Hi, Jakob. You're not in any kind of trouble. If it's okay, I'd like to get to know you a little bit. I hear that you've been really brave lately. I'm very impressed."

Jake shrugged and looked to me for approval or permission. Maybe reassurance.

"It's okay," I said.

"Sure," Jake told her.

I stepped back and started to sit, but Gertrude reached a hand out to forestall me. "Actually, Mrs. Jennson, I'm required to speak to Jakob privately. It won't take long, I promise."

Right, of course. She couldn't have me in the background pressuring him or leading his answers, else how was she supposed to discover all my foul misdeeds? I kept my face as neutral as I could. "Of course. I'll go get some coffee." I wasn't sure what I'd done with my last cup. Had I tossed it when I went after my stalker? That was proof enough that I needed more.

"I'll check in with you afterward so we can close this file," she said as I went to the door.

I gave Jake a last reassuring look. "Whatever she asks," I said, "you can answer honestly, okay? I'll be back soon to check on you."

"Okay, Mom," Jake said. He was already scooching up in the bed, messing with the controls to raise the back of it.

I left them to their conversation, my heart pounding unreasonably. Another trip to the upstairs café was out of the question. I would be too embarrassed to show my face so soon. Instead, I went to the common area down the hallway and filled a Styrofoam cup with the watered-down swill they had prepared there. I wasn't sure at this point that I even needed the caffeine as much as the distraction.

There were too many things on my mind for me to give any of them attention without feeling guilty about the others. I was sure that man had been following me. Private investigators were always better at staying out of sight on television, weren't they? But I couldn't think of who else it would be.

Even worrying about it felt selfish though. My son was in a hospital room, fighting the worst kind of sickness a child could have and doing it while he navigated waters with a woman who he wasn't aware was dangerous. What child didn't have something bad to say about their parents? Could Gertrude tell the difference between discipline and child abuse? Did she even have children of her own? I found myself prematurely furious with Child Protective Services for not hiring people with better qualifications. Until you had a child, you just couldn't understand what it was like being a parent and balancing a laundry list of critical needs with trying to raise a well-adjusted human being to adulthood.

My ruminating was interrupted by a polite clearing of a man's throat. "Mrs. Jennson?"

He was a youngish guy, maybe early thirties, in a suit rather than scrubs or a white coat. "Yes?"

"They said I might find you here," he said and approached with a hand extended. "I'm Henry Pullman. I'm with administration." After we shook, he fingered the ID badge at his lapel.

"Is there something I need to sign?" I asked.

"Not as such," he said, and shuffled through a file folder. "It's just that… there seems to be some discrepancy with your son's medical records. It's probably nothing serious but, you know, we have to dot all the i's and cross all the t's."

"What discrepancy?" I held my breath. I knew something like this was going to happen. When I saw Nathan again I was going to strangle him, we never should have lied to Dr. Saito.

"I understand that Jake was adopted," he said, "which is noted in your file here but when we received medical records, well… the thing is that there's a birth certificate? The odds are fairly long, but it's possible we have duplicate records, so I need to ask you a few questions."

Questions. Goddamn it. I needed Nathan here to be the one to lie. It wasn't my strong suit. "Is there any way this can wait? I know it's important, of course, it's just… I'm exhausted, you know. If we could do this first thing in the morning, that would be so much better."

Henry winced apologetically. "Gosh, I know, and I'm so sorry, but I can't really wait that long. I need to prepare the papers for the insurance company and, since we've been on such a tight schedule, we're already late, so…"

"Ok," I said. "I understand. Have a seat, or should I come with you?"

"Oh, this is fine," he said. "It'll be brief, it's only a few questions. Of course, I can't let you see the medical records until this is confirmed. Let's see…"

He flipped to a page and then turned to face me so that I couldn't see the contents of the file. "Do you recall at what age Jakob received his first MMR immunization? Mumps, measles, rubella?"

"He was a baby, I guess," I said. "And then… around kindergarten. Don't all kids?"

"You would be surprised," Henry muttered. "And was Jakob seen for a spot of the flu when he was four?"

I remembered that clearly. I'd been scared witless. It was also right before I had taken my first valium, hoping to damp down some of the anxiety. "No," I said. "We've never taken him to the doctor for the flu."

"And… lastly what was the name of his previous physician? Where you lived prior to Michigan." He looked up at me, face unreadable. I knew that I had given the wrong answer for the other question, shouldn't that have proven this was the wrong file? Started the process over again?

"Doctor… O'Leary," I said, snatching the name from somewhere in my memory.

Henry looked down at his file and frowned, then marked

something down. "Well… that is all I have for you. Sorry to inconvenience you, especially now."

"Is that it?" I asked. "I mean… what happens next?"

He waved his pen before he tucked it into his breast pocket. "Nothing you need to be worried about at all. I assure you, your insurance is already paying for Jakob's treatment—this is simply a formality for compliance. Handling these little hiccups is what they pay me to do. Have a nice day, Mrs. Jennson."

With that, he left. The hand that I held my coffee in was shaking, and I set the cup down. Any answer at all would have been better than nothing. Jake's birth certificate would have mine and Nathan's names on it. Surely, the odds of a mistake like that would be astronomical. There was no way Henry believed that they'd gotten the wrong records, was there? Two identically named families from the same hospital? Lying couldn't even buy us time.

I sent Nathan a quick text. *Admin asked about Jake's birth certificate.*

A few seconds after, a message came back. *Don't panic. Delete this text.*

Don't panic, he said. Don't panic? It was like he and I were living in two different realities. I did what he asked, though, and swiped the texts to delete them before I put my phone away.

My feet itched to take me back to Jake's room, to listen in on his conversation with Gertrude, but after witnessing me chase someone through the hospital halls, I was sure the staff thought I was crazy. I paced the waiting area instead and sipped my bitter, watery coffee until finally Gert came past the room, spotted me, and invited me to sit with her.

"So, is there something I need to sign, or…?" I asked.

Gert shook her head lightly and placed both of her hands on top of the briefcase on her lap. "Mrs. Jennson, Jakob seems concerned about the state of his parents' relationship," she said. "From his perspective, it seems like you and Mr. Jennson are experiencing some tension."

I stared at her. "We have a son gravely ill in hospital," I said coolly. "Are you married, Miss Olson? Do you have children?"

"I'm not, Mrs. Jennson, but I am—"

"Until you're married and have children of your own," I cut in, "I'm afraid you simply aren't qualified to comprehend what my husband and I are going through. I'm quite certain that my son did not indicate that Nathan and I are abusive or negligent in any way, so if you've had your fun then I'd like to politely ask that you leave now, and that we close this case so that I can focus on the very real problem of my son's health."

"Who is Hank Turner, Mrs. Jennson?" she asked.

My mouth worked, but nothing came out immediately. I had to

force it. "He... is the man who, along with his wife... abducted Jake when he was three months old. From our home."

"Are you aware that Jake has heard you and Mr. Jennson talking about Hank? Have either of you ever spoken to him about what happened?"

"Absolutely not," I said. "He doesn't need to know about that. It's history, and it's a very painful history, so I'd appreciate it if you left it alone, please."

Gert leaned toward me. "Children *listen*, Mrs. Jennson. They listen to everything and they often understand more than we think. I've been a clinical social worker in some capacity for almost thirty years. I may not have children, but I know how to talk with them and how to listen to them. All I am telling you is that your son is concerned about the state of his family —his security—at a time when he is already suffering a great deal of guilt and anger about his illness. Do you know what he said to me?"

I shook my head slowly, mortified.

"He worries that you and your husband are fighting because he's sick," she said. "That's when it started. When he came here, to this hospital. Now, it's true that there is no cause for me to be concerned about abuse or negligence, but that's not my only job here. My job is simply to see to the welfare of the children in our community. Perhaps you should consider sitting down with your husband and your son to discuss your challenges as a family together. I assure you, Jakob will listen."

Gertrude had thirty years to learn how to make a parent feel like the worst person to ever raise a child, I was sure. I was speechless and could only give her a shallow nod before I had to look away so that I could speak again. "We'll do that," I said. "Thank you for... for letting me know. I'm under a lot stress at the moment, I apologize for my outburst."

"It's only natural," she told me as she stood. "Please try to remember that I'm only here to help."

"I know," I said. "Thank you again. So, are we...?"

She sighed and shifted her briefcase from one hand to the other. "I'll see you and Jake both this time next week," she said. "And if possible, I'd like to see your husband as well. We can arrange a time. Good afternoon, Mrs. Jennson."

19

"Jesus Christ, Elaine," Nathan breathed when I unloaded on him moments after he finally returned over two hours late from his day. The only thing I had left out was that I had found out where Millie Turner was. If I'd told him that, he'd have made me swear not to go talk to her, and that's exactly what I was planning on doing. "Slow down, let me process all of this."

We sat in his car on the parking deck. I dared not have this conversation inside the hospital. Not when someone might be watching or listening—and that someone might not even be from the hospital. "What can we possibly do about Jake's medical records, Nathan? What is there to process? We need to tell them. Surely they'll understand if we lay out the whole story and help them see that we—"

"Absolutely not," he snapped.

I flinched.

Nathan ran his fingers through his hair and groaned. He stared out the window toward the hospital building as if he could see through the walls to watch Jake sleep. "Don't worry about the records," he said finally. "As for CPS, or DEFACS or whoever... we'll cooperate and they'll go away. All we have to do is pretend to be a happily married couple."

"Pretend?" I asked. "Is that where we're at?"

He folded his arms. "Isn't it? Tell me that you're happy right now. Tell me that you'd be happy if Jake was cured tomorrow and completely healthy."

I couldn't. How had we gotten here so fast? Or... had we never gotten to the other place to begin with? Suddenly I didn't know. I hadn't really had to think about it, it was just what it was. Before Jake got sick. Before I learned he wasn't really Jake. Before Nathan lied to Dr. Saito.

"You can't blame me for that," I whispered. "With everything that's happened, how could anyone be happy? How could you?"

"I didn't say I was," he said. "Did you, ah... did you say anything to anyone about the guy that you think was following you?"

"I didn't think he was following me," I said. "He was. He followed me upstairs and then back downstairs and then took off when he realized I noticed."

Nathan put a hand up in defense. "If you say so. I'm sure there couldn't be any other explanation in a hospital full of people coming and going at all hours of the night and day."

"You can save the sarcasm, please." I opened the door on my side to get out. "I don't care if you believe me or not. I know what I saw."

"Where are you going?" He reached across the center console and grabbed my arm as I leaned toward the door.

When I froze, he took his arm away as if I'd burned him. "I haven't slept in the past few days," I said. "Other than dozing off between coffee infusions. I'm filthy, and the shower here is terrible. I need some rest."

"Don't be gone long," he said. "Whatever is happening right now, I still want to be close to you. I need you with me."

I hated how that made me feel. Like this was all somehow my fault. I hadn't recognized our son. I had somehow failed to prevent him from getting sick. It was my action or inaction that had brought Child Protective Services to our door at this critical moment. All the pushing away was me, right? Not Nathan, who was just trying to do the best for Jake.

"I'll be back," I said. I got out of the car. "I, ah… I have an interview to get ready for."

He blinked. "An interview? How… when did this happen?"

"Before all of this," I said. "I can fill you in on the details later. Right now I need to be rested." It was a convenient excuse to be gone for a little while. And, in fact, the moment I said it I realized how close it was.

"You got an interview for a job and didn't tell me?" he asked.

I stood awkwardly at the open door and shrugged. "I wasn't sure I would get it. But I need to rest and print my resume, and... be ready for it. I can tell them what's going on. I don't have to start right away, but we need to be looking to the future, right?"

"Yeah, of course," he said. "But I thought..."

"What?"

He held his breath a moment and then let it out in a puff and waved a hand. "It doesn't matter, just do what you need to. But come back tonight, please."

"Fine," I said. Before he could say anything else, or my poker face could crack, I closed the door and went to find my own car, one eye scanning the parking deck for any sign of my stalker. If he was around, I couldn't spot him.

On the way, I called Linda. "Could you do me a tremendous favor?"

"Of course, hon," Linda drawled. "Anything you need, I told you that. Want me to bring some stuff from the house?"

"No, that's not necessary," I said. I winced as I asked my favor. "Do you think you could come by tomorrow in the morning to stay with Jake for a little while? I know it's a school day, but I think he'd love to see Tyler."

"Stay with Jake?" Linda said. "I mean... have you got some place to be?"

I hated lying. "Yeah, I've got this interview. Of course, I'll have to wait to actually start, but they want to get it out of the way and... it's a big deal for me, so..."

"Oh." There was a brief silence. "Well, if you need me to keep an eye on him, I certainly don't mind. I hate to keep Ty out of school but he'll be thrilled, if that's what you need."

I could hear the subtle judgment in her voice. Linda was terminally polite, and it was harder to tell when she was being critical than most of the other denizens of Avila Grove. Southern charm, maybe. I forced myself to ignore it. There was never going to be a good time to get answers, and if I didn't do *something,* then I was certainly going to come unhinged. "Thank you so much, Linda. You're a lifesaver, really. I owe you so much."

That softened her a bit. "That's what friends are for, sweetie. I guess I'll see you tomorrow morning."

"Yeah, I have to leave... pretty early. About seven or so, how's that?"

Another pause. "Of course. Sure. I'll bring pancakes."

"Great, Linda," I said as cheerfully as I could manage. "You're wonderful. See you then."

We hung up and I leaned against my car door, breathing hard as my heart rapped out a staccato against the inside of my chest and neck, echoing behind my eyes in a dull, rhythmic ache.

It was going to be a mess. But it was easier to ask forgiveness than permission after all.

I got into the car, looked up directions to Northgate Psychiatric Hospital on my phone, pulled out of the spot and then out of the parking deck.

It didn't *look* like anyone had followed me out.

I took a deep breath and headed toward the highway to make the six-hour drive into the past.

20

Even going ten miles over the speed limit the whole way, it took me until one in the morning to get to Jasper. I had taken money out of the ATM close to home and used it to stay in the cheapest motel I could find. I stayed up overnight staring out the window to keep myself from having flashbacks or dreams about Northgate. I had turned my phone off. The last thing I wanted was to hear it ring, or vibrate, or see text messages pop up all night and into the morning. Nathan must be beside himself, but if I told him where I was, for all I know there would be police showing up at my door.

I considered smashing my phone so that I could claim it had been broken, but that seemed like overkill and besides—who can drive more than an hour away from home without their phone these days?

The morning came both too quickly and too slowly. I showered and did my best to make myself look less like a junkie. No amount of foundation would cover the bags under my eyes at this point, though, so I resigned myself to more caffeine and the hope that it would keep me sharp enough to face Millie, if I got to see her.

That was a problem I had considered, and one that I decided I would tackle when it happened. To visit a patient at Northgate's criminal psychiatric ward wasn't much different than visiting someone at prison, or in the far nicer inpatient ward. You had to get on their visitation list. Millie Turner could very well tell me, though not to my face, to fuck off and die. And at this point I wasn't absolutely certain that I didn't deserve it. But I had to speak to her, so I was going to play the dirtiest card that I had in my hand.

God forgive me.

The front of Northgate was an inviting, if stark, façade of white marble and stucco. There was an intricate water feature before the main entrance, surrounded by lush green grass spotted with an array of colorful flowers, peonies, gardenias, and tulips. The fountain itself was a series of banded cylinders arranged in a crescent, so that water flowed down their sides as the bowls atop them filled and overflowed, while spouts pumped water from the shortest cylinder up the tiers to the top and then out in a shower that filled overflowing stone bowls below. It would have cost a fortune, and it conveyed accurately the sense of luxury that Northgate purported in their brochures.

That was, at least, the inpatient entrance, reserved for white collar folks like me who had suffered nervous breakdowns or, less commonly, made a suicide attempt, or a "cry for help" as the doctors and relatives inevitably referred to them. Not that they were necessarily wrong. If I had really wanted to do it back then, I suppose I could have.

Walking past the inpatient entrance brought so many memories back. I didn't exactly remember going into Northgate, but I remembered being there and I remembered the day I left. I remembered Dr. Amanda, who had the most patient, and somehow also condescending voice of anyone I had ever known. A voice that came out of a face that had undergone extensive plastic surgery; she looked like someone's drawing of a middle-aged woman, rather than the real thing. She was always beset with diamonds, and gold, and tasteful pearls. I had hated her at first.

I shook the memory away as the front entrance fled from view behind me and the criminal wing of the facility appeared.

It was white as well, but instead of stucco and marble it was painted cinderblock. Instead of a tasteful wrought-iron fence over a rustic looking stone wall, a plain chain-link fence, perhaps twenty feet high and topped with razor wire, walled the recreation yard off from the rest of the world. The eastern wing of Northgate was tucked politely away and out of sight like the dirty little secret that it probably was. I hadn't even known it existed until after I was discharged.

I pulled into a parking spot and found it difficult to let go of the steering wheel. Against my will, my body clung to the safety of the car, warning me not to go in, not to speak with Millie, and not to do what I was planning to do in order to get her to speak with me. I doubted that she would tell me anything I wanted to know, but there was nowhere else to get the answers I wanted.

I pried my hands from the wheel and left the car to approach the single gray metal door set into the side of the building near the end of the fence. The solid, single-small-window with a key-card and a buzzer with a camera kind of door. The entry to somewhere unsavory and dangerous.

I pressed the buzzer lightly and then had to lean into it. It was springy as if offering me a last chance to turn back. A moment later, though, the door made a loud buzzing noise, and I pushed through it to get inside.

Whatever distinction they made on the outside, the inside was largely the same. The room that the door opened into, at least, was painted that same neutral taupe, with the same bland white ceramic tile mottled with a hint of gray. Even the runner down the hallway matched the fancy carpet used in the offices. For a split second I was back there, walking down the hallway to see Dr. Amanda. I could even feel the dullness that had clouded my brain those months, like the memory of bad weather.

By the time I came to the check-in counter, I was hugging myself. The woman on the other side was a heavyset redhead who looked like she'd been here since the fifties with her horn-rimmed glasses and bright red lipstick.

"Yes?" she asked, one eyebrow raised.

"I'm here to… to visit Mildred Turner," I said. "I'm not on her visitor's list, she's not expecting me. But, she'll confirm me."

Nonetheless, the woman tapped away at her keyboard and scanned some records from behind her glasses. "It'll be a wait," she said. "You can come back later if you like or wait here."

"How long?" I asked.

She shook her head. "I can't predict that. She's in group therapy at the moment. Sometimes they stay after."

"I can wait," I said. There was nowhere else to go.

"Your name?"

I swallowed. "It's, ah… Elaine Jennson," I said as I produced the ID she would inevitably ask for. "If you could let her know that I'm here to talk about… to bring her news about Ralph." The name that she had given my son—I mean, *someone's* son —when she had him gave me a bitter taste in the back of my mouth like bile. For the memory of losing him, and for the pain that I knew this was going to cause Mildred.

If she'd gotten over the delusion that Jake had been her son, then that was an answer in itself and she may well send me away. If she hadn't, or if in fact Jake was her son, then there was no way she would turn me down.

The woman checked my ID, made an entry on the computer, and then gave me a visitor's form to fill out. I did, handed it back to her and when she tuned me out of her attention entirely, I looked around the empty room and took a seat in the chair furthest from the window. I looked down at my powered off phone only once and considered turning it on to text both Nathan and Linda that I was okay, but that I wouldn't be back for a while yet.

Before I could work up the courage, though, I put the phone back in my purse, leaned my head against the taupe wall behind me, and closed my eyes for a moment.

———————————

"Mrs. Jennson! Hello!"

My eyes snapped open, and I looked blearily around the room. Panic struck me immediately as the color of the walls, the patterns on the rug and the gray splotches on the tile all registered at the same moment. I hadn't dreamed, but I had dozed off. What time was it?

"Mrs. Jennson," the woman behind the window repeated impatiently. She huffed and waved me over when I finally settled my gaze on her and woke up the rest of the way.

I wasn't a patient, I was a visitor.

At the window she seemed irritated enough that I wondered how long she'd been calling my name. "Mrs. Turner has approved you for visitation," she said. "Hold your wrist out, please."

I did, and she fixed an orange paper band around it. "Don't remove this. In the event of a lockdown, this is how the orderlies and guards will identify you as a visitor. Please sign this release."

Signing was the only choice. Standard stuff—if Millie went wild and stabbed me in the neck with a crayon, I acknowledged that yes, I knew what kind of facility I was in and why people generally didn't visit.

I handed it back, and the woman flipped a switch well out of reach from the window to her left. The door buzzed and opened. A guard stood on the other side, holding the door open for me.

"Follow the guard," the woman behind the glass said flatly.

Although the door jamb was narrow and low, I nearly tripped going through the doorway. It was as if my foot caught on the very air, refusing to go any further. The guard very politely helped steady me with a gentle hand to my elbow. "Careful, miss."

"Thank you," I muttered. My throat was constricted. "Could I, ah… get a small cup of water on the way?"

"Sure," he said. "This way please."

He delivered, and I sucked down a small paper cup of cool water while he watched, probably making sure that I wasn't taking the opportunity to sneak anything in. I handed him the cup to inspect, just in case, but he only tossed it in the waste bin and gestured me along the wide, window-lined hallway to a room that came into view within a few yards to our right.

It became difficult to breathe when I saw her and I had to brace myself with a hand against the wall.

"Ma'am?" the guard asked. "Are you okay?"

I could only nod. The last time I had seen this woman, she weighed more, and she had more hair. Her face was softer somehow, with just that bit of extra that almost made it plump, though she'd had a few obvious lines around her eyes and mouth even then. That softness hadn't made the fury in her eyes or the spittle on her lips any less menacing at the time, I had thought.

That was then. Now, I missed it. Millie Turner had wasted down into a thing made of gnarled wood and sharp stone, her cheekbones and chin prominent, her eyes wide and sagging with bags that made me feel foolish for having worried about my own. Her wiry hair was cut short now, and there were one or two bald patches. Her shoulder jutted in the light peach shirt and pants they had her dressed in. She was handcuffed to the table, at least.

She turned her head and settled two black holes of loathing on me. I could almost see the fantasies playing out behind them. If this woman had the chance, she would kill me.

If someone had taken my son from me, and I was sitting across a table from them, would I feel any different? Had I felt different when I had first faced her and Hank?

I took a shaking breath and reached for the door handle with hands shaking so badly I fumbled it twice before the guard reached down and opened the door for me.

"Um… thank you," I whispered.

"I have to go in with you," he said.

I nodded. "I know, thank you."

Millie said nothing as I entered, only fixed those eyes on me and tracked me as I took a wide berth around her and sat down in the seat facing her.

"Do you, ah…" I couldn't look at her face. I looked at the collar of her shirt instead. "Do you remember me?"

My eyes flickered up when her lips moved, trembling. "What do you think?"

Of course she remembered me. I'm sure she couldn't forget me any more than I would ever be able to forget her. The urge to make small talk grew, but I pushed it away. No more time here than was necessary.

"Jake… ah… that is, Ralph… he's sick," I said, so quietly I

could barely hear it. I should have taken a cup of water with me. I spoke up a bit more. "Very sick. Cancer."

Millie made a small sound, like I had stabbed her and then garroted her in the same moment. "Oh God, no... my baby..."

That answered one question, then. She still believed he was hers. I started to reach across the table instinctively but stopped short of touching her hands. Her face had pulled into a picture of maternal pain so obvious that I knew that I had taken this woman's child. No one could fake that kind of emotion. Tears brimmed in her eyes before she shut them tight.

"You... took him from me..." she rasped. "You took him from me and now..."

"Millie, I didn't—"She opened her eyes and hurt became fury. Those dark pupils lit up with it and I thought she might very well burn me alive with them. She licked her lips and leaned toward me. "My Hank is free. You know that? He came to see me." She snarled and jerked her wrists against her handcuffs in an attempt to lunge at me. "And he's coming for you, you bitch! He's coming to take my baby back!"

"That's enough, Millie," the guard said, more gently than I would have expected. He shot me an accusatory look. "I think this visit is over, miss."

"Okay," I stammered. But as I stood I looked Millie over warily. "Did you take him? You have to tell me, Millie— where did you take him from? The truth."

"That's enough, ma'am," the guard said, sterner now. "I need to ask you to leave."

I skirted the table.

"He's coming for you!" Millie shrieked and then began to wail. "My baby! Oh, no, oh God, my baby boy!"

I stumbled backward out of the door while the guard spoke into his radio and then attempted to calm Millie. The sound of heels approaching at a clipped pace drew my attention down the hall where a tall man in a blue blazer marched toward me. "What is the meaning of this?"

"She j-just... I didn't know she would..."

He stopped in front of me and waved my visitor form in my face. "I know exactly who you are, Mrs. Jennson," he said. "What reason could you possibly have to come here and harass my patient? Do you have any idea how delicate her condition is? The progress we've made here? You've undone months of intensive therapy."

I staggered away from him until my back was against the wall and then took off down the hall toward the door. *Get out, get out,* was the only response I could think of.

"Mrs. Jennson," the doctor shouted after me. "I'm reporting this to the police!"

What on earth had I been thinking? I dashed to the door back into the waiting room and found it locked. Only after I had pounded on the door and mashed the button beside it a dozen times did it buzz loudly to let me through.

I ignored the complaints of the woman behind the counter, instead fleeing the building as quickly as I could to get to the open air outside where I could breathe again. She'd said her husband was coming to get me—that Hank was coming to take their baby back. Millie Turner was clearly disturbed, whether Jake was really her son or not. And I had to admit that if that was the case, and I was in her place, I wouldn't be any better off.

So, what about Hank? Did he share her fury? Enough to hire someone to follow me around, tell Hank where I was and where... *oh, God...* tell him where Jake was?

I turned my phone back on and waited for the series of alerts to come through from my no doubt panicked husband and my very cross neighbor while I made my way to the car.

Halfway there I stopped and peered at a tan and brown station wagon. Exactly the same kind I had seen before when I left the house. What were the chances? It wasn't the make of car you saw anywhere, certainly not in a neighborhood like Avila Grove. Twice in just a few days?

I snapped a picture of the license plate, monitoring the parking lot for any sign that I was being watched, and then hurried to my car, got in, and peeled out of the place with a promise to myself that I would never step foot near this building again for as long as I lived.

21

I had stopped for coffee on the way home, and when I finally made it back to the hospital that evening, I knew what to expect. Or at least, I thought I did. Nathan had left a number of voicemails that started out worried and crescendo'd right up to a threat to file for divorce if I didn't call him back, along with a matching set of text messages.

When I finally made it to Jake's room, my sister was there.

He had left that out.

I froze with my hand on the door handle as she looked up from Jake's tablet and in the space of a breath went from cheerful aunt to the judgmental sister I knew so well.

"Mom," Jake said, an edge of relief and worry in his weak voice. "You came back!"

I tore my eyes away from Diana's hateful gaze to smile at Jake. "Of course, honey," I said. "I had a few things I needed to do. How are you feeling?"

His forehead was warm when I went to the bedside and brushed his hair away from it to kiss him. "Okay, I guess."

"He's been sick today," Diana said. "He threw up a lot this morning, couldn't keep anything down."

"When did you get here?" I asked.

Diana put her auntie face back on. "We'll be back in a couple of minutes, kiddo. Don't beat too many more levels without me, okay?"

"No promises," Jake said. He looked up at me. "You're not leaving again, are you?"

I shook my head and swallowed a lump. "No, honey. I'll be right back."

Diana walked out of the room with me, then took a right to go down the hall, and ultimately went into the women's restroom. She held the door open for me.

Once inside, whatever demeanor she was maintaining evaporated. "What in God's name are you doing? Where the hell were you, Elaine? Do you know what Nathan said when he called me?"

"I can explain," I said. "I had to go—"

"Tell me the one thing that is more important right now than being here," she snapped. She went to the door and stood in front of it, barring my escape and anyone else's entry, arms folded over her chest. "Nathan thought you had run off. The way you did when Mom got sick. And you know what? I couldn't bring myself to tell him that he was wrong."

"Well, he was," I said. "I'm back now, and how dare you come here and judge me when you have no idea what I'm going through, no idea what's been happening here."

Diana stared at me for a moment before she leaned back against the door and shook her head with astonishment. "Are you fucking kidding me right now?"

I couldn't possibly tell her the truth. While I tried to come up with something else in its place, she laid into me.

"Who took care of Mom before she died? Who looked her in the eyes every day, never knowing if she would recognize who was caring for her? Which one of us endured the spitting, and the screaming, and the accusations of stealing her home, her car, and things she hadn't had for thirty years? Who do you think watched her slowly vanish, leaving behind a... an animal where my mother used to be? Huh? How very fucking dare you tell me that I don't know what you're going through, you selfish bitch." She was crying and shaking with anger. With one perfectly manicured nail she wiped tears one at a time from each eye. "Where the hell were you? Nathan said that you claimed to have a job interview. His words, not mine. You lied to him. So?"

"That's between him and me," I croaked. "I'll deal with Nathan when he gets back."

Diana's jaw fell open. "Did you change your mind?"

"What?" I frowned at her. "About what?"

"About leaving," she said. "You were, weren't you? You were going to bail on your husband and your son. That's what you do. Things get tough and you check out. At least you have a conscience these days."

"For your information," I said, and took a step toward her, "I left you to deal with Mom because you didn't want me around."

"That's absolutely—"

"No." I shouted the word and jabbed a finger at her. "You've said your piece, now I say mine. I left because from the very first day you were on me constantly about how I shouldn't be around her, about how nothing I did for her was good enough. It was bad enough having to watch her be taken away one memory at a time, but to have you on the other side reminding me that I was worthless on top of that? What was your excuse?"

Diana held up a hand and started counting off fingers. "You bailed on me when Dad died and left me and Mom to deal with the funeral on our own," she said, so coldly that ice should have formed on the bathroom mirror. "You left me when Mom got sick, and did you ever stop to ask if maybe the reason I was an absolute nightmare was because I was in pain, Elaine? And it didn't stop there. Being a fucking mother was so hard you cracked like an egg the very moment Nathan needed you the most so you could sleep away six months in a loony bin. And the second you get everything back, you check out of the psych ward and into a pill bottle. You run when things go south. You run."

My feet moved on their own, and I only realized I had slapped her when I felt the sting in my hand. The red in my vision drained away as Diana gaped at me, wide-eyed, one hand to her face where I had left a blazing scarlet mark visible.

Shock gave way quickly to that icy anger I had known my whole life. "You're a piss poor mother," she whispered, "a shitty sister, and pathetic excuse for a wife. Nathan is beside himself and he's drinking again, did you know that? He's completely alone; he has no idea who you are. You can be as mad as you want with me, Ell, but you need to get your fucking house in order. Go home."

"I came here to see my son," I said. "Get out of my way. You can leave."

She didn't move. "Where did you go, Ell?"

My hand ached. So did my heart. I shouldn't have struck her, and I regretted it. Part of me wanted to apologize, to hold my sister tight and be sorry for having fought like this. The other part, though, the part who hated how Diana picked on me and excluded and blamed me for everything, was willing to go to the grave before that happened.

But she couldn't know about Jake. No one could. "I was going to leave," I said. "You're right. And I changed my mind. I needed to sort things out for myself and I did."

For a long moment we watched one another. The last time we had done that was the day that I told her I needed a week away from Mom.

Eventually, she moved away from the door. "You look like hell," she said. "Like you haven't slept and got hit by a small train. Jake's worried about you. You need to get some rest. I've got him today, go tell him you'll be back and then go home and sleep. Please, Elaine."

She wasn't wrong. I had gone right through exhaustion in the car and was now fluttering high above my body on a second wind fueled in part by our shouting match. I wanted to collapse, but I wasn't even sure that I would sleep if I did. I had an apology to make to Linda. What's more, Nathan would be coming here in the evening. I wasn't sure I could face him yet.

But there was Hank, and there was the man that I was now almost certain he had hired to find me and Jake. "I'll go," I said. "But, ah… listen, have you seen anyone hanging around? A big guy, well dressed, kind of heavyset?"

Diana put her hands on my shoulders and locked eyes with

me. "Do you remember what you told the doctors when you were at Northgate?" she asked.

I pulled away from her, hurt. "This isn't like that."

"You have a history, Elaine," she said. "I need you to consider that… that it's possible you think you saw something but didn't. Just like with Jake."

Just like with Jake.

Maybe because I had recently returned from there, and the memory of the place was fresh, and I was so sleep deprived that the lines between reality and dream were bound to start blurring, I looked away from her and to the tile and for a moment I was back there again. I could hear my own voice echoing from somewhere far away, from Dr. Amanda's office.

"I didn't mean to do it," I had said. *"I didn't mean for him to die."*

"He didn't die," the doctor's voice reminded me, *"Jake isn't dead, Elaine, he's missing. You were here, there's nothing you could have done."*

I shivered and pushed Diana gently away. "I… I'll go say goodbye to Jake. I'll be back after I've had some sleep."

"Okay," Diana said.

I leaned against the door, my fingers on the handle. "Thank you for coming down, Dee. I'm sorry I hit you."

"I'll talk to Nathan," she said. "Get yourself together, whatever you have to do."

22

"Where did you go?" Jake asked when I returned to his room to check on him.

Lying to Nathan hadn't been exactly difficult even if it had made me feel terrible. I couldn't lie to Jake though. Trying made my stomach twist. "I… had to go see someone," I said. "Someone that I hoped would be able to answer a question."

"Oh," he said. His eyes dropped, and he picked up his tablet but didn't actually play with it. "Are you mad at me?"

"What?" I sat next to him and took one of his hands in both of mine. "Honey, of course I'm not mad at you, why would you ask that?"

He sniffed. "That lady asked if you got angry a lot. She asked if you ever spanked me. I told her you didn't, but she didn't believe me. She kept asking me, like you did when I broke the picture of Dad and Grampa and Gramma. But I didn't lie. I know you're not supposed to lie."

I bit the inside of my cheek and tugged him toward me for a hug. "No, baby, you're not," I said. "That lady is just doing her job. You did exactly what you were supposed to, and I'm not angry with you. You're the best kid anyone could ask for, you know that?"

He pulled away from me, and I wiped the tears from his eyes. "When can I go home?"

"As soon as you're all better," I said. "And I'm sure that'll be soon. How was your visit with Ty? Did you two have fun?"

Jake nodded but didn't look especially happy about it. "The robot contest is next week," he said. "Do you think I'll be out by then? Tyler wants to be partners like we were last time."

One of the hardest things about being a parent, the thing no one prepares you for, is having to choose whether to tell your kid a benevolent lie or a painful truth. I got stuck in the middle. "I don't know," I said. "Maybe. But what's really important is that you get well. Maybe Miss Linda can video the contest with her phone, and you can watch it on your tablet."

He sighed and lay back against his pillow. "I guess so, but it's not the same."

"I know it's not, baby."

Behind me, Diana cleared her throat quietly.

I glanced at her over my shoulder and then gave Jake my best everything-is-okay smile. "Listen, sweetie, I've got to go home and, ah… see if I can put something together for your room, okay? Dad will be back in a few hours, and I'll see you very soon. I don't want you to worry about anything. You are my very favorite little boy in the whole world. I love you so, so much, and I promise I'm not going to leave again."

"Pinkie promise?" he asked, holding up his pinkie finger.

I hooked it with mine and held tight. "Pinkie promise. Now you rest and be good for Aunt Diana. She can tell you all sorts of stories about me when I was your age, I bet."

We said goodbyes, and I left the room. Diana followed me out, and we stood some distance down the hallway away from his door. Her cheek was still red where I'd struck her.

"I'm only in town for a few days," she said. "I need to get back home to take care of my own family after that."

I nodded and kept my hands by my side instead of offering to hug her. The way she kept her arms crossed made me think it wasn't invited. "Of course," I said. "I'm sorry about before."

"Yeah," she said. Then she turned away and went back into Jake's room.

For a long moment I stood there staring at his door, wishing I had said and done things differently. Not just with Diana, with everyone. With Mom, when Jake was born. Hell, even when Nathan and I had separated. Everything would have been different if I had waited for him to come around instead of looking to Roger for comfort.

I forced myself to turn and leave, but as I left the hospital, going home didn't appeal to me. Linda was there, and I was certain she had been preparing a speech for me when I showed up. There would be no avoiding her until it was dinnertime, and she was too busy with her family to notice me coming in. It was the chickenshit choice to make but I couldn't face another confrontation. Not after Millie and Diana had both gotten their shot at me and knowing that Nathan was sure to be next in line.

So rather than going straight to the house I stopped in town during the first wave of post-work traffic to get coffee and something to eat. Sleep would wait. Or I'd lose my mind all together, one or the other. I kept replaying Millie's words in my head on repeat. *"He's coming to take my baby back!"* Maybe I could ask Roger to hire someone to keep an eye on us. He'd do that, I thought. And Roger knew those sorts of people; Nathan had always complained about Roger's insistence on hiring bodyguards because it made them look more important when they met with potential clients.

The combination of near-delirium from sleep deprivation and the fact that I was so consumed by my thoughts made me tune the rest of the world out, which is why I failed to notice when I came into the coffee shop that Linda was standing ahead of me with her two kids. It wasn't until she stopped in front of me and said my name that I refocused on the present and realized she was there, waving her venti skim no-whip sugar-free chai latte at me.

"Earth to Elaine," she was saying. "What happened to you?"

"I…" I froze and shrugged. Somewhere inside something checked out. "Sorry."

"Sorry," she repeated. She took a deep breath and then passed Ainsley to Tyler. "Baby would you take your sister to that table over there? Here"—she gave him her phone—"you two watch a video for a minute, please."

Tyler did as he was told and gave me a salty kind of look that Linda didn't remark on as he left.

"What on earth is going on with you, hon?" Linda asked.

I ran my fingers through hair that needed to be washed, certain that I looked a mess. "That's the million-dollar question, I guess," I said. "I had something to do."

"Not an interview," Linda said.

When you have a secret, there is nothing worse than having to keep it. I suppose that's why so many secrets come out in the end. They claw at your insides, begging to be let out. Sometimes that's because you just have to share it with someone and revel in the feeling of having a secret together—like when

Linda found out that Marie Pendleton was having an affair with her pool boy like some trashy soap opera character from the eighties. Sometimes, it's because the secret is eating you alive, and by sharing it you give it more to eat so that maybe, just maybe, it will take longer to finish you off.

And sometimes, you simply don't want to be alone with it. As if the darkness would be less frightening if there was someone in it with you to hold your hand even if they couldn't do anything more than you could to bring the light back.

"No," I admitted. "Not an interview."

"Well, then what?" she demanded. "I think you owe me that much. You should have seen Nathan. He thought I knew where you were and didn't believe me when I told him I didn't. I had to take Tyler out of there. And... well, I don't want to get between you and your husband, Elaine, but his breath was... you know... like he'd been at a bar. Not that that's any of my business."

Since when had that stopped Linda Keeler from putting her nose into anything? I would have to talk to Nathan, although I didn't know what leg I was supposed to stand on. That made two people who'd noticed his drinking. How bad was it getting?

Sometimes, you want someone to hold your hand in the darkness.

"I went to see Mildred Turner," I said.

Linda blinked. "I... who?"

"It's a really long story, Linda, and I don't have the time or energy to tell it right now," I said. "Can I, for the moment, promise you that it was really, really important, and that I had to do it? I'm sorry I didn't tell you before. I didn't tell Nathan either because... he wouldn't have wanted me to go. Believe me, I so badly want to tell you what's going on, but this isn't the place for it."

Her critical expression softened and turned to one of concern that brought out the wrinkles at the corners of her eyes and across her forehead. She held her breath a beat and then hugged me with one arm. I let her. God it felt good, for one second, for someone to give me a modicum of sympathy. "Alright," she said after she let me go. "I'm your friend, Elaine. Remember that, okay?"

"I will, Linda," I said. "Thank you, so much. It does matter to me, I promise."

She smiled and then whistled for her kids. "Alright you two little monsters, let's go. Hey, Tyler, do not let your sister chew on tables, what have we talked about?"

They left, and I got a final wave from Linda before I made it to the counter and got my cup of coffee, black and caffeinated, and then left. No telling who else I was liable to run into there. Certainly no one I wanted to talk to more than Linda.

Outside the coffee shop I looked down at my phone to check the time. Nathan would be off in about an hour, although if both Linda and Diana were right, he would hit the bar afterward. I made a mental note to talk to Roger about that before I talked to Nathan. Last time I tried to it had gotten very bad.

Someone ran into me. Hot coffee sprayed out of the hole in the plastic lid and over my hand, burning me, and I nearly dropped it. I turned with an angry reflex to tell the person to watch where they were going, please, and saw Hank Turner rounding the corner quickly to get away.

The coffee fell from my hand and I ran after him, turning the corner myself as my eyes frantically combed the sparse crowd. He was walking quickly down the sidewalk, his head down, wearing a ball cap I couldn't mistake. I wove through the knot of people between us, not bothering to apologize and caught up to him. I grabbed his shoulder to stop him. "You son of a bitch, I knew you were—"

The man who turned around gave me a shove. "Hey, what the hell is your problem, lady, are you insane? Don't fucking touch me, who the hell are you?"

I stammered and apologized as I stumbled backward from him. "Sorry … it was a mistake, I…"

The guy shook his head in disgust and hurried away, glancing over his shoulder once to make sure I wasn't following him.

Twice I had seen Hank where there was no Hank. Both times I had been dead certain it was him.

I fled the sidewalk and the stares I was getting, trying to

convince myself that I should go home and sleep and maybe even call Dr. Werner and see about getting back on my medication. Then again, maybe it was due to a lack of sleep. Either way, I had to get my bearings back. I went home and didn't even remember going inside or lying down. The next thing I knew, Nathan was waking me up and he was furious.

23

"Do you have any idea what kind of shit-storm you are calling down on us?" Nathan asked. "What the fuck were you thinking going to see *Mildred Turner*, Elaine?"

We stood on opposite sides of the kitchen, him leaning on the kitchen island, me holding a cup of lukewarm coffee.

"I thought she might know something, or say something, that would help me make sense of what happened," I said. It wasn't a lie entirely. "And she said that Hank was coming for Jake."

Nathan's eyes widened, and he leaned forward over the island. "She's in a psychiatric ward," he shouted. "She's insane, Elaine, why would you give anything she said any weight at all?"

"Because I saw Hank's station wagon," I snapped back, "here, in our neighborhood, and again at Northgate. He is here, Nathan, I can feel it."

"Like he was outside the toy store you went to with Jake?" He rubbed his face with both hands and groaned into them. "Did it occur to you that getting on any law enforcement radar might put our custody of Jake in jeopardy? Were you thinking about anyone but yourself for one second when you did this? When you *lied* to me and then ran off and scared the fuck out of me, Linda, and Jake? Even your sister was beside herself, she thought you'd run off for good. Do you know that?"

"You think I did this for me?" I gripped the mug tighter and almost threw it at him. "I went for Jake, and for the son that we didn't even know was still missing, you son of a bitch."

Nathan deflated. He turned and pulled one of the chairs away from the kitchen table and all but fell into it. He looked as lost as I felt in that moment. Then his face hardened. "If you're going to act like this, I don't want you around Jake right now."

"You can't keep me away from my—"

"What, your *son*?" He barked a cruel, mirthless laugh. "Which is it going to be, Elaine? You want to be his mom? Or some kind of suburban sleuth? Even if you didn't bring the police into this, how do you think you're going to find your son without losing Jake?"

"Our son," I corrected. "Our fucking son, Nathan, who is *gone*. He could be with someone else, thinking they're his parents, or he could be dead. Why do you not seem to care? Do you even care?"

"I've told you that I do," he said quietly.

I did throw the cup. It shattered against the far wall, spraying bits of ceramic and coffee everywhere. The sound of it was deafening and left behind a ball of rage in my stomach that burned until it hurt. "Then why the hell aren't you helping me instead of falling off the goddamned wagon?"

Nathan looked at the wall, and at the broken pieces of the mug. Wordlessly, he stood and began picking the pieces up.

"Say something," I said. "Say something, Nathan, anything to help me understand, please. You know what's going on inside me, but I have no idea what you're feeling."

Instead of answering, he took the bigger pieces of the cup to the trash and tossed them in, and then took the broom from the pantry to sweep up the rest.

I waited while he cleaned. Maybe I should have helped him; it was my mess, but there was a coldness radiating from him that I didn't want to get too close to. I could almost feel the connection between us being swept away as he brushed up the shards of ceramic and tipped them into the trash with the rest of the cup. When he did that, he stood over the can for a long moment before he put the broom and dustpan aside.

"Make an appointment with Dr. Werner," he said, bereft of emotion. "Get back on your meds, and *only* your meds. Do that, and you can see Jake again. I'm done being patient and understanding. You need to get your priorities straight, and if Jake and I aren't at the top of that list then that's fine—but you're not going to have it both ways, Elaine."

He'd said everything except divorce, but I could hear it behind the words. I was speechless. He couldn't keep me away from Jake, could he?

"Has it occurred to you," he went on, "that you might obtain answers you'd rather not know? That you might lose everything instead of gaining anything from this? And it's not just you. I could lose everything. Jake could lose everything. You're going to tear our family apart in our most vulnerable moment because you can't set this aside for a few months while our son fights for his life. I'm not going to let that happen. If I have to, I'll take Jake and we'll do this on our own. Do you understand me?"

He looked at me and I nodded. I still couldn't speak. My throat was closed and I could barely breathe through my nose.

"I'm going to the hospital," he said finally. "While you were off attracting the attention of the police and agitating a lunatic, I was talking to those dream room people, and they're coming tomorrow to make up Jake's room. Maybe you can sort yourself out by then and be there to see his face when he comes in and sees it."

"I…"

"If you can't," he said, "if you're going to sacrifice your

family for your quest, then don't come back. I'll tell Jake... I don't know what I'll tell him. I'll lie, though, because knowing that his mom had more important things to do would break his fucking heart and I'm not going to do that."

He went to the door and put his jacket on.

"Nathan, I—"

The door slammed behind him. On the other side of that wall, in the living room, something fell off the wall and broke. A picture—the picture we'd had taken together when we took Jake on vacation to Disneyland a couple of years before. I didn't have to see it to know which one it was.

My knees gave way, and I sank down to the tiled floor and cried.

24

They say that having a good cry can help you de-stress and even think more clearly. Something about stress hormones. I don't know if that's true or not, but I did feel a little more clear-headed when I finally pulled myself up to the counter and off of the floor, my knees aching from being pressed against the hard tile. I wiped my eyes, took several deep breaths, and made some decisions.

Whatever the state of our marriage was at the moment, it was important to me. Jake was important to me. Nathan wanted me to meet with Dr. Werner, so I called his office and moved my check-in appointment forward. I claimed an emergency and got an appointment for the evening though the receptionist warned me that my own doctor's schedule was very tight. Still, I didn't think the condition was that I see *my* doctor, just that I see someone. I sent Nathan a text with a screenshot of the confirmation email. He didn't respond.

After that, I walked myself through the last few days. Twice I had thought I saw Hank Turner when I hadn't. I had seen a station wagon—two of them, most likely—and let my imagination run away with me. It didn't make any logical sense. What was Hank supposed to do? Murder us and steal Jake? Millie wasn't getting out any time soon, especially not after I potentially made things worse for her. Was Hank going to take Jake and run and live as a fugitive forever? The more I reasoned it out, the more obvious it became. Even if he was planning something like that, Jake was sick—no father would take him from the hospital right now and it wasn't as though no one was there watching.

There was the other man, though—the man from the hospital, who I believed was also the man who'd been smoking in his car in front of my house. Then again, lots of people smoke. And any number of people had black town cars if I really thought about it, right? The five or six times that Nathan and I had ordered a car at the end of a flight, back before there were apps to do it on our phones—and before there were even smartphones for that matter—we'd been picked up in black town cars with tinted windows.

And Nathan wasn't wrong about that man being in the hospital. Saint Monica's was a big, well-known place. There were hundreds of patients there, and hundreds more people coming to visit them. For all I knew that guy was someone's driver. At the very worst he was a creep who'd been following me around because he thought I was hot. The idea of that was a little unsettling but less disturbing than being targeted by someone who meant to abduct my son.

Some instinct in me fought against rationality but I refused to let it win. There were only two things that I could say for certain, based on facts. Jake was sick. That was the most important thing. Second to that, no matter how much it tore my heart in half to admit it, was that my biological son had never been returned.

Where was he now? There could only be a few explanations. None of them could be tackled immediately unless I had the investigation re-opened and that would mean losing my family, maybe even going to prison. All I could do was hope that wherever my biological son was, it was a good place. If he was dead, nothing would bring him back. If it was some-thing worse than that...

Dwelling on it right now would only cause pain. I made a silent promise to myself that when Jake was better, I would find out everything that I could. Until then, I had to be a mother and a wife, in that order.

I let that sink in. A mother first, a wife second.

For the next hour while I forced myself to eat something, took a shower, and got dressed, I centered myself in rationality. There were things that needed my attention right now, real things, not delusions or figments of my imagination, or specters of my trauma. If I could hold on to reason, I could do them all one small step at a time. We'd be stronger for it afterward.

I put my coat on to leave but remembered that I'd spilled coffee on it when that man had run into me. It was one of my good coats and would have to be dry-cleaned. I set it aside, irritated with the accident all over again, and cleaned out the pockets to transfer anything important to my older, less stylish jacket.

From the pocket on the right side I drew out an unfamiliar square of folded paper. When had I picked this up? I opened it and then dropped it to the table as if it had bitten me. In a way, it had.

We must talk. I need to tell you the truth. Please meet me tomorrow night at the park in your neighborhood. I'm sorry about everything. H.

25

I was shaking when I knocked on Linda's door. It took a minute for anyone to answer, and I wondered if she had taken the kids to the park. It was close enough to walk to. But before I gave up, I heard her calling from inside.

"One second!"

The door opened a moment later and her face fell. "What's wrong?"

I handed the note to her. She read it without comprehension and handed it back to me.

"Can we talk?" I asked.

"Sure, hon," she said and stepped out of the way to invite me in. "Who's H'? Here, let me get you some tea."

In short order she had me sitting on her flower-printed couch with a glass of sugary iced tea in hand. It was a little too sweet for my taste but it gave me something to hold on to while we spoke. Linda's house was immaculate, just like her yard, and dotted with things to hold the eye. Aside from pictures of her happy family everywhere, there was an intricate quilt made up of yellow, green, and purple shapes that looked as though it was old and handmade. Here and there she had decorated the place with tasteful reminders of the south—a six-inch high wooden rooster on the mantle, a pair of landscape paintings depicting two red barns on either side of the large double-door entryway into the living room– and furniture that looked like classy, functional antiques.

"So, is this to do with why you disappeared?" she asked when we were settled.

I nodded and gingerly sipped the hummingbird food she called tea. "Yes," I said. "Linda... can I trust you? I mean, really trust you to keep a secret?"

"I'm not gonna pretend I don't gossip," she said, "but that doesn't mean I can't keep quiet, too. You're a friend, Elaine, I wouldn't spread your business around. I swear on my daddy's grave."

"This will be... it's the kind of secret that could do a lot of damage," I said. My hands began to shake enough that the ice in the glass clinked against the side.

Linda moved to sit next to me and gently took the glass from my hand to set it down. She held my hands in hers. "Where

I'm from, we take care of our own. Whatever it is, hon, I promise I'll do what I can to help."

I nodded and pulled my thoughts together. "Um… when Jake was born I… I had really bad depression. Post-partum, I was on medication for it."

"That happens to lots of women, hon," Linda said, her voice soft, more compassionate than I'd ever heard from her. "I had it after Ainsley, I know how hard it can be."

"I was pretty heavily medicated," I went on. "And, ah… one night I was bathing Jake and I don't really know what happened. I lost track of time, maybe blacked out a little bit? I was so spacey. He had a dirty diaper and maybe it was the formula, but it was atrocious. I had to wash him up when I took the diaper off, normally me and Nathan bathed him together, you know."

"Okay…" Linda squeezed my hands.

"The next thing I knew, Nathan was home. The water was still warm, it hadn't been long, but he went to check on Jake and found him in the tub." I sucked in a breath to keep from breaking down. "He… he was fine, you know, he was in his bath seat, but Nathan was so angry and I was beside myself. I don't know what I was thinking, but I locked myself in the guest bathroom and I just thought that maybe my medication wasn't working? So I took another pill, and then just kept going—I mean, I kept taking them. One after the other, I could see myself doing it and I knew that I shouldn't, that it was dangerous, but I couldn't stop."

Linda's grip was almost painful but something about that pressure helped keep me from drifting too far into the memory. I tried to be as dispassionate as I could, telling it like it wasn't my story but about someone I didn't know.

"I passed out. The next thing I knew, I was waking up in the hospital. I was cuffed to the bed, and I panicked and there was no one there with me and this... this horrible thought came to me. The last thing I remembered was putting Jake in the bathtub. And I... I must have dreamed that he..."

"Shh," Linda said. "It's okay. We all have dreams like that. It's scary, having kids, always being afraid they're gonna fall, or drown, or eat the wrong thing... you don't have to say it."

I nodded because I couldn't say it. I couldn't say that I woke up certain that Jake had drowned in the tub and that that was why Nathan had been so furious with me. It had been a dream, but at that moment it had felt so very, very real that I wanted to die. "I went into treatment immediately, suicide watch. No closed doors, constant observation. Counselling every day with this doctor. I don't even remember her last name. I call her Dr. Amanda because she insisted we be on a first-name basis. She said everything was fine, but then... I had only been there a couple of days when Nathan came to see me. He was a shell of person, he hadn't slept or eaten anything in days and he... he told me that Jake had been taken."

"Shit," Linda breathed. "Jesus, you poor thing… I'm so sorry. But you got him back."

"You have to believe me," I said quietly, "that I… I thought he was… the timing was right, they were in the area, they both had a record of theft, breaking and entering, and the baby was Jake's age." The last words came out as a strangled sound. "I thought it was him, Linda. I was so… I wanted him back so bad that I thought it was him and I was *wrong*."

Linda's grip loosened a little bit. Her mouth had fallen open. She closed it, swallowed loudly, and then took my glass to take a long sip of tea. She set it down afterward and I started to let her other hand go, but she held onto it and with her free hand turned my chin up to look at her. "Elaine… are you saying that Jake—the Jake that I know—that he's… not really your son?"

"And now I don't know where *my* Jake is," I said. "I lost him, and I stopped looking for him, Linda. God help me, I didn't know I was supposed to be looking for him."

"Jesus," Linda said. "Holy… come here, baby doll."

She pulled me to her and hugged me close. "God, you must be torn up inside, you poor, poor thing."

I unraveled in her arms, sobbing into her soft knit sweater while she let me. When it had passed, several minutes later, she straightened me up and handed me a tissue. Though still sympathetic, there was a set to her chin and shoulders that said she meant business now.

"This Turner woman," she said, "the one you went to see. Who's she?"

"The woman that I thought abducted my son," I said. "Her and her husband… Hank."

"Hank as in…?"

I nodded. "He slipped the note into my pocket yesterday evening, after you saw me at the coffee shop. I thought… well, I don't know what I thought now. I guess I did see him but he disappeared before I could get my hands on him. Millie went batshit when I saw her, said that he was coming after me. But the note…"

"It doesn't sound like somebody who wants to settle a score," Linda said. "Do you think Jake really was their kid? Why didn't they do some kind of DNA test?"

"They wanted to," I said. "The Turners wouldn't allow it on religious grounds, and no one wanted to get sued by angry parents after the trial. They were convicted on circumstantial evidence, their movements, location, timing, motive. They lived not too far from us. I was heavily medicated at the time, I don't remember much of the trial, and Nathan was there for more of it than I was. He and Roger handled everything, worked with the district attorneys, even hired their own private investigators. Everything pointed to an abduction, I believed. But now… I'm not so sure. And it's killing me."

"So, what do you think Hank wants?" She finished the tea for me and then held the glass up. "You want something else to drink?"

"I'm okay," I said. When she raised an eyebrow, I relented. "Water, maybe."

She was gone and back in a flash. "You gonna meet him?"

I unfolded the note and looked at it again. "I don't see how I can't," I said. "I have questions that I want answers to. I know it's a long shot but… what if he knows something about what happened to my son?"

"Well now, hon," Linda said with the tone of someone who hates to be the bearer of bad news, "what makes you think he would know anything about that?"

"I'm simply desperate, maybe," I admitted. The first sip of water I took from the new glass reminded me how thirsty I was, and I drank half of it in one go. "Thank you. I… I don't know what Hank could possibly have to tell me, but I have to find out. And I don't think I can meet him alone. I mean, I don't think I have it in me."

"You don't have to even ask," Linda said. "I'll go with you. Hell, I'll make sure we get whatever answers you want out of this guy."

The thought of Linda working someone over almost made me smile and provided a moment of relief. "I should meet with him on my own," I said, "but it would make me feel better if you were in the area. That you'd be nearby if I… had to run or something."

"You think it could be some kind of trick?"

"I don't know," I said. "That's what makes me nervous. Hank served his time, got out on parole. He's taking a big risk coming down here, much less meeting with me. So either he's got nothing to lose and means to even the score, or he's got something that he's waited eight years to tell me. I have to learn which it is, or I swear, Linda, I'm going to lose my mind. I thought I already was."

Linda didn't need long to think about it. She stood up as if were we leaving that moment. "Alright. When do we go?"

26

The hours between visiting Linda and leaving for the park were torture. I ran through every scenario I could imagine in my head, and most of them were terrible. Maybe Hank meant to kill me. Maybe he would inform me that he knew where Jake was and had proof that Jake was his son. What if he brought people? Linda intended to take her gun. A shoot out played through my imagination first, followed by a more realistic multiple homicide situation that I'd be unlikely to survive. I'm not built for that kind of thing.

Those possibilities made me want to go to the hospital to protect Jake, but I couldn't be certain that Nathan wouldn't cause a scene if I did. Instead, I was stuck here in purgatory, wandering the house in silence.

When the sun finally went down, Linda knocked on my door and I rushed to answer it.

"I told Malcolm we were having a girl's night," she said. "He owes me for last week when he played golf and assured me it would be over at eight. Turns out he and his buddies aren't all that good, they didn't get back in until eleven, and he was as drunk as a skunk on a weekday." She shook her head as if to say *"kids these days."*

"I don't know how long this will take," I said. "There's no indication of what time he means to meet. I'm not even sure why we're meeting at the park and not somewhere more populated. Maybe he doesn't want anyone to see him. Did you… did you bring *it*?"

Linda quirked an eyebrow and opened her purse to show a flash of gunmetal in its depths. "I don't mean to alarm you, but I always carry it."

After the week I'd had, I couldn't bring myself to criticize. I almost asked her how long it took to get a permit.

We left in her car, though the park wasn't far, and parked at the far end of the parking lot away from the children's area. There were still a few kids left on the playground, mostly older middle and high school students, probably getting up to no good away from their parents' watchful eyes. I found myself promising that when Jake reached that age, I wouldn't be the kind of parent who insisted on always knowing exactly where he was at all times. At the same time, the thought of him running free in the world—free to make terrible mistakes, free to make all the wrong decisions, free to be hit by a car when I wasn't there—was horrifying.

And saddening, as well. I honestly didn't know if I'd be there to see him grow up. He was in good hands at Saint Monica's, and I was sure that he would recover; he would live to see high school, to have his heart broken, to give in to peer pressure and have his first illicit drink or try weed and hopefully get caught and learn his lesson. But what if *I* wasn't there to scold him, or to soothe his tender soul when someone hurt him?

"Are you nervous?" Linda asked. She snorted and waved a hand. "Sorry. Of course you are. What does he look like?"

"He's in his mid-fifties now, I think," I said. "He had gray hair already when I saw him last. Weathered face. He and Millie were… blue collar, I guess you'd say. And they looked it. I'll know him when I see him."

"There should be rules for this sort of thing," Linda mused. "You know, like in movies when the government poo-bah meets with a spy, it's always by that big reflecting pool next to the big Washington penis."

I snickered.

"There, that's good for the nerves," Linda said. "My daddy always said that no matter how bad things are, you have to laugh. He was always making stupid jokes. Pretty sure the whole concept of 'dad jokes' started with him."

"Is he gone?" I asked. "I don't know why I've never asked. I don't really know much about where you're from, do I?"

Linda shrugged. "He passed away before you moved in. Heart attack. Dropped dead one day, just like that. Momma says it was bound to happen eventually, the man loved his bacon and didn't believe that cholesterol was a real thing. He thought it was made up to make more money for doctors. He didn't like doctors much."

"I'm sorry," I said. I watched a small cluster of teenagers gather and head toward the far end of the park, toward the south side of Avila Grove. "My dad never had any nuggets of wisdom for me. He was a quiet person. I think that's why my mom liked him. She was a personality that's for sure. Loud, obnoxious. She never missed a chance to embarrass me in front of my friends, or a boy. Especially boys. I think that was her plan for keeping me from dating until I was in college, pulling out those awful baby pictures the second a guy showed any interest in me. She drove me and Liam Winters to prom and the whole way there she made sure we knew about all the different kinds of protection we could use, and they regaled us with the history of the condom. You know, they used to use lambskin? You could wash it off and reuse it."

Linda made a face. "Thank God for the twentieth century."

"Later on they were funny stories," I said. "Things we'd get together and laugh about."

"Does she live close?"

At that moment, I missed my mother. It wasn't a loss that I had spent much time facing. I shook my head and was glad that it was too dark for Linda to see the tears in my eyes. "She died. Some time ago. Alzheimers."

"Oh. I'm sorry, hon." Linda squeezed my arm near my elbow.

"It went so fast," I whispered. "I thought there would be more time, or that it would be... I don't know, a magical bonding experience at the end of her life. They told us what to expect, but it didn't really hit me until I saw the way she lost herself. She'd never tell my sister, but I was her favorite. I know that, now that I look back on it. She pushed Diana hard. Straight As, college, a good career. Diana was the one who was going places. All my mom wanted from me was to be her little girl forever. Then she got sick and... she forgot."

"My grandmother got Alzheimers when I was little," Linda said. "I didn't get a chance to know her very well, and I wasn't there at the end, but they say that in the last few moments it's like it all comes back to them. My mother told me once that Gran hadn't recognized anyone for months, but when she passed, it was like she woke up for a second just to say good-bye. Did that... was she there, at the end?"

I wiped my eyes. "I ah... I don't know. I wasn't there."

We were quiet after that, but not for very long. Someone moved through the park. I couldn't be certain but thought it might be Hank. He stopped at the monkey bars and stood, peering at us, or toward us, straining to see.

"I think that's him," I breathed. "He's alone, right? Do you see anyone else?"

We both looked around. Linda shook her head. "I don't see anyone. You want me to come with you?"

If she did come with me, it was possible he would run. He didn't know Linda. For all he knew, I had brought a police officer with me. "No," I said. "But... be ready, just in case. I'll run if anything happens."

"What if he's got a gun," Linda asked. "Or a knife or something? You sure?"

"I'll have to deal with that if it comes," I said.

Linda took her pistol out of her bag and pressed it into my hand. "Take this with you. Tuck it under your arm and put your hand in your pocket." She flicked something near the handle. "The safety is off. Be *careful*. Only point at center mass—that's the chest and stomach; the torso. Don't try and hit something specific if you have to shoot. It's got a full clip."

The gun felt heavy and dangerous in my hands. Heavier than I imagined it would be. I almost handed it back to her.

But...

"I'll be careful," I said. I got out of the car and made my way toward the park—toward the man I had dreaded ever seeing again for the past eight years.

27

My eyes took a moment to adjust to the dark. When they did, and I could see Hank clearly, it seemed laughable that I had thought the man at the toy store was him.

He had changed. He was thinner, for one thing, his features almost skeletal. His shoulders were still as broad as I recalled but the thin windbreaker he wore, which was riddled with worn holes, fell over them in a way that suggested they were bony and almost frail. Prison had been difficult for him and I felt guilty for having put him there.

Other than his face and the shape of him, I could see nothing else clearly. His too large jeans were cinched tight around his waist, and he had his hands stuffed in his pockets. I tried to see if there was the shape of a weapon in one of them but couldn't tell if the loose denim hid anything.

He spoke first. "Missus Jennson. Thank you for coming. I know you didn't have to, maybe didn't want to."

I watched him warily in the weak light of the distant street-lamps, the way you watch a stray dog when you can't tell whether it's going to bite you or not. "I went to see your wife at Northgate," I said. "She said you were coming for me, and for Jake. You've been following me, haven't you?"

Not meeting my eyes, he kicked something on the ground that I couldn't see. "I know. I heard," he said. "She doesn't know what she's talking about. Millie is… she's been gone a long time now. I'm sorry if I scared you, that wasn't what I wanted."

I relaxed a little bit. "So why are you here, then, Hank? What do you want from me?"

He looked up. "It's not what I want from you, Missus Jennson. It's what you need from me."

The wind blew. It was unseasonably cold, the first hint of a winter that was supposed to be a couple of months away still. I wanted to pull my coat tighter around myself but with Linda's pistol under my arm, I couldn't move like I would have to. I endured it, my eyes watering. "Was Jake really your son, Hank? Is that why you're here?"

He sighed. "No. Jake's not ours. He never was."

One of the many knots that had tightened around my stomach for the past week loosened a little.

"But I know he's not yours either," he said.

Another knot tightened a bit more. "Where did he come from, then?"

Hank looked toward the car where Linda waited. "I can't blame you for not coming alone," he said, "but is that a police officer or...?"

"A friend," I said. "I didn't know what you'd do when I got here. I still don't."

He nodded slowly. "I get that. I promise, though, all I want is to tell you the truth about Jake, so you know where he came from. Millie told me you said he was... sick. How bad is it?"

I wondered if he really cared or not, but that seemed like a pernicious thing to ask at this point. "He's getting the care he needs," I said.

"Good," Hank said. "That's good."

"Who is he, Hank? Who was he before you took him?"

Hank leaned against the monkey bars and stared off into the night. "I don't know what his name was," he said. "Millie took him, from some infant day care up in Michigan that she used to work at. She had been fired a few months before. We only had one car, you see, and I needed it most of the time, so we'd go in early so I could drop her off. A few times, she ended up getting there late. I guess they had enough of it eventually and let her go.

"You know, we'd been married thirty years at that point." He smiled in a sad kind of way. "We'd known one another since grade school. Same small town, you know, everybody knows everybody in those places. I was sweet on her since the fifth grade. Got my shot in high school but her family was deeply religious. Her papa hated me with a passion, thought I was out to corrupt his sweet little girl. Nothing could be further from the truth; I loved Millie's sweetness. I never wanted to see it change.

"We got married right out of school. I had a decent job at a factory outside town, and Millie, well, all she really ever wanted was to have a slew of kids. Six, she said. Six kids, I don't know why." He gave a quiet laugh. "Never was interested in college or anything like that. Her mama had stayed home with them, and she was a good woman. I think Millie wanted to be like her. She had that instinct. So, once I was sure we were more or less secure, we started trying to have kids."

As much as I wanted him to get to the point, I couldn't bring myself to interrupt him. There was a hollowness to his voice, like he was giving a eulogy. I had a sinking feeling that I was going to regret listening to him.

He maybe sensed my impatience and gave me an apologetic look. "I know it won't change how you feel," he said, "but for eight years I lived with the guilt of what we did, and the knowledge that people believed we were monsters. That they still do, of course. And there's no real excuse for what we did but I want you to understand. I want you to know that my Millie… she's not evil. She did something terrible, but out of desperation. And I went along with it out of love."

"Okay," I said. "I… keep going."

He looked back into the night, or the past. "We had a hard time getting pregnant. It took a year the first time. She miscarried three months in. God's will, she said. He's got a plan, and she knew, without a doubt, that whatever it was it meant something. So we tried again. We lost three more before I finally got us on insurance and cashed out our savings to see a doctor about it. Turns out she just wasn't built for it.

"It crushed her. For years, we kept trying. We fostered a few kids, but we weren't the sort that anyone wants to let adopt a kid. Lived in a double-wide trailer, barely got by. She loved those kids, though, and she was good at being a mother. We tried to adopt, but we got turned down, over and over again. For her, it was like losing more babies. Time kept passing, she got older, and once forty passed us by, well… she changed. Whatever hope she'd had left, I think she lost it. Lost her faith, too. Stopped going to church, stopped saying her prayers when we went to bed or over dinner. I was never all that religious, but it worried me."

He slumped a little and glanced at me. "I should have done something then," he said. "Should have gotten her some help, maybe taken her to get on some pills. She slipped a little bit further away. We stopped fostering. I think that was the last thing she could stand to lose. Millie was sad, all the time. I worried she would hurt herself but, you know, suicide is a mortal sin; no redemption from that, she believed. So she suffered.

"But then she got the job at that day care," he said. He smiled from the memory. "Changed like that. She started talking again, started telling me stories about all these little babies. It was a specialized kind of place, you see, only infants and very young kids, all under two. And she loved every one of them like they were her own. I had lost my job when the factory closed, though, and had to get work pretty far away. I guess it was my fault she lost that job. I should have been able to get us another car or make some other arrangement."

He was quiet for a moment as the wind picked up again, hard enough to make his windbreaker flap loudly. As it died down, he stood from the monkey bars and looked me over. "You cold? You can have my jacket if you want."

"I'm alright," I said. "When she took Jake, why didn't you say something?"

Hank bobbed his head. "I should have. She went to get her job back. We didn't know if it would work out or not. So, I waited for her. She wasn't in there long. She came out in a hurry, got in the car. She had a bundle with her and I… I knew it was one of those little babies. Just drive, she said. Maybe I was in shock. Worried, too, about what would happen to her, to us. So I pulled away and… kept driving.

"I don't have a good reason for you, Missus Jennson. I was in love. After everything we'd been through, I was as madly in love with her as I was in the fifth grade." He shrugged and made a rueful laugh. "I kept telling myself I had to take the boy back, but the thought of breaking her heart like that... I knew that if I did it, she'd die. I couldn't lose her again, not like that—not by my own hand. First the hours got away from me, every one of them with me saying that I would call the day care or the police in a little bit. Then it was days. There was a news story by that point, and one of those amber alerts. I knew they'd find us, eventually."

"But they didn't," I said quietly. "You ran. Right?"

"Yeah," he breathed. "Yeah, we ran. No one pays folks like us much attention. You quit your job and move, and it's like you never existed. We'd lost our parents already. I was an only child, and Millie's siblings had all been pushed so far away she might as well have been alone. They never asked after us, in any case. Millie was so happy to finally be a mother. Except... after a couple of months, once we'd found a new place—where we were when the police picked us up thinking we had your son—she started saying things... stuff that really worried me. We were at a new church, see, and she had made a few friends, other mothers. They were impressed she had a baby so late, she was forty-three at the time, and she started coming up with all these stories about being pregnant and giving birth and... at first I thought it was just a cover, you know?

"But it wasn't, she believed it. She wanted to have another

baby, she begged me, said that she'd loved being pregnant." Hank took a shaky breath. "I knew something had broken. She felt guilty about what she'd done, you know? She was a good person. Always wanted to do right by God. Maybe the only way she could feel whole was if she made up this fantasy."

"Hank," I said, "I need to know—who are Jake's real parents? Where are they? Do you know?"

He hesitated but reached into his inside coat pocket to pull out a folded piece of paper. I took it from his outstretched hands but didn't open it. I had a sudden, terrifying sense that the knowledge inside would commit me to choices that I wasn't ready to make.

"That's everything I know," he said. "It's what I remember from the news, not that I could ever forget it. Look, I know I can't ever fix any of this; the damage is done. But I want to do right by that boy, if I can. That's all."

"Thank you," I said. But, I needed more. Knowing where Jake's parents might be, that was good—it was painful, but I needed it. The location of my biological son though—that was what I needed to know most. "I know this is a long shot… but you… you don't have any information about my son, do you, Hank? Anything at all?"

He bowed his head. "I'm so very sorry, Missus Jennson. I don't know a thing. The first I knew of you and your husband was when we went to trial."

"Why didn't you say something then?" I asked. "During the

trial? If we had known he wasn't ours, we wouldn't have stopped looking. We thought we had him back. You could have changed that, Hank, you could have told us the truth."

"I know," he rasped. "I know, and I think about it all the time. What I remember of the trial is that the whole thing just … took a turn. Not that I thought we deserved to get off, but our attorneys started pressuring us to change our plea, and it was like everyone had decided how it was going to go. That's why it was over so fast, I think. I was so deep into it that I couldn't even think straight. I … I wanted the truth to be what Millie wanted. I don't know if you can understand this, Missus Jennson—but I'd have done anything for Millie. Anything, you understand? If it meant seeing her smile, there was nothing I wouldn't do. If we could somehow make it out of that trial and still have each other, it was worth it. That's what I was thinking."

"Afterward, then," I said. "After he was taken, and you were convicted."

"Millie may be the one at Northgate," he said quietly, "but make no mistake, Missus Jennson, we're both broken. Millie broke the day they took Jake away from her; I broke the day they took her away from me. I'm still broken. I don't know why I didn't speak up. I thought about it, but… my world had become a dark, lonely place. It still is. But I think maybe I don't have a lot of time left now that I've seen my Millie. Just can't live without her, you know?"

I hated how he'd made me feel. The ache in my chest felt like a betrayal. I pocketed the paper. "I'm sorry for everything that happened," I said. "To both of us."

"Me, too," Hank said. "I hope that you find your son. And I hope that Jake gets better."

I took a step back to leave. But Hank stopped me with a final word. "Oh, and there's something else you should know."

"What's that?"

He looked toward the parking lot. "I followed you for a little while," he said. "Like I said, I'm sorry that I couldn't get up the nerve to come to you straight away. But the thing is... I don't think I was the only one."

28

"Are you okay?" Linda asked when I got back in the car.

I shook my head but held up the paper. "He gave me this, though."

She took it carefully from my fingers. I let her open it; I still hadn't worked up the nerve. "Little Bright Day Care," she read. "Ralph Hayes, Norman Hayes, Gayle Hayes. Detective Paul Aaronson." She turned it over. "Just names. That's all, what is this?"

I closed my eyes and pressed my hand to my forehead. There was a headache brewing behind my skull there. "I think it's the day care where Jake was taken from," I said. "The Hayeses, I think, are the family he must belong to, and I guess Aaronson was the detective who was on the news at the time."

She handed the paper back to me. "What are you gonna do?"

"For now," I said, "I don't know. Go back to the hospital. See Jake, try to make something work with Nathan."

"And these people? Jake's parents?" she asked.

I caught a tone in her voice, almost accusatory, as if I'd already decided not to tell them anything. "I'll find out what I can about them," I said.

"Of course," Linda said. "But then, of course, you'll tell them, right? I mean, after eight years they have to think the worst."

"It's not that simple, Linda," I said. I shifted uncomfortably in the seat. "I know it's the right thing to do but… right now Jake is at Saint Monica's getting good treatment and it's not cheap. Who knows what the Hayeses' finances are like, for all I know they couldn't possibly take care of Jake the way we can."

She said nothing as she started the car and began to pull out of the parking space.

I watched her. She was avoiding looking at me. "Linda," I said softly, "you have to trust me on this, okay? I can't hand Jake over to strangers—"

"His parents, you mean," she said.

"Yeah. His parents," I agreed, "who don't know him because he's been away from them for almost a decade. How would you feel if you lost Tyler and got him back only to find out he was deathly sick? Wouldn't that be worse pain than if you never saw him again?"

"I honestly don't know, Elaine," Linda said, "but I know that you can't pick and choose when to do the right thing. You either do what's right or you don't. If you only do it half the time, when it's convenient, then you're never really doing the right thing at all."

That hit me in the gut. I looked out the window as we drove back to her house. When she pulled into the driveway, she left the car on and waited for me to look at her. "Talk to Nathan, I guess," she said. "It's your business. I'm your friend, Elaine, and I want what's best for you, and your family. Really, I do. I know you'll do what you need to."

"And what about my son?" I asked. "My baby? I still don't know where he is, where he went, who took him. Who's going to do right by me?"

"Hurting someone because you got hurt is how the world falls apart," Linda said. She turned the car off. "Think about what you would want, if you were these people, these Hayeses folks —if you were Gayle Hayes, and you knew that somewhere out there was a woman who was raising your son like he was her own, but you couldn't do anything about it. If you were powerless to get him back; how would you feel?"

I couldn't meet her eyes. I knew exactly what that felt like, now.

"I should go," I said.

"I'm here when you need me," she said. After a second she

reached over and took my hand in hers, squeezed it, and then let me go.

I let her go inside and made my way back to our house where I sat on the porch. I did need to go to the hospital, but before I did, I had to see what else I could find. Looking for the Hayeses' information online was easy enough, and I confirmed who everyone was. Ralph. That was the name they'd given Jake when he was born, the name I'd never known or called him by. There were articles from a place called Cassopolis, in Michigan.

Infant missing five months, the one I pulled up read. *Police investigation flagging.* A picture of the Hayeses was off to one side. They were a young couple, maybe in their mid-twenties. A little further down was a picture of the lead detective, Paul Aaronson, in front of a copse of microphones during an interview that looked unofficial.

Police have cleared suspect Andrea Williams, 24, who worked at Little Bright Day Care but was fired over suspected child abuse only a week before Ralph Hayes' disappearance.

There was a picture of this Andrea woman as well, it looked like it had been taken off Facebook – she was smiling and her friends had been blurred out. She was pretty, she had a beautiful smile. God, to think that they'd been so close. If they'd dug a little deeper, looked at everyone who had ever worked for the day care.

If they had, I wasn't sure how our life would have gone. We'd have kept looking, I suppose. Maybe we still would be. There was a hair's breadth of fate that separated the Hayeses and the Jennsons. Merely a bit to the left and they might be us, we might be them. They would be the ones worrying over their son's hospital bed, and we'd be the ones doing whatever they were doing now.

Waiting, probably.

It only took a little more digging to find a number. Not for the Hayeses, their information would be private by now. Nathan had gotten no end of calls and tips when he publicized a reward for finding our son. It had gotten so bad that he'd changed his number after the police arrested the Turners.

The number I found was for Paul Aaronson. No longer a detective, he was a private investigator with a website and everything. I saved his number and then stared at it on the phone. I don't know why, possibly guilt, but… I tapped it. I didn't put the phone to my ear though. I waited until I heard it ring and then ended the call. Then, just in case, I blocked the number.

Even that little brush with "doing the right thing" had started my pulse pounding. I put my phone away, caught my breath to calm down, and went to see my husband and son.

The hospital was quiet at night. I half expected Nathan to be asleep but when I got to Jake's room, I saw him sitting up in the recliner, watching over our son.

The dream room people had apparently come and gone. As I opened the door, I could see the difference they'd made. There were posters all over the walls of Jake's favorite Avengers, and his bed was now covered by a blanket showing off the Guardians of the Galaxy. He lay his head on a Black Panther pillow. They'd gone all out, apparently.

Nathan looked around the place. "You should have seen him when he saw what they did," he said quietly. "The look on his face…"

"I wish I'd been here," I said.

"Me too."

I closed the door gently behind me, went to Jake's bedside to make sure he was properly tucked in, and sat on the window bench near Nathan. "Did you get my message?"

He nodded. "I expected you to be back sooner. What were you up to?"

My instinct was to lie. To say that I had taken some time to decompress or take a girl's night with Linda. Somehow, I couldn't muster the will to do it, though. "I… I met with Hank Turner."

Nathan stiffened. He turned to me with a look of utter disbelief. "Say that again? You… what?"

"Let's talk somewhere else," I said. "I don't want to wake Jake up. Or for him to hear anything."

Nathan stood and stalked out of the room, leaving the door open for me to follow him. In the hallway, he leaned against the wall, his fists tight, and breathed hard. When I followed him out, he gave me a look that was half anger and half abject fear before he waved me to follow him and leave the pediatric cancer ward.

We didn't say a word until we were in the courtyard. No one else was there, and with the walls of windows around us I suppose we'd have known if anyone was approaching. Once Nathan seemed satisfied we were alone, he sank onto one of the benches near the fountain in the middle. "You met with Hank Turner," he said. "Face to face, you mean? You were in the same room as him?"

"We met at the park, actually." I sat on the other side of the bench.

"Why didn't you call me?" he asked. "Jesus, Elaine, he might have done anything, what were you thinking? Did you go alone?"

"Linda was with me," I said.

He breathed a curse and then took a deep breath. "What does she know?"

Right now wasn't the time for him to lose his temper and get distracted by it. I swallowed. "Nothing," I said, my voice shaky, "I didn't tell her, and she didn't press the issue. She only wanted to be supportive. I'll figure something out later."

Nathan bent forward, his elbows on his knees, his face in his hands. He groaned softly before he rubbed his face and then sat up again. "What did you and Hank talk about?"

"A lot," I said. "But the main thing was that he told me who Jake's parents are."

"We're his parents," Nathan growled. "We are his mother and father; we raised him, we taught him, we're the ones here—"

"I know that," I said. "I mean, the people he was taken from. They're this couple from Michigan. He gave me the name of the detective who worked the case, and the day care facility that Millie Turner took Jake from."

Nathan stared at the windows and then at the fountain in front of us.

"He also said that someone else was following me." I tugged my coat closer around me. "I wasn't wrong about that."

"Elaine," Nathan whispered, "you have to get rid of that information. You have to drop this and not pick it up again. I want you to hear me, and to understand something."

"I haven't decided to—"

"Be. Quiet." He looked at me with a harder face than I had seen on him before. His shoulder trembled. "We can't fix this. We can't give Jake back. It was a terrible mistake, but it's done now, and it's been done for eight years. We can't change the past and if you try…" He squeezed his eyes shut.

"I don't want to lose Jake," I said. I reached over and took his hand. "Nathan, really—I don't. I don't know what's supposed to happen, but what I do know is that we can't even start looking for our baby, the one that we lost, if we don't do something about this now. We can't reopen the investigation, we can't fix anything. If we go to these people, the Hayeses, and we explain what happened, then maybe we can work something out. Jake deserves to know where he came from and these people deserve to have their life back."

"No," Nathan said.

I held his hand when he tried to pull it away. "I know that you're angry with me," I said, leaning closer to try and find his eyes with mine, "I know that I've been on the edge, that we both have, and I know that you don't want to lose this family. But how can we possibly live with ourselves if we don't do this? We can't just forget. We can't move on from what we lost, and from what we've taken whether we meant to take it or not. Believe me, Nathan, it is tearing me into pieces to think about this but… I don't think I could ever look our son in the eye again and tell him that I love him if we choose to hide this from him."

"You don't understand," he said. "God help me… you don't remember…"

I let his hand go, but he caught it and held it and turned on the bench to face me. "You need to know—"

One of the doors opened. A woman came into the courtyard and answered her phone.

Nathan and I sat in silence as she had a terse conversation that sounded like it might involve a babysitter. All the while, Nathan gripped my hand as if I were going to flee any moment. The light wasn't much, but it was enough for me to see the sheen on his forehead and the glisten under his eyes. He was barely holding himself together.

When the nurse finally went back inside, it was like we could both breathe again.

I broke the silence. "I'm going to do whatever I have to do to see my son again," I said. "There's nothing you can say to convince me otherwise, Nathan. And fixing this is the only way to get there."

"You can't," Nathan said.

"We can wait until Jake is better before we—"

"No," he said, more firmly. "No, Elaine, I mean you can't see our baby again. You can't find him, you can't... he's not out in the world somewhere. I should have told you before."

I pulled my hand away from his and stood from the bench. I nearly tripped over the edge of the fountain. "What do you mean? What do you know? Nathan, what do you mean by that?" My knees grew weak. My chest tightened.

Nathan stood and reached for me but I backed away.

"Tell me, goddamn it." It came out a rasp.

His arms fell to his sides. He looked back to the bench. "Please sit."

I did so, numb.

He sat well away from me. "Elaine… you're never going to find our Jake. He's not… he was never taken." He took a shuddering breath, and all the light and warmth drained from the world when he found his voice. "He's dead. He died in the bathtub. Drowned, when you left him alone."

29

I was standing in our bathroom, leaning against the door. Outside, Nathan was pounding on it. "Elaine, open the door. I know you can hear me. Goddamn it, Elaine, open the door right now or I'm calling the police!"

I was sobbing. I remember that much. I had done something terrible. And some part of me wanted to pay for it. There was a prescription pill bottle in my hand. It opened, or I opened it, and then I was swallowing one of them. Then another, and another. Nathan stopped hammering on the door. I finished the bottle and then went to the medicine cabinet and took out another. The label didn't matter. These pills were orange. I swallowed handfuls of them.

Then I was floating or falling. Slumped against the door, I prayed that I would die. Not that it would be fast, or painless.

Just that, after whatever came next, everything would go black and I could finally rest.

The problem with that memory is that I remember it two ways.

In one version, I can hear Jake crying somewhere in the house. Even as the world turned inside out and began to swallow me, I could hear his piercing cry. Even when I couldn't hear Nathan's voice, I could hear that, clear on the other side of our condo.

In the other, there is nothing but a sense of guilt and dread that is heavy in the air, as if it were a real, tangible thing that had laid down on me and was pressing me to the ground.

One of them is a dream, one of them is real. Or they're both dreams, and neither is real.

I couldn't move or think or breathe as Nathan's words slipped between the fissures in my already cracking sense of reality and set to churning a storm of memories and half-forgotten dreams. I found myself searching for the memory of Jake, of seeing him in the tub. I couldn't even remember putting him down for a bath. There was a vague sense of having picked him up from the bedroom… and then I was shutting myself in the bathroom.

"Elaine," Nathan said. It *hurt*. I know that sounds strange. But hearing my name on his lips hurt me, physically, like a burn. When he moved toward me I pushed him away.

"No," I rasped. My vision blurred. "No, I… I didn't—it didn't happen that way. They told me, at the hospital, they told me that he was okay. I said that I thought he was gone, but you *told them*, Nathan. You said that I was delusional. And then… and then the police, the *police*, Nathan! They would have found him, found his body, I would be in prison now or dead. You're lying to me. Why would you lie about this?"

"Let me explain, please," Nathan begged, and again he tried to touch me.

I bounded from the bench, hugging myself, but I couldn't stand. My knees collapsed, and I barely let my arms go in time to catch myself on my palms. Grit from the pathway around the fountain bit into my palms and fingers. Tears dripped onto the back of my hands, adding to the fine mist that the fountain put off. "Go away. Don't fucking touch me."

His feet shuffled toward me and I swung an arm at him to warn him off. If he had touched me, then I would have screamed. I wanted to scream, but it was locked inside me, eating away everything behind my ribs.

"That night I almost lost both of you," Nathan said. "You have to hear me. You didn't mean to, baby, you were out of your mind. I couldn't lose you both. They took you in the ambulance and I… I had to…"

The scream inside finally clawed its way to my throat. "You should have let me die."

"Is there a problem here?"

I looked up to see an orderly at one of the doors, peering at us with concern.

"It's been a rough night," Nathan said. "We'll keep quiet, I'm very sorry. Our son is here."

The orderly looked at me, both eyebrows raised. I realized it was Jake's friend, Mark. The one with the tattoos. "Are you alright, Mrs. Jennson?"

I pushed myself to my feet and dusted off my knees and hands. I was still shaking, there was no way I could have hidden it. "We're fine, Mark. Thank you... we're... just stressed."

He nodded, gave Nathan another long look, and left us alone.

Nathan put his hand on my shoulder.

I turned and slapped him across the face. Hard enough that he staggered back. When he recovered he spat and touched his lip. Blood came away on his fingers.

The urge to do more damage was almost overpowering. The only thing that tempered it was the emptiness in my stomach that had begun to suck me down into it.

"I covered it up for you," Nathan said. "I knew that we could... try again or move on. We staged the abduction, thought that there was nothing to find so—"

"*We?*" I shook my head. "What do you mean 'we'?"

"I meant…" Nathan's jaw worked a moment and then clenched. "I misspoke, my head's still spinning."

"You said 'we'," I whispered, as more of the world around me came into light. "Did… did Roger know about this?"

"He…" He sagged. "You think I don't know about you and Roger? How he felt about you? Feels about you, maybe? How you felt about him?"

"I chose *you*," I said. "The two of you… I wish I'd never met either one of you."

I turned to leave, and Nathan grabbed my arm. "No, Elaine, you have to—"

"I don't have to *anything*," I said and tried to shrug him off. When he wouldn't let go, I jerked harder and had to catch myself to keep from falling when his hand came loose. "Don't you dare lay your hands on me again. I have to… go. I can't… I just can't."

I practically ran into the hospital to get away from him. Everything felt unreal, and I seemed to be watching myself like some puppet, being pulled along with unseen strings. I floated over my own head, watching my own back as I walked through the hospital to the elevator. I had parked in the deck. The lights were too bright inside. The carpet was too hard under my shoes. The buzz of halogen lights that made it more than obvious that I was a wreck struck my ears the wrong way and made me want to break them.

When I found the car, I didn't leave. I couldn't have driven. Instead I crawled into the back seat, closed and locked the doors, curled into a ball and sobbed until every thought, every emotion, left my head. Until I was empty, and numb, suspended in some moment of anguish that had stripped away all sense of time and self. I was nothing but loss.

When I emerged from my stupor, I knew three things.

The first was that I was not fit to be anyone's mother. How could I be, if I had let my own child drown, blocked it out of my memory—or, so I thought—and then mistaken someone else's child for my own?

The second was that whatever had driven Nathan, or Roger, it didn't matter, I could no longer summon anything but contempt for either of them. It seemed in that moment impossible that I would ever be able to again.

The last was that I had choices before me and they had become clearer. I had to make contact with Jake's real parents and reunite their family. It was more than simply the right thing to do. I couldn't leave Jake without a mother.

I fished a package of tissues out of the glove box and cleaned myself up in the mirror as well as I could. My eyes were bloodshot, and my eyelids were puffy. There was a hint of red around my nostrils. There was a hair tie in the console that I used to pull my hair into a pony tail that at least hid the fact that I had been laying on it. What I needed was a shower, but it seemed like a distant, trivial need, and I had no real impulse to fulfil it.

Once I was confident I wouldn't be mistaken for a transient, I went back into the hospital. There was light in the sky outside. It was early in the morning. My phone told me it was just after six thirty, and that it was about to die. I tucked it away and wondered if I should wait just a little longer to avoid seeing Nathan, but I couldn't bring myself not to go inside. I hoped that Jake was up so that I could see him before whatever happened next.

When I made it to the room, Jake was alone. He stirred when I opened the door, and when he rolled over and saw me he gave me a weak smile and sat up. "Hey, Mom. Are you feeling better? Dad said you were sick."

"I was," I said. "Still am, a little bit, but seeing you makes me feel better. Sorry I was gone for a while."

Jake shrugged. "It's okay, I guess."

I bit my lip as I sat next to him. "How do you like your new digs?"

He plucked at the Guardians blanket. "It's pretty cool. I miss my own room though."

"I know, sweetheart." I raised one arm so that he could snuggle close. His shirt was damp.

Jake had grown pale. I had missed so much time with him that

I hadn't seen it happen gradually, so noticing it then was abrupt, as if it had happened overnight. The machines by the bed beeped quietly as we snuggled, and I found myself rocking him gently to the rhythm of his own heart. I thought about the day my own son was born, and the times that I had rocked Jake to sleep. The memories were inseparable to me.

It was as though I had lived two different lives. In one life, I had given birth to my son, raised him, and been connected to him for all but a brief period. In the other, I had lost my child —lost my baby by my own actions.

Murdered through negligence. That was the truth of it.

My phone buzzed in my pocket. I pulled it out with the intention of setting it aside but there was a number on the screen from Michigan that I didn't recognize. My stomach tried to turn inside out. Had Hank reached out to the Hayeses? Had he told them where their son was? I tried to make my thumb swipe the screen and answer, but before I could force myself to do it, the call ended. I set my phone aside.

"What's the plan for today?" I asked. "Want to watch some movies? I could go and get us something if you've seen everything here."

Jake shrugged and then squirmed for a moment. "I have to…" He didn't finish but threw his blanket off and slipped out of bed and headed toward the bathroom. I rushed after him when he forgot to take his fluid drip along and rolled it to the door. Jake had ducked inside and bent over the toilet to throw up.

I clung to the doorway while he did. Bent over as he was, I could see the bumps of his spine under his shirt, see his hip bones. He was wasting away. That was the point, of course—what the medication did to him. It was in there, in his blood, killing off part of him.

When it passed, I went to him with a warm cloth and helped wash his face. Some vomit had gotten on his shirt, so I took it from him and got a new one, helped him put it on.

"Rough morning," I said when we finally got back to the hospital bed.

Jake nodded, looking sullen and miserable.

There was a knock at the door. Signey was there. I thought it was to check in and maybe bring Jake something for breakfast until I made sense of the expression on her face. "Uh... Mrs. Jennson, there's someone here to see you."

"Sure," I said. I kissed Jake's head. "I'll be back in a second, okay?"

Jake nodded. "Tyler said there's a new robot movie," he said as I left him. "We could watch it, if you want."

"Yeah, baby," I said. "I'd like that. I'll go pick it up later."

He smiled and lay back against his pillow as I left the room.

Signey looked nervous. She turned her back away from the end of the hall where a group of people were gathered and watching us. "It's the police," she said. "Some detective."

My heart skipped a beat. The police? I knew, a second after I realized what was happening, that Linda had called them. Her and her goddamned moral compass. I should never have gotten her involved. If the last week had taught me anything, it was that you could not trust anyone. No one at all.

"It's okay," I said to Signey. "I'm sure they just have some questions. I've had some… problems lately. Nothing to worry about it. Where's my husband?"

"He left a little earlier," Signey said. "With the other two gentlemen."

The two officers left a pair of nurses and began to walk in our direction, a Latin woman, maybe in her forties, a bit shorter than me, and a much taller black man; both of them with hard looks on their faces. The nurses peered past them at me. I locked eyes with Signey. "Two gentlemen? Who? Was one of them Roger? Tall, handsome, interminable flirt?"

Signey nodded. "That's one of them. The other was a big guy. Kind of rough in the face."

I paled. "Did you hear what they—"

"Elaine Jennson?" the female cop asked, she had a hint of an accent. She held up a badge. "I'm Detective Amalia Spinoza and this is my partner Detective Michael Truman. We have a few questions for you."

I looked from one to the other, and then at Signey. I gave her a little nod. "It's fine."

When she left, I looked over my shoulder to see that Jake was staring at us. "Can we step over there, please?" I asked. "My son is watching."

They both stepped aside so that I could pass between them, which I did. In the rest area there were a few other people sitting, reading magazines or on their phones. I kept my voice down. "What is this about?"

Detective Spinoza watched me for a second, her eyes studying me. "Mrs. Jennson, we've been made aware that there are some discrepancies regarding your son's medical records."

Part of me was almost relieved—Linda hadn't called me in after all—the other part was in an instant panic. It was the administrator who'd reported us, it had to have been. And he had whatever evidence they might need. "Those are confidential," I said. I glanced toward the nurses' station. People were still staring at us.

"Yes, they are," Detective Truman agreed. "That is, unless those discrepancies suggest a possible abduction."

I had to put my hands in my pockets to keep them from shaking. It didn't help with my stomach, which quivered with nervousness. Spinoza seemed to take that in, her eyes flicking down at my hands, and then seemingly looking for other signs of something—probably deception. There was no way my lies would convince her, I could tell that. But it didn't stop me from doing so on sheer reflex. "Abduction? I'm sorry, I don't know what you mean. What's this about exactly?"

"I think it would be best if you came to the station with us," Spinoza said. "You might be more comfortable answering our questions in private."

I took a step back. "Sorry, am I under arrest?"

"No," Truman said quickly, "you're not under arrest. We don't have a warrant, and we were hoping we wouldn't need one."

"But if we do need to obtain one," Spinoza said, a hard edge in her voice, "we can do that and come back here with uniformed officers and handcuffs. I don't think you want that."

Some of the people in the waiting room were trying to look as though they weren't paying attention. I looked around to see that a number of other hospital staff had gathered to watch us as well. I swallowed hard and felt the slight coolness of impending sweat sweep over me. "Okay," I said, "I will go with you but … could we wait for my husband to come back? I'd rather not leave my son alone."

Spinoza tilted her head a bit to one side. "Mr. Jennson is already at the station," she said. "We picked him up outside this morning and he didn't make a fuss. I suggest you do the same. If you've got nothing to hide, Mrs. Jennson, it won't take long."

"Don't make this harder than it needs to be," Truman said.

Spinoza came to me, put a gentle hand on my arm and urged me toward the hallway.

I knew it was the wrong thing to do, but I couldn't help jerking away from her touch. "You don't need to touch me," I said.

She stiffened. "We have a car downstairs."

"Fine," I said. "I'm coming with you, please... let me say goodbye to my son first."

They followed me to Jake's room and waited at the door while I assured him that I would be back soon and that I would pick up his robot movie while I was out. He was already bleary-eyed again.

"Signey will watch out for you, okay?" I said.

"Who are they?" Jake asked, looked toward the door.

I glanced back at them and forced a smile onto my lips. "Just some people who want to talk to me," I said. "Nothing to worry about. Dad and I will both be back soon, I promise."

Jake nodded, but watched the two detectives warily, perhaps instinctively sensing my own nervousness. It occurred to me that this could end up being the last time I saw him. For all I knew, they would find out everything, Nathan and I would be arrested, and Jake would go into the custody of the state. I pulled him to me and squeezed tight until he was groaning.

"Mo-om," he complained. "I can't breathe."

I let him go and wiped my eyes. He frowned up at me. "What's wrong?" He eyed the detectives again. "Mom? What's happening?"

I shook my head and kissed him. "Just rest. Please. I love you. I'll see you in a little bit, okay? Get some rest."

He lay back, and I left him to go with the detectives.

As we made our way down the hall and toward the entrance, Spinoza walked ahead of me and Truman behind. Both had weapons in clear view and anyone would recognize them as law enforcement officers.

Everyone, including Gertrude Olman as she entered the hospital with her briefcase in one hand and a coffee in the other. I tried to duck my head out of her sight but the look on her face was undeniable: she'd seen me.

Her and everyone else. I knew how this went. No matter how this went down, everyone would know one thing for sure: whether I was convicted or not, I was a criminal. Because only criminals got marched out of hospitals by law enforcement, right?

The worst part of it was that they were right. And I knew, deep down, that when we got to the station, that it would be the last time I saw the outside world.

30

I had seen police interviews and interrogations on television, but the reality was very different. I expected to be taken to a room with a single table, two chairs, and a two-way mirror. I figured that Nathan and maybe Roger were in other rooms, being told that I had spilled, turned over on them, and that the best thing they could do was turn on me in kind.

Instead, however, Truman left us when we entered the station, saying something about paperwork, while Spinoza led me to her desk and asked me to have a seat. It was a busy place, but quieter than I expected. There were no hard criminals being frog-marched across the office in cuffs, no crop of uniformed officers gathered around a water cooler eating donuts. Presumably they did that in a staff room somewhere like they did in any other office environment. It was almost unsettling.

"You're aware that your son's birth certificate indicates that he is your natural child," Spinoza said as I took my chair, "but that he is apparently not a genetic match to you or your husband, Mrs. Jennson?"

I wanted to know if I was under oath here, but that seemed foolish to ask. I couldn't claim not to be aware, and I had no idea what Nathan had said to them already. Honesty and ignorance seemed like the best choices. It did occur to me that I might just tell her the whole story, let her sort it out. It was what I had planned to do myself, really—there was no way that revealing Jake to the Hayeses would be a quiet affair, after all.

"I was made aware by the administrator, or one of the admin staff, I guess, at the hospital, yes," I admitted. "They said they thought it might be a … mix-up or… something."

"Maybe that was the initial assumption," Spinoza said. "But that person did some digging, made a few calls, and it seems there was no mix-up. Now, I'm having a hard time coming up with a reasonable explanation for it."

"Me too," I said. "I… don't know what it means."

Spinoza leaned back in her chair and appraised me. She clicked her pen twice and then glanced at her computer screen. "Do I understand, Mrs. Jennson, that your son was abducted at three months of age, and was missing for—if my information is accurate—approximately six months?"

"That's correct," I said. My voice wavered. I took a slow breath to try and calm myself. She was going to pin me down if I lost control. Spinoza was looking for a crime, and there was one to find. I suddenly felt very alone.

"And, it looks like there was a conviction—Mildred and Hank Turner, is that right?" She looked back to me. "Those are the couple who were arrested, charged, and convicted with first degree abduction of a minor, as well as breaking and entering, and a short list of other charges. The people who served time for abducting Jake, correct?"

"Y-yes, that's correct." My mouth was dry. "Could I get a glass of water, or something like that?"

Spinoza's lip twitched up at the corner. She nodded and looked around briefly. "Murphy," she said, "could you grab some water for Mrs. Jennson here?"

"Sure, Spinoza," said one of the other officers, a barrel-chested, olive-skinned man who didn't smile when he looked at me. I wondered how many of the officers in the room knew why I was here.

"Thank you," I said.

"Certainly," Spinoza replied. She leaned forward again, bracing her elbows on the table. "What do you think that I ought to know, Mrs. Jennson, so that this odd series of events makes a little bit more sense? Is there some part of the story I should be aware of? Because, I'll be completely honest, right now it looks pretty bad."

She looked over my shoulder and raised an eyebrow before she sighed.

I had opened my mouth to say something—what, I didn't know, words were tumbling out of my mouth without me really considering them, or what they might cost me. But before another word could come out, a man spoke up behind me.

"Detective Spinoza," he said, his voice a smooth baritone, "what a pleasure to see you again. If you would be so kind, I'd like to consult with my client before you ask her any further questions."

I looked up to see a man I had never laid eyes on before. He was hook-nosed, immaculately shaved and dressed, and reminded me a bit of Roger—the way he made an effort on every little aspect of his appearance. He looked expensive.

Spinoza's jaw muscles flexed, and she looked to me. "You understand, Mrs. Jennson, that you're not currently under arrest?"

"I do," I said. I looked up at the alleged attorney. "Nonetheless, I think it's a good idea to speak with my attorney, if that's what he thinks is best."

She drummed her fingers on the desk and nodded. "Of course. I'll arrange a conference room."

"Thank you so much," he said. "Please ensure our conversation is confidential."

"Absolutely," the detective said. She stood and led us away from the office area and to a hallway where we passed a number of closed doors before she stopped in front of one of them and knocked. When there was no answer, she opened it and held it open for us.

I entered first at the attorney's insistence, and he followed me in. A moment later, and we were alone.

"Please," he said, "have a seat, Mrs. Jennson."

"Who are you?" I asked. "Did Nathan hire you?"

"I was retained by Mr. Walton," he said. He extended a hand. "My name is Ethan Crux, I'm with Logan, North and Crux."

I shook his hand. He had the soft hands of a person who moisturized often. The name was familiar. Why? I sat in the chair on one side of the table while Ethan sat on the other side. It came back to me as he drew a folder from his briefcase and set it on the table.

Logan, North, and Crux had been part of the investigation into Roger and Nathan's business—the investigation started by Diana's husband when he'd been let go. He pushed the folder across the table toward me.

"In this folder you'll find the relevant documents to confirm custody of your adopted son, Jakob," he said. "Including the death certificate of your biological son."

My mouth fell open. "I'm sorry... I don't..."

"These documents," he repeated, "confirm your custody of Jakob. The hospital had an unfortunate mix-up, but it's all being cleared up. If you'll please review these documents, we can clear this business with the police up right away and you can get back to him. I apologize for the inconvenience. We weren't notified of the predicament until half an hour ago."

"You got these together in half an hour?" I asked.

Ethan pushed the folder a little closer to me. "If you'll review them, please."

I opened the folder carefully and paged through the papers inside. My sense of what was real began to dissolve as I pieced through them. Adoption papers for Jake. A death certificate as well. The same name was on both documents though—Jakob Peter Jennson. I looked up. "These papers say that Jakob was adopted... and that... that he passed away?"

Ethan spread his hands. "It's not my place to comment on you and your husband's choice of names. I can certainly understand that in a moment of grief one might seek to recapture such a devastating loss."

I looked down. The date of the adoption was just a week after Jakob's birthday. On the death certificate...

"This says Jakob was stillborn," I whispered.

"I'm very sorry for your loss," Ethan said softly. "Now, when I invite Detective Spinoza in to clear this up, I need you to let me talk. If she asks you a question, I will answer on your behalf. It's very important that you do not speak without checking with me first. Understand that anything you say during this interview can be used to incriminate you if not now then later. My colleague is with your husband at the moment in one of the nearby interview rooms, speaking with Detective Truman. I'm very sorry that you were brought in like this. But we'll be out of here very shortly. Okay?"

All of these papers were lies. And it was inconceivable that they had been fabricated in half an hour. I thought about Jakob, though, and closed the file. "I understand."

Ethan gave me a sympathetic smile and then stood, straightened his tie, and knocked on the door.

An officer opened it, and Spinoza came in a moment later. She took the chair from the corner of the room and brought it to the table where Ethan took his seat with a muttered, "Thank you", before she pulled the other chair away from the table and sat in it.

"So," she said. "You should both know that as of now the camera is on and this interview is being recorded."

"Certainly," Ethan said. He picked up the file and handed it to Spinoza. "As you'll see, this has all been the product of a terrible misunderstanding and the unforeseen complications arising from a choice of name for the Jennsons' adopted son, which, I'm afraid, neither of them could have anticipated. My client doesn't intend to seek remuneration from either the hospital administration or your department. It was an unavoidable and unique set of circumstances."

I had to bite the tip of my tongue to keep from reacting. Even if I spoke up and agreed, there was no way I could do so convincingly. Instead I folded my arms and tried to make myself sit completely still.

Spinoza opened the file and went through the documents. Her expression remained neutral. There was no sudden realization evident on her face, nor any appearance of outright skepticism. If she wasn't buying the papers, she was keeping it to herself.

After she'd gone through it twice, she closed the folder and laid it on the table and slid it across to Ethan. She looked to me. "Do you attest, then, that these documents are genuine?"

I opened my mouth, and Ethan's knee very gently bumped mine. I looked to him, and for a moment, our eyes met. He gave a slight nod.

"I do," I said. "If I had—"

"If the Jennsons' weren't in a state of abject fear for the health of their son," Ethan cut in, "they would no doubt have presented these documents to administration at Saint Monica's. However, they were under no legal obligation to attempt to predict any difficulties administration would have in parsing through an unusual case like the Jennsons'. So, if that's all, I'd like for my client to be released so that we can reach out to Saint Monica's and ensure that this complication causes them no further emotional distress."

"Emotional distress," Spinoza repeated quietly. She pursed her lips, gave me a long look, and then gave us a nod as she placed her hands on the table and pushed herself to her feet. "I hear you loud and clear, counsellor. By all means, you are both welcome to go. I apologize for any inconvenience we've caused."

"You're just doing your job," I said. The words didn't feel like they'd come from my own throat. "No harm done, of course."

Ethan smiled sublimely up at Spinoza before he scooted his chair back and stood and held a hand out to me. I barely felt his fingers as I stood. When Spinoza knocked on the door and then stood aside, we walked out and I kept my mouth shut as we left the station. Ethan didn't look around, didn't seem at all nervous or concerned with the fact that we had just presented documents that were certainly fraudulent to a detective in the course of an investigation. That had to be some kind of crime —obstruction of justice? Perjury, maybe? Had I been under oath in some technical sense? I didn't know.

Outside, Nathan was waiting for us with an older, equally sleek attorney, as well as Roger. I stopped cold. They were with the man who'd been following me. He gave me a brief look, winked, and then turned his attention back to the attorney who was with Nathan and Roger.

"You've got nothing to worry about," he was saying. "If you have any other problems, just call me directly at that number. We'll ensure that we make the necessary arrangements with the insurance company as well, so don't give that another thought. The papers are one hundred percent legitimate, I assure you."

"Thank you for your help, Rich," Roger said, and shook the older attorney's hand. He looked at me as he let the hand go. "How are you doing, Ellie? You must be shaken up. Come on, let's get back to the hospital and see that boy."

I nodded dumbly and shook Ethan's hand again when he offered it and said his goodbyes. He and Rich left, and Nathan led me down to a black town car—the same one that had been watching the house. Roger opened the back door for me and I hesitated before I got in. I looked to the stranger, and then to Nathan. "What's going on, Nathan?" I looked to the stranger again, and then to Roger. "Who is this? Why was he following me?" And to him, "You were following me, weren't you? I saw you at the hospital, and in front of the house. Someone tell me the truth."

"If you'll get in," Nathan said, "we can do that. But not here in front of the police station. Let's go."

In my gut, there was a visceral resistance to getting into the back seat of that car, as if I could sense some malevolent aura around it. I had to quash the feeling just to take a step closer and practically hold my breath to get in. Nathan followed. Roger and the other man got into the front, with Roger on the passenger side. We pulled away from the steps of the police station in short order before anyone said anything else.

"Why was he following me?" I asked when we were moving.

The man driving glanced at me in the rearview mirror. I looked to Roger. "Does he work for you?"

Roger didn't immediately answer, and Nathan cleared his throat. "He was hired to keep an eye out for you," he said. "When we heard that Hank was out of prison. Just in case."

"We were just looking out for you, Ellie," Roger said. "Mr. Quincy is an old friend. Very capable. Sorry that I didn't say anything; I didn't want to make you nervous."

In the mirror I could see one corner of what looked like a smug expression on "Mr. Quincy's" face. Something about it didn't feel right. Whatever was going on, though, my gut told me to go along and keep any cards I thought I might have out of sight until I learned more. "Fine," I said. "Nice to meet you, Mr. Quincy."

"Nice to meet you," he said in that gravel-barrel voice. "Sorry if I spooked you. Just doing my job."

"Sure," I said. I leaned on the door so that I could no longer see his face in the mirror.

Nathan didn't look at me. He was watching the back of Roger's seat with focused intensity, almost pointedly, as if he were specifically avoiding looking in my direction. Something brushed my fingers, and I looked down to see his hand barely touching mine. As I pulled my hand away, his fingers pressed down on mine briefly before he withdrew it.

At the hospital, we got out at the front entrance—Roger,

Nathan, and I. Nathan drew me away from the car, but before Roger closed his door, I heard Mr. Quincy saying something to Roger.

"We'll be in touch," he said. Or, at least, that's what I thought I heard. It was barely audible. Whether it was that or something else, Roger was stock-still for a moment before he closed his door and turned to us looking just a bit stiff.

"Glad that's sorted out," he said, and plastered on a fake smile that I had seen before. "I'll head up with you, say hi to Jake real quick before I take off. Lots of work left to do."

I let him pass me. Nathan did as well. As Roger went through the front doors, Nathan put a hand on my shoulder.

"It's all going to be okay," he said. "But… you have to hold it together, okay? It's important."

"Nathan," I said, and brushed his hand away, "what the hell is going on? How long have you had those documents? Stillborn? I gave birth to our son, I remember it, believe me, and you told me that he… what happened that night. So what the hell is the truth?"

Nathan clenched his jaw and made a visible effort to relax. He looked toward where Mr. Quincy's car had driven off as if checking to see if it was really gone and then ran his fingers through his hair with a sigh. "The truth is that we've dealt with the problem for now. So… let's just go in and see our son. You don't have to like me. I understand how you must feel. But you do have to look like everything is fine. Do you understand? Anyone who's watching needs to think that everything is fine."

All I could manage was to nod quickly before I watched him go inside. Once I'd regained control of my feet, I followed him. The feeling of someone's eyes on me was a sensation I couldn't shake though, and at the door I turned compulsively to scan the parking lot.

Anyone who's watching? I'd been certain that someone was watching me, and I'd been right. Now I knew who that was. So... who the hell was Nathan talking about?

31

We hadn't been gone long enough for the staff to turn over, and they had not forgotten. As I made my way across the lobby two detectives brandishing badges and guns in plain view had escorted me through only a couple of hours earlier, I could feel the eyes of Saint Monica's staff on me. I had an urge to stop and tell each one of them that it had all been a terrible mistake but, of course, that would have been a lie and I was in no condition to deliver it convincingly. Moreover, I was tired of lies. So very, very tired.

Nathan had gone ahead of me though not by much. When I turned a corner that he'd only just disappeared around, I stopped—he'd encountered Gertrude. That woman had waited for us to return, or possibly wondered if we were even going to return. They were too far away for me to hear them clearly, but I heard Nathan say something that sounded like "paper-work" and "documentation."

I smoothed my shirt compulsively, ran my fingers through my hair and decided to reset my ponytail, but there was nothing I could really do to make myself one hundred percent presentable. Leaning against the wall, I took several deep breaths and tried to calm the trembling that hadn't really left me since Nathan told me about what had happened. It was no use, of course. All I got was vaguely light-headed.

Waiting indefinitely would be foolish—Gert would eventually leave in this direction. So I rounded the corner and approached them with as much confidence as I could.

"Miss Olman," I said as I reached them. "I see you've met my husband."

Gertrude assessed me quickly—I could see it in her eyes, the once up and down and a subtle tightening of her lips. "Yes, I… thought it would be best if I hung around when I saw you leaving," she said. "Just in case Jakob had any worries or questions."

"Well," I said, "we're back now. I'm sure Nathan told you what happened."

"That it was all a terrible mix-up," Nathan said. He put a hand on my back, between my shoulders as he gave me a sympathetic look. "It's been a really rough morning, Miss Olman, as I'm sure you can understand. Maybe we could do this later? I'll be back here after six tonight."

Gertrude looked from Nathan to me and back and finally gave a patient smile. "Well, I suppose waiting a few hours can't hurt. How about seven? It'll be after hours but, well, you're never really off the clock in my business anyway."

"Don't I know how that feels," Nathan said. His smile was more genuine than Gert's was. It made me wonder how many times he'd given me that expression and whether I had believed it when I saw it. It even reached his eyes.

They shook hands, and then Gert and I shook although I didn't quite process it when she offered me her hand. There was a moment of panic—if I didn't shake it would seem standoffish, or like I had something to hide, which I did. If I did take it, then the moment of hesitation would seem equally as strange. God, it was like I could feel multiple pairs of eyes judging my every move. I could not convince myself that every small action I made wasn't being analyzed.

I let her hand go and mumbled my own goodbye as she left.

"We need to deal with her tonight and be done with all of that," Nathan said. "The last thing we need is DEFACS breathing down our necks."

We. Our. Like we were a team or something, in this together. I realized then that… we weren't. Or, at least, I didn't feel that way.

"Wait," I said as Nathan turned to go into Jake's room. Roger came toward us with three cups in hand.

Nathan stopped, glanced down the hallway, and then gave me a hard look. "Not right now. If you need to get your head straight, then go home. Everyone here is already staring, now isn't the time to make another scene."

"Nate, Ellie," Roger said as he came close. "You'll have to take your drinks. Americano on the left for you, Nate, and I got you your shot in the dark, Ellie."

I took mine from him and Nathan took his. Roger sipped the last one for himself and then pursed his lips as he looked us over. "I... interrupted something. Should I go?"

"I'm going," I said. "I'm sure I look terrible."

"Never," Roger said. He checked his watch. "Well... Nathan doesn't really need to be in the office until about one. That's a few hours, yeah?"

Roger was so... calm. So upbeat. He knew everything, Nathan had said as much. Did he not know that I knew? Was he still keeping up the charade?

"Everything okay, Ellie?" he asked.

I realized I'd frozen, staring at him, and had to shake myself. "Zoning out. I should go, I'll be around in a bit. When Jake wakes up, tell him I love him."

Nathan's face became unreadable. "Don't be gone too long. And keep your phone on, please."

"Of course," I said, and gave him a kiss on the cheek. Roger came in for his and I flinched away before I chuckled nervously and then pecked him as well.

I rounded the corner and stopped.

I listened. Nathan could be soft spoken, but Roger never was.

"She's not alright," Roger said.

Nathan said something I couldn't hear and Roger grunted. "I'll give it some thought," he said. "We may have to give her what she wants."

What I want? What did Roger know about what I wanted?

"Let me make some calls," Roger said. "Mind if I say hello to the tyke?"

Their voices disappeared entirely, and I tried to imagine what Roger might have meant. What calls could he make that Nathan wouldn't, or couldn't?

I got to the car and plugged my phone in to let it charge on the way home. By the time I pulled into the driveway it was on and had chimed to let me know I had missed three calls and had a voicemail from a number I didn't recognize. But, it was the same one as before—the one from Michigan. I listened to it on speaker, breath held in my chest.

"This is Paul Aaronson," the man said. "I had a call from this number on my office line. Initially I didn't think anything of it, but, well, I'm professionally paranoid, you see, so I traced your number and did a little research. I found a few news articles and I think you know the ones I mean. And I think that I know why you called me. Maybe you want to talk, maybe you've changed your mind. But I would like to meet. I'm not with the police anymore. Call it... call it an old wound that never quite healed over. You can reach me at this number."

I hung up and nearly deleted the voicemail.

Nearly.

Who knew if I could trust Aaronson? At this point, I didn't trust anyone. The problem was that I wasn't sure if I even trusted myself.

I sat in the car for a long moment and then looked across Linda's lawn to see her through the bay windows of her dining room, hauling a basket of laundry across the house. Probably, I thought, no one trusted me, either.

All I had left were sins, and I was so very, very tired of carrying them with me everywhere I went, waking or sleeping. I craved something like absolution even if I could never really get it. So I went inside, showered and changed clothes, and went to Linda's door in a wide-brimmed black hat with my hair tucked under it, a leather jacket that was just a little over-sized, and wearing my largest pair of sunglasses.

She didn't speak right away, uncertain of what to say either because of what she knew or how I looked. I didn't need her to speak though.

"I need one more favor from you," I said, "and then you never have to see me again if you don't want to."

Linda sighed. "Don't say that," she said. She waved me in. "Come on. What do you want to get me into now?"

32

I peeked through a small gap in her blinds and watched as Linda made her way across the lawn in my hat, jacket, and sunglasses, her hair pulled up and under the hat just as mine had been. She walked quickly and then got into my car. A moment later she pulled out of my driveway and sped off down the street.

I waited and watched.

Only a few seconds later, a car followed her. I couldn't be certain it was actually *following* her specifically, but if there had been someone watching, it would have been them. Linda had not obeyed the speed limit.

After another minute, I took her keys and took her car as we'd arranged. She hadn't been keen on the idea right away, but when I explained what it was I wanted to do with it, she gave in. Trust Linda Keeler to be supportive of doing the right thing. She'd hugged me and told me that whatever happened she would be there for me.

She'd also insisted that I take her gun. It made my purse heavy and when I got into her car, I stuffed it into the glove compartment with a silent prayer that I wouldn't be pulled over.

I considered calling Nathan, but if I told him, he might talk me out of going.

I made the call on my way north. Aaronson answered after only two rings.

He gave a sigh of relief, or maybe despair, before he spoke. "Is this Elaine Jennson?" he asked.

It was unsettling; both that he knew my name, whether he'd looked me up or not, and the tone in his voice. I felt like a ghost, haunting someone who only just realized who was responsible for all the noises they heard at night.

"It's me," I said. "I'm on my way north."

"I found an address," he said. "Tricks of the trade. No reason for you to come all the way up though. Meet me at a place called the Fishbone in Fort Wayne."

"Why not meet in Cassopolis?" I asked. "Will the Hayeses be with you? Do they not live there anymore?"

He hesitated a moment. "It'll just be me. Let me know when you're close. I'll be there."

The call ended. I checked Linda's gas. Fort Wayne was only two and a half hours away. It would save a lot of time. I plugged it into my GPS and gripped the wheel with white knuckles all the way there.

———

I had been to Fort Wayne once before, during a business trip with Nathan and Roger. We had brought Jake with us, he was five at the time. He'd remarked then that Fort Wayne was "red." Until that moment, I suppose he thought that every city was like Dayton—green from a distance. We had been there in time for some festival for Johnny Appleseed and gotten Jake a raccoon skin hat there that he refused to take off for weeks. The majority vegan moms I had only just started having to deal with at the academy had been utterly scandalized, which was why I didn't push too hard for him to take it off. Come to think of it, that was about the time that Linda and I really began to bond.

Strange to think that even then, everything I knew was a lie. My memories weren't less happy because of it, this one still holding a store of happiness for me—as if I could reach in and ladle some out to alleviate the pit that I could feel myself falling into. I wondered if it were possible to shovel enough happiness from those memories to completely fill it in.

But, alongside the happiness, there was a bitter taste now. At every happy turn, I saw Nathan's face, heard his voice. Roger was there, too, now. Both of them, acting as if everything was fine when it wasn't. All these years. What must that have been like for them?

The Fishbone was a divey little bar and grill off Jefferson Boulevard, a part of the city I vaguely recalled driving past. Roger had pointed out where Fort Wayne's minor league baseball field was and suggested we might be able to get tickets to some game that was playing while we were in town. Even then, Jake had not liked sports, and I certainly wasn't a baseball fan. Still, he and Nathan had ended up going with a client. Business, they'd said. Even that was questionable now.

I walked into the Fishbone after having sent Aaronson a text. It didn't look like the kind of place you'd set up a sting operation. I took one of the several empty booths and asked only for a glass of water when the middle-aged waitress came by to put a menu on the table. She didn't seem pleased.

My phone rang. I answered it without looking. "Hello?"

"Ellie?" It was Roger.

"Yeah," I said. "It's me. Hi, Rog. Is everything okay?"

"You tell me," he said. "Listen, ah… where are you now? Close?"

"Just getting something to eat," I said. I winced. It was stupid. There was nowhere I could legitimately be that would take two and half hours to get back from. Never mind however long it took me to speak with Aaronson. "And then I have to…

to go help Linda with… some errands. To say thank you for watching Jake and being so helpful, you know."

"Linda," he said. "That's your neighbor, right?"

"That's the one. I'm sure you've met her before, at a dinner party or something."

"Right," he said. "Sure, of course. Are you eating at home?"

Panic set in. At about that time, the door to the Fishbone opened, and a tall, broad-shouldered man in a cheap suit came in, scanned the tables, and then headed toward me. Aaronson, it had to be. He was walking purposefully and watching me as he approached. No one was with him. "I'm not, actually," I said. "I went out. Listen, Rog, can I call you back? My food just got here and I'm starving, so…"

"Sure," he said. "Whenever you're done. Just wanted to have a chat about some things, see how you're holding up. Nothing serious."

"I'd like that," I said. Aaronson stood over me for a moment before he sat down, frowning. I grimaced as I pointed at the phone and mouthed the word 'sorry.' "I'll call you soon, Rog."

We hung up and I put the phone down. My hands shook so badly that the phone rattled against the table before I let it go and clasped my hands together, then reached out to offer Aaronson a hand instead.

He spent some time looking me over and didn't accept my hand. I withdrew it and clasped both hands together in my lap.

"Are you...?" I asked.

"Paul," he said. "Paul Aaronson. And you're Elaine Jennson. Husband Nathan Jennson, son Jakob Jennson. One child, as far as I could tell. You live outside Dayton, Ohio."

I shifted in my seat. "Is that how you introduce yourself to everyone?"

Paul gave a soft snort and finally seemed to relax. "You're not the kind of person I expected."

That threw me off whatever balance I'd had. "I don't think I have a lot of time, Mr. Aaronson—"

"Paul," he said, "please. Mind if I smoke? This is the only place in town where you can smoke inside. Reminds me of the old days kinda."

"If you want," I said.

While I waited, he tapped a cigarette out of a pack, searched for his lighter, and then lit it. He waved for the waitress with the lit cigarette, and she turned to fetch an ashtray from the bar. Once she'd come and delivered it, and taken his order of water and coffee, we sat for a moment while he took a few drags and worked something out behind his eyes.

"After eight years," he said, finally, "I'm wondering why you finally started looking."

"Looking for what?" I asked. I knew, but I wanted to see what he thought of me.

He breathed out a plume of smoke that stank—I'd never liked the smell of cigarettes—and shook his head slowly. "We both know why you're here, why you called me, what you were looking for. You know about the Hayeses. So, you know that Jake isn't yours. I want to know why it took eight years."

"You said you found the news articles," I said. "You know about the Turners. About the... the abduction."

"Is that what it was?" he asked. He ashed his cigarette with an alarming slowness. "You mean to tell me you really thought that boy was your son?"

"It's complicated," I said. "He was... the same age, the right size. He had the right hair, the right eyes. I had been medicated out of my mind while he was gone. When I saw him I *believed* he was Jake."

"So, what changed?"

"We just met," I said, "and I'm not even sure that I trust you, to be honest. This... cloak and dagger, dive bar stuff makes me nervous. I just want to know where I can contact the Hayeses."

He raised an eyebrow. "You want to give him back?"

I opened my mouth, closed it, and had to blink through the sudden burning in my eyes. "I did lose a child," I said. "I know what that feels like. I keep thinking of Gayle Hayes and what she must be going through. What she must have gone through. If I was her, and someone brought my son back to me after eight years… it would be like getting my soul back. And right now, maybe he needs her more than he needs me."

Paul puffed his smoke again and then put it out. He sipped his coffee and then sighed as he reached into his pocket and pulled out a folded bit of paper. Not notepaper, or some scrap. He handed it to me, and it was a newspaper clipping.

I opened it and wasn't sure how to feel about what I saw.

"I'm afraid you're a little late," he said.

Gayle Hayes, the newspaper clip read, *May 28, 1974 - March 29, 2015. Abigayle Lucy Hayes was born May 28, 1974 in Crookston, Minn. She joins her husband, Norman Peter Hayes. There are no known relatives.*

I looked up. "What… what is this?"

"An obituary," Paul said gently. "You're a few years too late, Elaine."

33

"I was the detective on the Hayeses' case," Paul said, after he ordered something a bit stronger and I relented as well. The whiskey was cheap, and it burned going down but at least it gave me something to anchor myself to. "The investigation went on for about a year, but after just one month the pressure was on to put it on the back burner. It's still technically open, you know, but it's a cold case now. You know that once the first three days have passed, these cases typically go unsolved? Once those days have gone by, the situation is clearly more complicated than normal. There are about half a million missing persons cases a year in this country alone, and all but a couple of thousand resolve in those first few days. Usually, it's as simple as someone close to the family, or a misunderstanding."

He sighed and shook his head. "And then, sometimes, it isn't."

"What happened to the Hayeses?" I asked.

He sipped his whiskey, grimaced from the burn and then set it down and ran his finger along the lip of the glass, back and forth, his eyes distant. "I had to drop the case. Of course, it was still active, but there were other cases that were fresh, that needed eyes on them right away. That's something they don't usually tell civilians—we do what we can to find out what happened, to solve a case, but there are other things that need our attention and there are only so many of us on a force." He was thoughtful for a moment. "The Hayeses didn't take it well, of course. No one would. I was the one that had to sit down and have the conversation with them, tell them that until there were new leads, the case was no longer a priority.

"It broke them, I think," he said softly. "I remember hearing Mrs. Hayes... how she screamed like I told her we found a body. They didn't give up right away though. She and her husband poured just about everything they had into looking for their son. They hired a private investigator, sold their house, their car, everything. When they turned up nothing, they had nothing left."

I swallowed hard. It could have been me. If the Turners had gone somewhere else, anywhere else, then the last eight years would have been a pit of suffering. I might have still crawled into a pill bottle to get away from it, but without Jake, I would never have climbed back out. "How... did they die?"

"Norman started drinking," Paul said. "He lost his job, leaned on unemployment for a few years. I'd see him at a bar occasionally, he'd turn and walk out. One night he walked out, got into his car and ran a red light. Died at the hospital a few days later. Gayle lasted another year."

"Before?" I knew what he was going to say. I imagined myself in the same position—having lost my son and then lost Nathan. I know what would have happened.

"Found her in her apartment." Paul finished his whiskey. "She'd left a note. Nothing long or complicated. It just said '*I can't anymore.*' She took pills, we still don't know where she got them. Some opioid, maybe bought on a street corner somewhere."

I went cold. "She… did they, ah… have any relatives? Siblings, parents?"

Paul frowned. "No, not a single one. A few distant cousins, but they weren't around during the investigation. I gather they weren't close."

"So what do I do?" I asked.

Paul lit another cigarette. "Tell me something," he said around it as he put his lighter down, "is Ralph happy?"

It took me just a moment. Of course, he'd have known Ralph by his birth name. "He is, I think. He's sick right now but fighting. He's sweet, and kind and smart. We put him in a private school, an overly designed place called Greenway Heights. They've got this Robotics Club that he loves, and I swear he's going to grow up and change the world one day. I don't even understand half the stuff he can do. He has good friends."

"Then I guess it could have been a lot worse," he said. "You know, my pet theory at the time was a black-market adoption. There was a big ring up here a couple decades ago, some hill-billy mafia business, a little after I first joined the force. They'd buy or sometimes steal infants and then sell them off to rich families that had the kind of skeletons that made traditional adoption impossible. Or sell them overseas, sometimes. Busted them up in the eighties, but those operations never really go away. We recovered about half those kids, but by that time some of them were teenagers in high school. Some were adults. Some we never found and there's no telling where they are now."

It made me sick to think about it. What kind of person *bought* a child? "I don't think the Turners could have afforded that."

"No," Paul agreed. "So, I guess all that just leaves the question of what happened to your son, right? To your Jake?"

"It's, ah…" I nodded and had a hard time looking at Paul in the eyes. I occupied myself with another small sip of whiskey and then stared into it. "I'm still trying to find that out."

"What do you know so far? Anything?"

I shook my head. What could I possibly say?

Paul rested his elbows on the table and caught my eye. "I know it can seem hopeless," he said, "but I looked for Ralph for years. And long after I'd given up hope, I heard from you. I know it's hard, Mrs. Jennson, but you can't give up. Even if someone tells you that you should. If I could take back anything, just one thing—it would be what I said to the Hayeses."

I wished it were that easy. That I could just believe. I wanted to; I wanted hope, a comforting lie that I could cling to. A part of me reached for it. "How would I even start looking?"

He leaned back again, lips pursed, and gave a long sigh as his eyes searched the table for a moment. "I take it you haven't involved the police," he said.

"No, we... they did get involved, but..."

He raised an eyebrow. "But?"

My mouth was dry again, and I was out of water. Another sip of whiskey it was, then. It didn't help.

Paul rubbed his jaw. "You don't have any reason to trust me," he said. "I understand that completely. Let me tell you this— you seem like a nice lady. I did a little looking into you and your husband. Professional habit, you understand. Seems to me that Ralph—Jake—could have ended up in a worse place. A lot worse. Some of these kids end up overseas, in terrible places, and we barely find any of those. I won't even tell you what condition they're in when we do. But Jake? It looks like you've given him a happy life. I think you're probably a good mom. And the Hayeses... they checked out a long time ago and now there's nothing to fix, okay? You wouldn't have called me, or come and met me, if you weren't loaded up with guilt. All this—it wasn't your fault. All I can say to you now, is that I'm just glad to know that he's alive, and that wherever he ended up, it was better than where most of these kids go by a long shot. I'm not interested in getting the police involved."

"Then what do you want?" I asked. "Aside from closure, I mean."

"That's just the thing," he said. "I don't really have it, do I? If I had kept looking, followed the right leads, maybe, or interviewed more people... I don't know, done something a little different, I might have gotten Ralph back to his parents. And if I had, maybe you would have kept looking for your kid and maybe you'd have found him. I guess I feel responsible. Not directly, but indirectly."

"You couldn't have done anything," I told him.

He nodded. "Maybe, but perhaps I can now. Anyway, it's entirely up to you. Tell me, or don't. I understand either way. But I want to help make it right and the last thing I want is to destroy another family."

We sat in silence for a moment. The waitress finally came back, refilled my water and eyed us both. I wondered what she thought of us. Silly of me, but she had one of those faces, you know? The kind that appear to be judging you. She couldn't have known Paul, but he had a look about him—like he might be the sort that digs up dirt. Maybe she thought my husband was cheating on me.

Just distractions. When she left to refill Paul's glass at the bar, he spread his hands, the offer open and almost literally on the table. "I know a thing or two about a thing or two," he said. "That's all."

I did have questions. Things that I couldn't ask Nathan, or Roger, and which didn't quite add up. Things that made me wonder, but that I hadn't given as much thought to as I should have. After all, what was there to wonder about? I had let my own child die and taken in another. Now he was sick. Like a changeling, I thought, those old silly stories. How many of them were like mine, in truth?

"The hospital caught a… detail, I guess you'd say, in Jake's medical records," I said slowly. "Someone reported it, I guess, and we ended up being interviewed by the police."

"Shit," Paul muttered. "Are they pressing charges?"

"No," I said quickly. "That's the thing… my husband produced papers. Adoption records, and ah… a… a death certificate. For my son—my biological son. There was a story about how he had died and we had adopted Jakob, and that he was the child that was abducted and that we got back."

Paul frowned and started to speak but closed his mouth when the waitress returned. He watched her until she was out of earshot and then lowered his voice. "You can fake those kinds of documents," he said. "I've seen it done. Whole identities, brand new people sometimes. There's always someone who knows a bureaucrat somewhere who will sign something or hit a few keys at a computer. It doesn't come cheap, though, but I guess someone like your husband could afford it. Have you looked at your bank statements?"

"I haven't. I didn't think to…"

"Like I said, professional habit." He swirled his drink but didn't sip it again. "How long between when you found out and when that interview took place?"

I counted days in my head. "I don't know… maybe… a week? A little more?"

He grunted, eyebrows raised.

"What? What does that mean?" I asked. My heart started to race.

"I can't say for absolute certain," he said, "but… in my experience those kinds of things take a while. See, you can't just make this stuff up on the fly. It has to be entered into all the right systems and it has to be done just the right way, by the right people. Organizing all that takes time. When we busted this illegal adoption ring, we found a lot of this stuff. We ended up making six arrests on corruption and conspiracy charges at the state department of Indiana; all of them directly involved. They'd been paid off."

"You're saying that these documents were made up in advance," I said. That tracked, of course. If Nathan knew what had happened to our child, what I had done, then he and Roger might have gone about preparing for the inevitable discovery.

Even if Jake hadn't gotten sick, it could have come out some other way. I wasn't ready to grasp onto any kind of hope just yet. "That just means that my husband knew about it. And... he's admitted that. He kept it from me to spare my feelings, he says, but that doesn't prove anything."

"Well, here's the thing," Paul said. He swirled his drink again. "Your average private citizen doesn't have the infrastructure to make something like that work. But if they've got the money, and the connections, they can get the people who *do* to work it all out."

"Like corrupt police, or...?"

"Like what we in the professional business call 'organized criminal actors.' The mob, or mafia or whatever you want to call them." He shrugged. "There are other ways, but, see, it's not as simple as paying the right people. You have to cover that money up, launder it, get it into the right hands in a way that people like me can't figure out what's going on. You need a whole operation for that."

He rested his gaze on me, a pointed look on his face. "What do you know about your husband's business dealings, Mrs. Jennson?"

34

Fifteen years ago, long before Nathan and I had separated, and having a child was anywhere on our radar, Roger and Nathan's company had been struggling. In an effort to save their business and share resources, they had purchased my brother-in-law's specialty software company in the hope of expanding into the financial sector and away from social apps.

For a little while, it had worked out alright. Lawrence brought with him small clients that Roger used to get larger clients while Nathan began leading Lawrence's customers toward banking apps that acted more intuitively. Most of it was stuff I never really understood, but the end result was that things picked up and we began to climb the socio-economic ladder much faster than we had before.

Three years in, however, the three men had some kind of

falling out. I always thought that it had something to do with my and Diana's growing conflict over our mother's care; that Lawrence had been directed by Diana to put pressure on the company so that I would cave. It was precisely the kind of manipulative tactic I expected of my sister, to be entirely honest. She'd always been like that, ever since we were kids.

But it very quickly got serious. Nathan came home one night and declared that Lawrence was out—that they were firing him after they'd promised he would have a permanent position in the new company, managing the branch that he had started himself. "It just isn't working out," Nathan said at the time. "Lawrence is holding us back, getting between Roger and the clients and making trouble. We lost a big client because of him, and they aren't coming back into the picture until he's gone. It's for the good of the company, our employees. And us, Ellie. I hate it, but Lawrence will get severance pay and a good reference from us. Enough to start over on his own if he wants, I promise."

The next thing that I heard about the situation was absolutely preposterous.

"That weasely son of a bitch," Roger said over dinner a few weeks later when he and Nathan had brought work home to discuss away from the office. "Having us investigated for fraud. This is all because we had him resign when he damn well knew he was hurting the company. How else were we supposed to comply with our own bylaws? It's not like he didn't know what they said."

Fraud sounded like a big deal. But when I raised the question, the two of them had dismissed it like they'd made a joke. "There's nothing there," Nathan assured me. "Lawrence is just putting pressure on us. We'll comply with the FBI and the IRS and this will all go away. Our books are immaculate. But it's a damned inconvenience, and it makes us look bad. Any clients that hear we're being investigated are at the very least going to hit pause on any work we have with them and at worst they'll find another firm."

Roger was far less concerned. "He's just trying to ruin us but it won't work. The way these things go," he said, waving a fork with a piece of steak on it, "is that everyone gets a little nervous at first, until the investigation is over, and then when it's done, confidence goes way up. Call it a tempering experience. A little bit of fire won't burn us down, it'll just make us stronger in the long run."

"Why would he accuse you of fraud to begin with?" I asked. "I mean, why that specific accusation? Isn't he afraid of a libel suit?"

"We're not going to countersue your brother-in-law," Nathan said when Roger seemed like he was about to threaten that very thing. "He's been through enough. He just used the right buzz words, that's all, and the FBI had to take him seriously."

"Buzz words," I said. "Like 'fraud'?"

"Like 'organized crime,'" Roger corrected. He rolled his eyes. "He's claiming we're in bed with the mob. Like this is nineteen twenty-something Chicago, and mobsters rule the streets. It's complete bullshit, I can't believe anyone took him seriously."

Nathan soothed my worries away with a hand over my then much longer hair. "Don't give it any thought, Ellie," he said. "There's nothing to any of this. Really. It'll all go away, and we'll be fine."

Now I found myself wondering just how much I should have been concerned. It did seem, at the time, completely insane to suggest that Nathan could have anything to do with "The Mob", as if we were in some *Godfather* movie. But as Paul went on about modern organized crime, and how things had changed in the last century, I began to think about Lawrence and question why he'd really gone after my husband's company.

"See, it used to just be drugs, or maybe alcohol during the prohibition," Paul was saying. "But it had to get bigger than that. These days, mobsters had their fingers in everything. And it's not like those old mafia movies, you know—*Godfather*, or *Serpico*, all that stuff. These are white-collar folks. They even deal with digital crimes now, hacking people's identities, taking computers hostage, blackmail, that kind of thing."

"You think that my husband is involved with the mob?" I asked. It seemed impossible, even laughable—some kind of conspiracy theory. Paul may as well have been telling me the earth was flat, or that my husband was a lizard person.

At the same time, it rang too many old bells. How had Nathan and Roger gotten those documents? How had they managed to fabricate an entire identity for Jake?

"I don't know what to think, Mrs. Jennson," he said. "But if he were… well, it depends how deep into it he is, and how valuable his interest is to them, whether they step in to take care of their investment. These people are all about money, and only money. For them, money is power, see? If they can make more money by intervening than by staying out of it, they intervene. If it'll cost them too much to do that, they don't. These aren't petty crooks, they're business people. Profit comes first."

I shook my head. "I don't see what that has to do with Jake. I'll admit that… I would be concerned if all that were true but this doesn't help me."

"Maybe not," Paul admitted. He pushed his empty glass away and clasped his hands as he leaned his elbows on the table. "But if there was something you could do to find proof; some paper trail, or a contact they've got that you've maybe seen around; anything suspicious. You start pulling that string, maybe let me help you pull it, and the whole thing unravels. It could be big."

For a moment I searched his eyes. The light started to dawn on me, a bit at a time, and my stomach sank. "How does this help me? Or Jake?"

Paul gave me a long look and then shook his head. "At this point, it's about justice, isn't it?"

"If I wanted justice, Mr. Aaronson, I would have called the police." I opened my purse to pull out a twenty, hoping it would be enough to cover my drinks. "I should go. Thank you for the information about the Hayeses, I appreciate your taking the time."

He frowned as I stood up. "Now, listen, Mrs. Jennson," he said, "they could be dangerous people. You think they won't know if you're digging around, finding answers?"

"All the answers I might find only make things worse for my son," I told him. I stepped out of range when he reached for me. "We're done here. I don't know what you think you know, but I know everything I need to. What I know is that I'm all my son has left. Me and his father."

"It would be a shame if the police knew about our conversation," Paul warned.

A flare of anger briefly made me see red. "Are you threatening me, Mr. Aaronson?"

Paul narrowed his eyes, but eventually softened. "Of course not." He reached into his pocket and withdrew a card. I looked at it as though it might be poisoned, but after a few moments of considering it, I took the thing and stuffed it in my purse. "If you feel like you need my help, you call me. No charge, alright?"

I sniffed and noticed the handful of patrons in the bar that were staring at me. As well as our waitress. I looked back to Paul. "I don't know that I will need to," I said quietly. "Until I do, just… forget that we spoke. Please. My family is broken enough as it is. We can't take another loss."

"What about your son?" Paul asked. "Your first son, I mean. The baby."

"He's long gone, wherever he is," I said. I closed my eyes against both the sudden sting of tears, and the distant echo of a baby crying. *Ghosts,* I thought. *Just ghosts.*

"I couldn't find the Hayeses' kid," Paul said. "But I might be able to find yours. Missing persons was my beat. Let me help you, Mrs. Jennson."

"I'd prefer if you didn't," I said. But something… something made me pause before I walked off. An ache that I couldn't ignore, couldn't let go of. An irrational desire to change the past. "My husband can't know of this meeting, or anything we've talked about. If you have to look, no one can know. I'll be honest, I don't have much faith that you'll find anything, Mr. Aaronson, but… if you feel compelled to look, I can't stop you."

"Don't you want to find him?"

"More than anything," I whispered. "More than I've ever wanted anything. But some things may be better left alone. If I've learned anything these last weeks, it's that."

He turned away from me. "You go back to your family."

I left him there and stepped out into the afternoon sun feeling exposed and raw. I would make it back to the hospital before

Nathan was supposed to be off work. I didn't know if he had stayed home or not. I had been with Paul for just over an hour. And, I had told Roger that Linda and I had gone out to run errands, hadn't I? I couldn't remember if I'd been specific. And it seemed strange that he had called me. I decided to call Linda, just in case, to see if I needed to amend my story somehow.

With no time to waste, I left the parking lot and pulled onto the main street. The gas gauge was nearly empty. I had passed a gas station on the way into the city and decided I could wait until I got there to fill up. A crazy thought occurred to me that my clothes might smell like cigarette smoke from the bar, and that there were no smoking bars in Dayton, and that maybe Nathan would know I had left town the moment he got close enough to smell it. Nathan wasn't the type that noticed little details like that, it was a paranoid thought bordering on delusional. Still, I found myself paying close attention to every breath, hunting for any out-of-place scents.

At the gas station, I stepped out to fill the tank up. As I was about to swipe the debit card, I stopped. Maybe Nathan didn't notice little details but maybe it depended on the detail. I dug into my wallet to see how much cash I had left. Fifteen was enough to make it home, at least.

I hated this. I hated the secrets, the hiding, needing to be careful. I hated that I had chosen to leave Jake to get these answers and that in the end it had been pointless. What had I really learned? Only that the guilt I felt was going to be with me forever. There was no way to fix what had been broken. Every direction I could possibly turn would end the same way—destroying Jake's life. At this point I didn't even care what happened to me, or to Nathan. But there was no out for Jake.

I paid the attendant inside, avoiding eye contact. That fifteen dollars was the last of the cash I had on me. I couldn't even afford to get coffee and I desperately needed caffeine. I mumbled my thanks and returned to the car to pump gas.

It wasn't until I had taken the nozzle off of the pump that I realized I wasn't alone at my car.

"I'm trying to figure out," Detective Spinoza said, nearly causing me to drop the gas nozzle, "why you would leave the state and come to Indiana, of all places, when there is so much on the line, Elaine. Care to enlighten me?"

35

I put the nozzle in the gas tank and locked the handle into place, trying to act as though I wasn't as startled as I had been. "Detective," I said. "I didn't realize I was being followed."

"Do you normally worry about being followed?" she asked.

I ignored the question. I suppose I had gotten a little too relaxed when I thought Linda had gotten Roger's tail off of me. "We're outside your jurisdiction," I said. "And it's not illegal to cross state lines. Unless you have charges pending?"

Spinoza shook her head and folded her arms as she leaned against the pump. "But you know, I bet this car holds more than fifteen dollars. And I bet that a woman like you has at least, what, two credit cards? Even if the bank was bone dry, I think you could fill up. Unless, that is, you didn't want someone to know you'd been here. Using a credit card would leave a trail. So, what I wonder is—who is it you don't want to know you're here?"

"Maybe with all the medical bills we're a little tapped out," I said. "Or maybe I'm having an affair."

She clicked her tongue, squinting at me as though trying to see through whatever mask I was wearing. "You don't seem the type," she said. "I bet you've never once cheated on your husband. Even if things were rocky between the two of you… I'm betting you'd never do that to your son." She pursed her lips and raised both eyebrows. "But then again, I could be wrong. While I was waiting for you outside the bar, I did a little digging. Nothing special about this place. It didn't come up in your background check, you've never lived here. So, you were meeting someone. Who were you meeting, Elaine?"

Frustration got the better of me. "Am I under arrest?"

Spinoza smiled, mirthless and cool. "No. You're not under arrest. After all, the paperwork is all above board. As far as the state is concerned, the story is just what your husband and his team of lawyers says it was."

"Well, then, I'm sorry you took the time out of your day to stalk me all the way to Indiana," I said. The gas pump stuttered, slowed, and finally stopped. I took the nozzle out and replaced it in the pump, then screwed the gas cap back into place until it locked. "If you'll excuse me, it's a long drive."

But the detective didn't immediately let me go. When I started to open the door, she intercepted in a few steps and rested her hand on it before I could. "Here's something to think about," she said softly. "That doctor who signed your son's death certificate—turns out he lost his license a few years back. You know why?"

"I don't even remember his name, detective," I replied. "I didn't keep up with him."

"He was arrested in connection to human trafficking," Spinoza said. "Real bad stuff. He took twelve children from parents. High-risk pregnancies. Switched them for stillborn babies, doubled up on the paperwork. That's just twelve that we know of, over eighteen years. Made a fortune. You know how much a baby is worth?"

My stomach knotted. All I could do was shake my head and keep my hand from trembling on the door handle.

"A quarter of a million dollars," she whispered. "Now, here's something that's really, really interesting. A coincidence, you could say. Your husband's company filed for bankruptcy once, about eight years ago. And then, like magic, it seems the company got a cash infusion from an angel investor. Saved the day. I want you to tell me how much this benevolent soul invested all at once. You could look it up if you wanted—it's public record, filed with the IRS and the State Department. Guess."

"Am I under arrest?" I asked again. "Because if I am, you're welcome to follow me back across state lines and arrest me back in Ohio, back in Dayton, where your badge is worth something."

She searched my face. We both stood there, waiting for the other to move, or crack, or do anything.

I couldn't really call it a win, but she blinked first and stepped away. "The thing is, Elaine," she said as she walked slowly backward, toward the back of the car, "when someone dies, there's a whole trail involved. A complete trail. Want to know what I found on your son's trail? I mean, the baby, the one you lost."

"Good day, detective," I said and opened my door.

But I heard her voice again before I could make myself close the door.

"Nothing," she said. "That's what I found. Nothing but the death certificate. No cremation, no burial, no permits for either, no logs at a morgue or at the hospital. Nothing. Almost like it didn't happen."

I watched her in the rearview as she returned to her car. It was non-descript, a car you'd see anywhere, all the time. I supposed that was the whole point. Roger's bodyguard suddenly seemed like a rank amateur, driving around that *Godfather* car.

I knew without Detective Spinoza having told me, that if Nathan and Roger had really been saved by some investor, the number was two-hundred and fifty thousand dollars. She wouldn't have brought it up otherwise.

But Nathan told me that he and Roger had covered up my baby's death. Of course there wouldn't be a trail. All there would be was the fraudulent death certificate.

How would they have known what doctor to go to for that?

36

What Detective Spinoza told me followed me back to Dayton, to Avila Grove, and to Linda's door. It seemed like there were two stories unfolding, finally coming together, but which one of them was real? I knew the one that I wanted to be real. But wanting it didn't change reality.

"Honey, you got problems," Linda said when I delivered her car. She pulled me inside quickly and peeked through the door before she closed it, then leaned against it as if she thought someone was about to come charging through.

She looked worried. No, *scared.*

"What happened?" I looked around instinctively for something out of place. Had she been broken into? It didn't look like it.

Linda bit her lip. "I got caught. When I left here, sure enough someone followed me. I just went into town, I had to get some groceries anyway, but I was watching him, right? This big fella, just like you described. He parked a few spots down from me and I waited inside the Great Foods store in their café to, you know, see if he'd come in."

"Did he?"

Linda shook her head. She stood from the door, locked it, and went into the living room. It was a mess, but I was hardly in a position to say anything, much less judge at all. Linda's place was just normally so immaculate. "He waited outside," she said as she picked up a glass of something and drank half of it in one go. "I thought maybe he'd just left. I didn't see his car out there, so I went back to your car after I got a few things and, well, he was there, at the car waiting. He was a little confused. He didn't say anything to me, just left. I saw him call someone."

"When was this? How long after I left?" I sat when she did and took the glass when she offered it but put it down on the table.

"Must have been two, two and half hours? I ran him around town a little first and then waited in the store about forty-five minutes to an hour." She shuddered. "He looked mean, Elaine."

Poor Linda. I couldn't very well tell her that he was, supposedly, one of Roger's people. For that matter I wasn't sure that would make any difference. I put my hand on hers. "I'm so sorry, Linda."

"Now that he's seen me—"

I shook my head quickly and squeezed her hand. "No, no, that shouldn't matter. He was supposed to be following me and when we gave him the slip, I think he just had to call his boss."

Linda's eyes widened. "Elaine, sweetheart… what trouble are you in?"

"Honestly, Linda, I wish I knew." I let go of her hand and leaned back on the couch. Instantly, my eyes started to grow heavy.

"How long have you been up, hon?" Linda asked.

"Too long," I muttered. I forced myself to sit up and suppressed a yawn to keep Linda from getting any more concerned than she already was. Bad enough she was worried about her own safety now. "I'll handle my tail. You just take care of your family, okay? I have to get back."

She reached out to hold me in place as I began to stand. She leaned in, her eyes intense, brow knit. "Sugar, this is getting out of hand. You need to call the police, file a report. Do something. With everything you got going on, you can't take chances like this."

"Right now is the worst possible time to deal with the police." I sighed and rubbed my forehead. "Believe me."

Linda took her hand away and then looked away from me and

to the mess around the living room. She wrung her hands as a tension grew between us.

Of course, she could never just come out and say that she needed to be done. I might have been hurt or felt just a little more lost... but I was so unbelievably tired. All the emotion felt drained from me, and I couldn't yet bring myself to scrape up anymore. "Whatever comes next," I said softly, "I can handle it. I don't want to put you, or your family, at any kind of risk. Thank you, Linda, for everything you've done for me. I've really needed it. I don't think I could have gotten through this in one piece without you."

She wore a tight smile as she finally met my eyes again. "You know I think the world of you, hon," she said. "And I love that little boy of yours. I don't care where he came from. I just have to watch out for my own family, my own kids, you know?"

"I do," I said. "I really do. I should go. Jake's got to be wondering where I am."

She walked me to the door, and we had a brief, quiet goodbye before I went back to my own driveway to retrieve my car.

Linda had been my one confidant, my one ally. Paul was too far away to make any difference and in any case, I wasn't completely sure that he counted as anything but someone with an axe to grind. That left me with no one. Jake, I supposed. Signey? But Jake needed to be kept far away from all of this, and I could hardly expect Signey to do anything that might put her job on the line.

No. In every direction now there were only lies, secrets, and the people who were keeping them. Whatever happened next, I knew that I was on my own. Alone.

37

R oger called again just as I entered the hospital. I found myself looking around to see if his guy was in sight before I answered.

"Rog, hi," I said. I didn't bother to hide my exhaustion. "Sorry I didn't call you back, I haven't really been myself."

"I can't exactly blame you," he said.

There was an awkward, tense silence.

"Roger?" I asked. But I could hear his breath on the other end of the line.

"Where are you now?" he asked.

"I just got to the hospital," I told him. Which, I was betting, he damn well knew. "I'm about to go in and see Jake. Why?"

"Can we meet in a little while? Just you and me. There are some things I need to talk to you about, things I need to ask you."

My gut instinct was to tell him that we would never again be alone together if I had my way about it. "I'm not sure, Roger," I said. "With everything going on right now I… I really would rather just stay with Jake until this is all over, you know?"

"It's about your son," Roger said. He let that hang in the air.

I couldn't keep from saying something anymore. "I know what you and Nathan did."

"Me and Nathan?" He gave a snort. "Is that what he told you?"

Whatever balance I had held onto slipped out from under me. I rocked on the bench and had to steady myself with a hand. "What's that supposed to mean, Roger?"

"I'm still at the office," he said. "Nathan is here, too. The police came by earlier, that detective, the man—Truman. I don't know what Nathan said to them, but he looked worried when they left. Will you please just meet me this evening? I want to protect you, Elaine. You have to believe that."

"Protect me from what?"

"Seven o'clock," he said. "Not at the hospital… there's a little park down the road, toward town. Well lit, you can't miss it. Meet me there?"

It turned my stomach, just as if I'd leapt off a cliff and was plummeting fast to jagged rocks below. But if Roger was going to be the one to flip? It was worth it to hit those rocks if it meant getting answers. "If I do," I said, "you answer all of my questions. I have a lot of them."

"Everything you want to know," he promised. "I'm so sorry for all of this. You have to know that all I ever wanted—and I think all Nathan ever wanted—was to get you back."

I swallowed hard, and it hurt. "You know that he might have been yours. You know, don't you?"

"I'll see you tonight," he said. "I'll make everything better. I promise."

He hung up, and I composed myself before I stood and went inside. I got all the way to Jake's door, and could see him dozing in his bed through the window when Spinoza's partner stopped me.

I groaned out loud. I didn't mean to; it just came out. "Please, can this wait? I already spoke with your partner."

Truman shook his head. "Just a few questions. We can do it here, or down at the station. Your pick."

I pressed my forehead against the window and watched Jake for one second longer before I closed my eyes and steeled myself for what I hoped would be the last hoop I needed to jump through tonight. "Lead the way. Let's get this over with, please."

38

"I know you were approached by my partner," Truman said when we tucked ourselves into the far end of the café. "I spoke with your husband today. He had some interesting things to say."

I kept my fingers still around the paper coffee cup in my hands. "Detective, I'm too exhausted physically and emotionally to do the back and forth any justice. Do I need my lawyer here?"

"That's your right," he said. "If you want to call him, I'll wait."

"Just tell me what you want," I said. "I'll decide afterward."

"Can I quote you on that?"

It was hard to tell which of the two of them was supposed to be the good cop and which one the bad cop. "My son could wake up any moment and be alone," I said. "Again. Is this about the doctor? The one who wrote the death certificate?"

"No," Truman said. "This is about your addiction. And the suicide attempt. And the claim that you may have made a mistake when caring for your son and that as a consequence he died."

Nathan. That son of a bitch. Was this him trying to throw me under the bus? Why? He'd go down with me, he had to know that, and what about the two of us coming together to keep the secret and take care of our son?

I measured my next words carefully, weighing each one before I spoke. "I did spend some time in a… an institution where I believed that was the case, but as I'm sure my husband told you, it wasn't."

"You can see how it might call your credibility into question, though," Truman said. "In the event of, say, a prosecution."

I blinked. "A… prosecution? I was under the impression I wasn't under arrest, detective. Has that changed?"

"Honestly?" He leaned back and shook his head. "I'm not sure yet."

We were quiet as I did a quick mental calculation. He wanted something, and not from or about me—at least not yet, it seemed. Otherwise, I would be in handcuffs. So, it was Nathan or Roger, or their company, maybe. Paul Aaronson and Detective Spinoza both seemed to think there was something going on, and Spinoza certainly discussed the case with her partner. I was beginning to think they'd coordinated these two encounters together.

I couldn't come right out and ask if he wanted me to turn on my husband. That would imply there was something to turn on him *about*. Which, as it turned out, there probably was, but it was nothing I had anything to do with.

My brother-in-law, however; it was entirely possible he did know something.

"Can you tell me something, detective?" I asked. "If it's not… I don't know, classified or something."

He raised an eyebrow at me, maybe amused. "I can certainly tell you whether I can or not."

"Do you and your partner think that my husband and his company are involved with some kind of organized crime? Or that they were? That's what she made it sound like."

Truman spread his hands. "You tell me. Is he?"

"I don't know what my husband does," I said. "When he does talk about work, it's technical things, or some new contract that means more income. Honestly, I have no idea how the company works, just that it does. I've never been employed there, never had anything to do with it. Nathan has never expected me to be involved—just to raise our son. He hasn't even been that keen on the idea of me working." I stopped, closed my eyes, and sighed. "Shit."

"What?" Truman asked, leaning forward a bit.

I waved a hand at him. "No, it's nothing… I had an interview. I completely forgot about it with everything going on. Jesus…"

"It's understandable," he said. "If you did know anything, Mrs. Jennson, and felt the need to clear your conscience, you should know that we can protect you."

"All I have to do is wear a wire and get my husband to say something about his involvement with the Corleones, right?" I propped my head up on my hand. I was so, so tired.

"If it's true that your husband doesn't talk about his work much," Truman mused, "then I don't think wearing a wire would help."

"Then what would?" I asked. "What could I possibly do even if it were true, which I'm not saying I believe."

He drummed his fingers on the table. "When your lawyer came to meet you at the station," he said slowly, "Spinoza said you looked surprised. When he handed over the paper-work for Jakob, she said that you looked liked you had no idea what was happening. You know what I think, Mrs. Jennson?"

"I really want to know, detective," I said. "I mean that. Lately it seems like everything has two faces and I'm only seeing half of each. I just want my life back, you know? I had a direction and now…"

"Hard to know where you're going when you can't see the road," he said. There was sympathy there. Genuine, even, though maybe I was too tired to know the difference. Probably part of his job was making people like me feel understood. This was an interrogation—I hadn't lost sight of that.

"Something like that," I said. "So, what do you think, Detective Truman?"

"I think that whatever's going on here, it's not on you," he said. "I think you were surprised at the station because you didn't know, because it's your husband, and maybe his partner who did the work."

"The work?" I wondered. "The allegedly faked documents?"

He smiled. "Allegedly, yes. But much more than that. We have reason to believe that Roger Walton has connections that go beyond crooked doctors. We did some digging, made some calls. Turns out he and his father both have a history of, shall we say, near misses with the law. Now I don't know if your husband is directly involved with anything or not. And you may not know anything about that—but if you could convince your husband to work with us, we might be able to cut a deal for both of you. And as for the paperwork, well… it all looks legitimate. Our chief would never clear an investigation. Not with only what we have now. But we do know at least one thing."

"That is?"

Truman narrowed his eyes, his nostrils flaring as he thought something over, weighed up some decision. On what basis, though, I hadn't the faintest inkling. "One of the big red flags that tells us, when we see it, that there might be some kind of crime happening, is when money changes hands. As soon as something comes up, we start looking for the money. Who got paid, who took a hit, which bank accounts suddenly closed or opened." He watched me carefully. "The Turners' public defender bought a new house right after the trial. Public defenders do hard work for not enough money. I know; we always expect a conviction or at least a plea deal when we go up against them in court. There's no clear proof, yet, but Spinoza thinks maybe she got paid off to… throw the case. She could have insisted on a DNA test, convinced her clients how critical it was. But she didn't. And honestly, your case wasn't that strong. Not really, not enough that she couldn't have won. But I'm guessing you don't know anything about that."

"I was indisposed," I said. "For almost all of it. I wasn't discharged from Northgate until the trial was almost over."

"Yeah," he said, "I'm aware of that. But that just means that if it did happen, it was someone else—someone with a vested interest. Either in your family, or in your husband's business. See where this is going?"

"Aren't you tipping your hand?" I asked. "That's your lever-age, isn't it?"

Truman nodded. "I guess it is. But Spinoza told you about the payments. About the doctor."

"She did," I said.

He leaned forward. "Then let me ask you this, Mrs. Jennson. What exactly do you think they got paid for?"

39

I managed to get back to Jake's room before he woke up. It was past six. Nathan wasn't back yet and hadn't called me. Maybe he was angry, or maybe he was avoiding me. After all, he'd spoken to the police, told them about my past. I tried to get inside his head. There was a time when I thought I could do that; when I felt like I knew him.

Instead, I had to think it out like he was a stranger. He had to have told them about me in the event that I turned on him. Maybe I didn't know Nathan anymore, but he knew me —knew that I had a conscience. Or, at least, that I used to have one. Watching Jake sleep, and holding tightly to my love for him, I realized I wasn't sure I really *did*. If a person does something terrible, and gets caught, and admits what they did was wrong and asks forgiveness, that's a conscience.

When you didn't get caught, though, and so you don't ask forgiveness or admit what you did…

I thought of Hank Turner, of how he'd kept quiet for the sake of his wife. The more I had time to reflect on him, the more I found it impossible to hate him like I had in the past. He was just a man who was lost in his love for his wife. In some macabre way it was almost romantic even if it was heart breaking.

What exactly do you think they got paid for?

Two hundred and fifty-thousand dollars.

That's what an infant was worth, Spinoza had said.

Two hundred and fifty-thousand dollars.

"Mom?"

I emerged from the fog and focused on Jake's face. It was dark in the room, the only light coming from the machines around him and filtering in through the blinds from the hallway. But I could see him clearly as if it were broad daylight. "Hi, baby," I cooed, and brushed his face with my fingertips. "You slept pretty hard, huh?"

He nodded and started to push himself up. As he did, he put a hand to his mouth and nearly fell back down. I'd seen that face before. I dove for the bucket under his bed and put it in place just as he began to heave. In a moment, he was empty of whatever bile had gathered in his stomach. There was no sign of food.

The episode was violent enough that when he finished, he was crying. It was a weak, high-pitched, thin sound. Like a baby bird, I thought—fallen from the safety of the nest and injured.

"I'm sorry," he said between two sobs.

I set the bucket down and pushed it out of the way, but not so far I couldn't reach it again, and slid onto the bed beside him so that I could gather him up close in my arms. "Ssh, shh, you have nothing to be sorry about." I rocked him and let him cry into my chest.

All at once, memories came to me. Every time he'd been sick. Every time I had held him close just like this, and checked his temperature, and given him lemon water with honey in it to soothe his throat. It was as though I could feel his form against mine at all those different ages at the same time. From when he was small and colicky, and lay on my chest, just shy of twelve months old, to the time he got chicken pox and Nathan had to stay the week at Roger's place because he'd never gotten them as a child. Then, Jake and I had been together twenty-four hours a day. He'd slept in my bed the whole time he was sick, and I'd had to stay up and keep him from scratching in his sleep.

"When am I gonna be better?" he asked, his voice muffled by my shirt.

"Soon, sweetie," I said. "Really soon. Just one day at a time. After this is all done, it'll be just like when you had chicken pox. Remember how miserable you were?"

He shrugged against me. "Kind of."

"It'll be just like that," I said. "You'll always remember, but you'll forget how it felt. You just have to keep taking little steps forward. Just keep going and don't stop, and before you know it, you're through. Okay?"

He didn't respond. I looked down and saw that his eyes had closed. The monitors didn't show anything was wrong, so I didn't panic. I just continued to rock him, hoping that somehow, he could just sleep through it all and wake up better on the other side of it.

And I desperately hoped that I would be there to see it.

Nathan never showed. I left the hospital just after seven after trying to decide whether I wanted to meet Roger or not. In the end, there was nothing worse that I could have learned, nothing he could have told me that would be worse than what I had already been told or what I suspected after talking with Detectives Truman and Spinoza.

As I walked down the sidewalk to the park near the hospital, I sent a text to Paul. It was short, and I deleted it afterward. *Anything you can do to help. Don't respond. I'll call you later.*

I spent the next ten minutes getting a handle on my nerves. Between the lack of sleep and, well, everything else, the fading light turned every shadow into someone watching me out of the corner of my eye. There was no sign of the black town car, of Roger's bodyguard. The sidewalk was empty other than someone in maroon scrubs carrying a backpack toward the hospital. She was young, maybe new to nursing, or some kind of tech. I hadn't learned what the different colored uniforms all meant yet. Her face was lit by her phone, and she had a bounce to her step—not quite dancing to whatever was piping through her earbuds.

Is it strange that I was jealous of her? Just for a moment. Then again, she had problems I couldn't see from looking at her. Everyone does, right?

Roger was already at the park when I arrived. He hadn't sat down. His arms were folded and he was pacing. Wondering why I was late, I'm sure, and if I would come. There was a pensive, worried look on his face. He looked up just after I saw him, and his expression changed to relief as he approached. "There you are. Did you get held up?"

"Couldn't quite remember which way the park was," I said. He came in for a hug and I took a step back, slow and apologetic. "Not now, Rog. I just… I can't right now. Why are we here?"

"I wasn't sure when Nathan would be back at the hospital," he said. "I didn't want to run into him. He comes from the other direction, from the office."

"That's not what I meant," I said.

"No," he agreed. "No, I know that. You should sit down.

Here." He led me to one of the benches that dotted the park's walkways.

I sat, but he didn't. Instead, he paced back and forth in front of me for a moment while I groomed my patience. When the silence didn't break, I broke it for him. "I missed my interview."

He shot me a quizzical look, confused until realization dawned on his face. "Oh. Right. It's no big deal, we can find you something else. Or, I can make a call. They'd have to understand, with everything you've been through."

Funny how he could imagine a future where that was going to happen, given what he said next.

"Elaine…" He held his mouth open and then closed it. He started again. "You know I loved you. Right?"

"Roger, I don't—"

"It's okay," he said, "I know you didn't feel the same way. That's alright. Funny how different things could have been though. You know, that night that Nathan talked to you after the concert, when you were with those friends of yours? We'd argued over which one of us would be the one to do it. I told Nathan that night that you looked like the marrying type. Old fashioned, I know. Thing was, so was Nathan. And I wasn't. I knew that. Hell, I'm still not. I don't think I ever will be."

"I know the story," I said. "Nathan's told me."

"It's just," he said, "these little turns life takes. That's all. Everything might have been different."

"You and I might be together?" I asked. "Is that what you mean?"

"And maybe we'd have a son," Roger said. He shook his head. "No. I'd be a weekend dad. You'd have divorced me, most likely for cheating on you. I'm the cheating type. I don't think I've ever had a girlfriend I didn't cheat on. So that's why I told Nathan to go talk to that girl with the pretty eyes, who was talking to her friends about Proust. I told him you were too smart for him, but that he should try it anyway. I'd just screw it up. And I guess I did."

"What we had was never a relationship, Roger," I said. He nodded agreement and opened his mouth to speak again. I held a hand up. "I'm sorry about what happened. I was hurt and lonely. I shouldn't have used you like that."

"That's… not what I meant," he said. "I need you to listen and not say anything yet. This is going to be hard to hear. It won't make anything better, except… except maybe to give you back your life. Maybe. I don't know. But you need to know."

"Roger," I said quietly, "what do I need to know?"

He began pacing again. "I wanted us to do well," he said. "Nathan and me. It was important to him, and I love Nathan like a brother. I really do. And he's brilliant. He comes up with things so innovative that I'm not sure we'll ever really bring everything he thinks of to life. But he's bad with money.

Christ, is he bad. That first couple of years I barely kept us out of bankruptcy on my own dime, and my father's. But I knew that if we could just last long enough, make the right deals, we could both have the life we wanted. And the life he wanted for you. So I found someone who could give us that early start-up money. A loan. Enough to get off the ground and then, between me and Nathan, we could pay back double what we took."

He shook his head. "Dad warned me. Nathan was nervous about it, too. But I thought it would be fine and for a while it was. You remember—Nathan was busy all the time. It was right before you two separated. Because he was distant. He was, too, but not because he'd fallen out of love with you, Elaine. He was just working himself to the bone to try and make it work. And we got so close."

"Who did you take money from?" I asked.

Roger turned away from me. "People who don't put up with late payments. We held them off for a while. Made deals, did jobs. But it wasn't enough. It's never enough. They get their hooks in, and then they won't let go. I knew better."

"So, what hap—"

"They made Nathan choose," Roger said. I could barely hear him. He still wouldn't face me. "They made him choose between you, and… and the baby."

He turned to me. "He chose you, Elaine. Of course he did. And I think he knew, maybe, that it wasn't his child."

"You're saying," I said, my voice hoarse, "that… some kind of mobster… killed my—"

"No," Roger said quickly. He sank to his knees and reached for my hands. When I wouldn't give them, he put them on my knee. "No, Elaine. That's just it. These people don't kill anyone; not unless they're some kind of risk. People are a commodity, you see? Either for who they know, what they know, what they can do or… what they're worth to the right people."

I stood, so quickly that Roger nearly fell over. He caught himself, though, and stood up as well, and followed me as I walked. My body was shaking, I couldn't have sat still. I was sick, and angry, but somehow inside all of it I was… elated.

And crushed.

"You son of a bitch," I huffed, unable to take a full breath. "You… Nathan said that you helped him with the body, that you covered it up."

"They'd have killed you, Elaine," he said. "We had to do something."

"So you *sold my baby?*" I would have screamed it, loud enough for anyone in the park to hear. But it came out like razor blades in my throat and I choked it off with a sob that wouldn't let me howl frustration in dignity. I bent over at the waist, felt coffee and bile rising, and had to rush to the bushes and flowers nearby to empty my stomach.

"You don't have to forgive me," Roger said. "Or Nathan. I'm not asking for that. I'm not asking for anything, Elaine. Here."

He handed me something smooth, cotton—his pocket square. I wiped my mouth with it and tossed it into the bushes. "Then you had better tell me what you do want while you have a chance," I growled. "Because I'm going straight to the police after this and I am telling them everything, and I will watch from a distance with my boys while you and Nathan rot in a goddamned cell for the rest of your lives."

Roger regarded me for a moment, calmer than he should have been. But then, that was Roger. Calm under pressure, always self-assured. Bastard.

He reached into his coat and pulled something out. Small, rectangular. Photo sized.

And that's what it was. He handed it to me. Only the street-lamps that lit the park provided any light, but it was enough.

It was a picture of my son. Eight years grown.

40

To anyone else, maybe the boy in the picture could have been any child. He looked tall for his age. He had the same narrow nose that my sister and mother had, and bright green eyes. Not like mine, or Nathan's. Like Roger's.

I *knew* him. Instantly, without a doubt. It was possible, of course, that I was only seeing what I wanted to see. Again. I wasn't infallible, clearly. But something about this boy grabbed me by a thread connected to something deep, visceral, and pulled on it until I felt I would turn inside out.

"Where...?" I couldn't get the question out.

Roger kept his distance. "I had to make some calls. I don't know where exactly, that's not something they'd just tell me. They're a wealthy family, though; well connected."

I cut my eyes at him. "To the same kinds of people you are?"

Roger shrugged. "I don't know."

"I want him back." My fingers nearly crushed the precious photo. "You can make another call, right? Sort this out? If it was between getting me my son back and turning them in then—"

"Absolutely not. If that was the choice, they'd make you disappear is what they would do." He took a long breath. "And think about it. How would Jake feel if his parents showed up one day and took him back? Do you think he'd just go with them, happy to be back with his family?"

"Why are you telling me this, then?" I waved the photo at him. "Why show me this and then tell me he's out of reach?"

Roger raised his hands. "They didn't tell *me*," he said. "But… the gentleman who's been on the lookout for you—"

"Watching me, you mean."

"Yes," Roger admitted. "He's a different story. If you play ball, if you stay calm, then… he can take you to your—*our*— son. You won't be able to meet him. And if you breathe a word of this to the police or anyone else, that'll be the end of both of us."

To say that I was skeptical would be a gross understatement. I considered walking away. I had the photo. I could take it to Spinoza and Truman, maybe to Paul Aaronson, and between them they could find my son.

And yet I couldn't make my feet move.

"If you want this," Roger said, "I can make the necessary arrangements. You have to wait though; you have to stay in one place and let me make the calls and assurances. These people only care about one thing. As long as we don't threaten their money, they can be gracious."

It was more than the Hayeses ever got. They'd died believing Jake—Ralph—was gone forever, his body hidden somewhere. If they'd had the chance to see him again, and they had seen him with me, seen what a happy, sweet, intelligent boy he was, and how loved he was... would they have taken him from me knowing it would destroy his life?

Roger was offering me what I wanted. Roger knew how to play people. I'd seen him do it, heard him talk about manipulation in everything from sales to picking up women. I knew he was playing me. I *knew* it.

But how could I have said no?

"How long will it take?" I asked.

Roger's smile was small, sympathetic. Well-crafted, maybe. "Not long," he said softly. "Keep the picture. If the police come to you again just ask for your attorney. Okay?"

I nodded and looked at the picture again before I slipped it into my pocket. "I should get back."

"Don't mention this to Nathan," he said. "I went around him on this. There's no telling what he would do."

"Whose idea was it?" I asked. "You, or Nathan?"

"Elaine, that won't—"

"Tell me," I said. "It's done now. I can't forgive either of you. Ever. But I want to know."

"Nathan chose," Roger said. "He didn't have any real choice, though. You have to believe that. No one could have made that decision with a clear conscience."

"You can tell yourself that until the sky falls down," I said. I didn't wait for a response, just turned and left him there, one hand in my pocket as if I might lose this one thread if I let go of it. Roger didn't follow.

When Nathan eventually did show up, he wasn't alone. Diana was with him, but had a suitcase with her, her coat draped over one arm. Whatever they were talking about coming in, it stopped when they saw me. Roger had told me not to say anything to Nathan, and I didn't intend to—but the moment I saw him, I couldn't help wanting answers. If not about my son, then about what he was up to trying to throw me under the bus with the detectives.

"Back from your trip?" Diana asked. "I was just about to go to the airport."

"Thank you for coming out," I said.

Diana gave me a blank look, then shook her head and turned to Nathan. The two of them embraced, and Diana went to Jake's bedside to give his pale, damp forehead a kiss. "Hope you feel better, Jakob."

She gave me another icy look before she passed by Nathan, put a hand briefly on his shoulder, and then left.

I stared at the door and then at Nathan.

"My sister?" I asked. "Really? I guess it didn't need a hard sell."

He looked like I had hit him. Again. "Christ, Elaine, it's not like that."

Jake stirred. I stood and stalked past Nathan to the door. "Let's not wake him up."

"I don't feel like—"

"Let me tell you how much I don't care what you feel like doing or not doing right now," I said. "I talked to Detective Truman. He told me about your interview with him, about me. You have some explaining to do, so you're going to do it."

He gave Jake a long look, then ran his hand through his hair and sighed. "Fine."

Once we were away from the room I turned on him. "What the hell were you thinking?" I asked. "You said you wanted to be in this together, that we had to protect our son. How does throwing my history out there with the police help that?"

"How does driving off to god knows where, again, help?" he countered. "Where did you go? You went to a lot of trouble to hide it. Having an affair with someone else?"

"I went to find out about Jake's parents," I said.

Nathan's jaw dropped. He closed it and looked over his shoulder before he stepped closer and lowered his voice to a harsh whisper. "Are you out of your goddamned mind?"

"They're dead," I told him. "Both of them, a few years ago. There's no one for Jake to go home to."

His posture relaxed, and a shadow of pain crossed his face. "I guess now we know. No one's going to come looking for him."

"Do you even have a conscience?" I asked. "Has this good guy thing been an act all these years?"

"I never claimed to be a good man." He clenched his jaw. His hands balled into fists. "All I ever claimed was to put you and our family first, and that's what I've always done."

"Is that why you paid off the Turners' attorney?"

The question staggered him. Realization and then worry followed. "Who told you that? Roger?"

"Detective Truman," I said. I watched the panic widen his eyes. "They know, Nathan. Or they think they do. How long before they find all the evidence they need?"

He closed his eyes and leaned against the wall. "So that's it, then," he breathed. "You couldn't just be happy with what we have. You had to tear it down? Why?"

"What we have?" I gaped at him. "What *we* have? What do I have, Nathan? You took everything away from me and gave me a lie to replace it. This was about you. It was about some illusion of a life that you wanted. It was never real. I don't know what's going to be left after this, but you and me? That will be gone, and if you think that after everything you've done I'm letting you step a foot near that poor boy whose parents *died of grief*, then you've got another thing coming."

His eyes flashed open. "Now hold on a minute," he said. He reached for me.

I stepped out of range, and he followed, until his hand clamped down on my wrist. If I hadn't been nursing my anger for hours now, I might have been terrified. Instead, I tried to pull my arm away from him.

"Calm down," he ordered.

When I couldn't get free, I clawed at his arm. He spat as lines of red blossomed, and he gave me a shove before he let go. "What the hell is wrong with you?"

Fury took me over. I flailed at him, my vision red. "You took my son from me!"

I barely registered the shock on his face as he raised his arms to defend himself.

Someone got between us. I almost struck the stranger as well but stopped when I saw Diana. Her suitcase was toppled over a little behind her, and she was white in the face. Her phone was already out, her free hand held out toward me to keep me at bay.

I had enough time to realize that there were security officers coming up behind her before she spoke. Not to me—into the phone. "Yes, I'm at the Saint Monica's Pediatric Hospital," she said quickly, her voice taut and pitched, "there's been a domestic incident. Diana Feldman. It's my sister, Elaine Jennson..."

The rest faded as I staggered back. I couldn't be arrested. Not right now, not if Roger was about to arrange for me to see my son. I looked to Nathan, but he only turned his face away and said something to Diana. Our address.

The security guards sped up as I began to walk backward. I turned, finally, and fled down the hallway, toward the main entrance. I wouldn't make it to the parking deck.

Diana had seen me lose control, and not so long ago I had slapped her as well. The security guards had seen my outburst; there was no telling who else. What had I been thinking?

I hadn't. I should have known better than to face Nathan knowing what I did.

But I was thinking now. I ran out through the front entrance, and back toward the park, already pulling up Detective Spinoza's contact on my phone. When she answered, I ducked into a shadowed copse of trees.

"Detective," I said, breathless, "we need to talk. Please. I'll tell you everything."

41

It was late when I took an Uber to Linda's house. I had nowhere else to go. If the police began looking for me, I couldn't just sit around town. As much as I knew Linda wanted nothing else to do with all of this, all I could come up with was to throw myself on her mercy and hope that she caved.

She answered the door in a night robe. "Elaine? What are you—"

"I need to come in for a bit," I said. "Not long. That's all, and then I won't bother you again, I swear."

She didn't invite me in, instead filling the small space with her body. "The kids are asleep," she said. "I'm sorry, hon, but I just can't be involved in it, whatever it is. I really wish that I could help but…"

I pulled the picture out and handed it to her.

She took it hesitantly and had to turn on the porch light to look at it without comprehension. "I don't know what I'm looking at, Elaine."

"Jake," I said. "It's Jake."

She eyed me warily. "This isn't Jake, sweetie. Listen, if you're on something, I understand, after all you've been through—"

"*My* Jake, Linda," I said. "My baby. That's him."

Her eyes slowly widened. She looked back down at the photo. "Are you sure?"

"I promise I will be quiet," I told her. "I'll be out of your hair in an hour, at the most."

Linda chewed her lip, but finally stepped away from the door. That she might regret it was written all over her, but she let me in.

"Do I want to know what's going on?" she asked.

"If you don't," I said as she pulled out a chair in her dining room for me, "that's okay."

She filled an electric kettle and set it to boil. By the time it did, and she brought us both a steaming mug of water and some kind of herbal, floral tea, she had apparently decided she couldn't stand not knowing anything.

"So... what's happened?"

Linda's cup was still full by the time I told her everything. She hadn't touched it, just listened to me, frozen in place with her mouth parted in abject horror.

"If it were me," she said when I told her about having gone after Nathan—but not about the police possibly looking for me, "I'd have killed the son of a bitch. So, did you call the police? Do they know? Why are you here?"

"I can't just turn them in," I said. "If I do, I'll never see my son. Neither of them. I have to know where he is first. And besides, I don't have any proof except for this picture."

Linda's brows pinched together skeptically. "So you really trust Roger to, what... arrange a visit or something?" She shook her head. "You need to get the right people on this, hon. This is a really bad idea. I don't think you're thinking clearly."

"I'm not," I admitted. "I know that. Not where my son is concerned. But right now, Nathan and Roger hold all the cards. Even if I told the police everything, they could investigate, but police can be paid off. These people are good at covering their tracks. Right now, they want me to play ball. So... I have to seem like I'm doing that. Think about it, Linda. If it were Ty, what would you do?"

She softened. "Anything. Take a bullet if I had to."

"That's what I'm doing," I said. "Anything that I can."

Linda tapped her finger on the table a few times while she chewed her lip again. She focused on me, sat up straighter in her chair, and held her hand out. "Give me your phone."

I hesitated but handed it over. I gave her my passcode when she asked. Of the people in the world likely to do me some kind of harm, Linda was nowhere on the list at this point.

"If you're going to go," she said, "then at the very least you need to turn on your GPS. Lynn Beasely showed me how to do it a few days ago—Tyler wants a phone because all his friends have one, and she was saying that you can switch the GPS on and then you always know where your kid is. It made it seem like maybe it wasn't such a bad idea. Not that Tyler ever runs off, you know, but give it a few years and if he's anything like me, there's no end to the trouble he'll get into. I'm no dummy. There."

She handed it back to me, then went to the kitchen counter and unplugged her own phone, spent a moment messing with the screen and then held it up for me to see that there was a little dot on a map with my name and an old contact picture Linda took after we first got to be friends.

It was like looking at a picture of a stranger. I tried to ignore that.

"Now," Linda said, "wherever you go, it's tracked. Just in case."

"Thanks, Linda," I said, "but they'll think of that, surely. No one's going to let me bring my phone."

She snorted. "Honey, you have got not a shred of guile in you and I love you for that. You *hide* it, sugar. Don't you watch TV?"

I was only there another half hour or so before I got the call. It wasn't Roger. When I answered, a gruff, deep voice was on the other end. Lloyd Mason, Roger's watchdog. "I'm outside," he said. "Mr. Walton made the call. Come on out, I don't want to alarm your pretty friend."

"I'm on my way," I said. I hung up and locked eyes with Linda. She walked me to the door, away from the bay windows in the dining room, and handed me her phone. I tucked mine into the back of my pants, both the ringer and the vibrate switched off, courtesy of Linda's forethought. I held hers in my hand as I left her house and headed toward the black town car with its lights on, parked at the curb.

As I approached, the passenger side window rolled down. Lloyd's blockish face peered out, and he pointed to the phone in my hand. "Leave that."

"Where?" I asked. I looked around. "Just on the ground?"

"Telling me you can't afford another phone?" he asked. "Drop it or the deal's off."

I made a show of considering the phone for a long moment

before I finally dropped it. Hopefully, it didn't break. Though, I owed Linda more than a phone at this point.

"In the back," Lloyd said.

The car doors unlocked, and I cast a final look back toward where I hoped Linda was still watching before I opened the back door and got in. Experimentally, I tested the handle from the inside. The child lock was on.

"Buckle up," Lloyd said. "Wouldn't want to get a ticket. It's a long drive."

I did as I was told. When I'd buckled in under the supervision of Lloyd's dark eyes in the rearview, he pulled away from the curb. Whatever was going to happen next, there was no turning back.

42

We drove west but avoided the highway. Periodically, Lloyd looked in the rearview mirror at me, but he said nothing for the first hour we were on the road. The radio was on, but it was quiet. Some classics station.

"Where are we going?" I asked when I couldn't quite take the silence anymore.

"Don't worry about it," Lloyd said. "If you need to stop, say so."

"That's kind of you," I said.

Lloyd glanced at me in the mirror. "Just don't want a mess in the back seat."

"How long will we be on the road?"

Another glance, this time with a quiet sigh. "A while. You have to be patient. And quiet."

There was a dangerous tone in his voice. I found myself wondering what else he'd done for Roger, or for whoever he worked for if it wasn't directly for Roger. The tinted windows reflected my face more than they showed the scenery outside, narrowing my world down to just what I could see through part of the windshield.

Whatever route we were taking, it was off the beaten path. Occasional streetlamps eventually became a rarity, and the houses that dotted the roadside were gradually swallowed up by trees. There were a few big national forests well west of Dayton, but without taking my phone out to look at the map—which would certainly give away that I had it on me—I couldn't be certain where we were. Far from home, certainly.

"Can you turn the radio up?" I asked.

Lloyd did so without comment until something country that I hadn't heard before began to play. Something about a dance, sung by a man with a prominent steel guitar in the background. It seemed out of place for the moment, but then what was the appropriate sound track for something like this?

My mind wandered in the monotony. I wondered how Jake was doing. Whether the police had issued a restraining order or a warrant. For me, or for Nathan or Roger. Spinoza had taken everything that I told her down, supposedly, but she hadn't sounded entirely convinced that I wasn't involved myself. I suspected that if they did go after either one of them, Lloyd would get a call.

I kept one eye on Lloyd, waiting for him to check on me again. He did, at length, and once he looked away, I shifted in the seat to reach my phone. Lloyd glanced at me, and I arched my back until it cracked. "My back hurts a little," I explained. "It's fine."

He put his eyes back on the road.

I pulled my phone out from the back of my pants and slipped it over the edge of the seat to the floorboard, pushing it under the back of the passenger seat with my foot. Just far enough to be out of sight.

"Are we avoiding the highway to avoid the police?" I asked. "Do you know if they are looking for me?"

"Mrs. Jennson," Lloyd said, "Mr. Walton only gives me the details I need. I got a good gig. I do what I'm told and don't ask questions."

"But you know where we're going," I said, "and why?"

"Yeah," he said.

It sent a shiver along my spine. "Can you ah... can you call Roger and just find out if everything is okay at the hospital?"

"Out of cell range," he said. "Maybe later."

I kept my face placid, but my heart sped up. Out of range? If that was true, my phone wasn't tracking where I was. Maybe, if it picked up a bar here or there, it would update? I wished I hadn't asked. Knowing that there was some lifeline connecting me to the world outside that car had given me the confidence to stay calm. If I was cut off…

"When you get a chance, maybe we could stop," I said. "Don't want to make a mess back here, like you said."

"Sure," Lloyd muttered. "It might be a little while, unless you want to go in the bushes."

I could barely see the corner of a smirk on his face.

"I can wait," I said. "Just… when we see some place."

He bobbed his head slowly, once. "Just try to relax," he said. "Won't be too long now."

"I thought it was going to be a long ride," I said.

He glanced in the rearview again and shrugged. "Depends on what you call a long trip, doesn't it? You'll know when we get there."

I settled into the seat and had to wonder: was it really possible that all this time my son had been just a few hours away? Or was my gut right when it told me there was a reason we had driven so far out of the way and it had nothing to do with going to see him?

When the car finally came to a stop, it wasn't in front of a house, or a neighborhood, or somewhere to relieve myself. It was some kind of gravel landing off the side of the road, surrounded by tall pines on all sides. There was a single old streetlamp to light the place in dim yellow pallor. There was also another car, the same model as mine.

When Lloyd got out and came around to open my door I thought we were transferring for some reason. Then I got a good look at the car and the license plate. It wasn't the same model as my car.

It was my car.

"Why is my car here?" I asked.

Lloyd closed the door, and I saw the gun in his hand. Cold fear sank into me, and I had an immediate, feral instinct to run.

Before I could act on it, Lloyd held up his phone. There was video playing on it. It was a view through the window of Jake's room. "You run," he said, "and I make a call. Don't be more trouble than you're worth. And it won't just be him."

"You were supposed to take me to my son." My voice quavered, unsteadied by the shaking in my stomach. "I just wanted to see him. That's all. I won't make trouble, I just need to know he's okay, that he's happy."

Lloyd waved the pistol toward the tree line. "If you want, I'll tell you all about him. Walk. There's a trail, just between the railing."

"You don't have to do this," I told him. He waved again, more insistently, and my feet began to move of their own accord. When was the last time I ran any distance? A long time ago. But Lloyd was a big man. Something told me he wasn't the type who could keep up if he wasn't running for his life.

But he had eyes on Jake. And the boy who should have grown up to be Jake.

"I just… I just want to know," I said as Lloyd followed behind me, rattling quietly with something in his pockets. Bullets, maybe? How many did a hit man need for one woman? I swallowed hard, my mouth dry from fear. "You're going to kill me?"

"Just walk," Lloyd said. "Think about your kids. It's better that way."

43

I did. Hard as it is to believe, the adrenaline in my veins made my mind race. As we marched along the trail, I thought back over Jake's life—all of it, with a strange kind of clarity of detail that I had never experienced until then. Maybe it was the nearness of the end, that moment when your life flashes before your eyes. I thought it was supposed to happen when you were dying, but then again, that's what was happening; just in slow motion.

I remembered giving birth. Jake had been a big baby, over nine pounds. God, the pain. It had drowned out everything, except this spark of excitement that my son would finally be with me and I could hold him close. It seemed strange, looking back on it, that those two feelings could be so fused together. Then there was the rush of relief when he was finally out, and the nurse handed him to me for the first time.

Even the dark months that followed came back more clearly than they ever had before. I saw the memories as if I was watching someone else's life. Just short clips in stark relief. I had been jealous of Nathan. Whether I was especially hard on him because of it is hard to say, but I hated that I was always exhausted and miserable, and that he could come home from work and enjoy fatherhood. I had all the guilt for not being able to smile all the time, like he did when he was with Jake, and what did he have? A carefree couple of hours a day playing with the baby before he finally fell asleep. It was always me who woke up through the night to feed him.

When did Nathan begin to wonder if Jake was his? I remembered when I did: the day that I took the pregnancy test. I should have been overjoyed, that's how expectant women always look in commercials, right? No one is ever portrayed as being scared out of their wits, thinking of everything that's about to change, or the grueling nine months ahead. I was beside myself. I threw up, right then, everything I had for lunch that day.

But then, there was Jake. And then the night that I left him by himself in the bathtub. The bright orange and blue of the pills I took. The months of wasting away at Northgate while Dr. Amanda tried to decide whether I was ever going to recover. That pit that opened up inside me, tried to swallow me down, and then *almost* closed up again when Nathan came to me and told me the words that made all those jagged puzzle pieces I had become begin to fit back together.

"We found him, Elaine."

Had I known that it was a lie? Had there been some subtle clue that I should have seen, or that I did see but chose to ignore?

All of it rushed past me, and I was Mom again. Better this time, with a little help that had turned into more help than I needed. I don't think Jake ever knew what was wrong with me. No reason he should have—I was fun, finally. Maybe not for Nathan. But those days were some of the brightest memories I had of Jake. Me, high as a kite on Valium or whatever else I could get my hands on when my prescription ran out and wasn't due for a refill yet; Jake, full of energy that I could finally match without feeling like I was drained all the time.

"This is fine," Lloyd said.

The night returned. My visions of the past dissolved, leaving me more acutely aware of the present. Of Lloyd. Of his gun. It was unbearably quiet here, despite the sounds of night birds and insects that buzzed like static in the background of the forest.

Lloyd moved to a large tree with great roots that formed a little hollow at the base. Some kind of ancient, massive fir tree I thought. Not that I knew that much about trees. "Sit," he said.

I sank into the spot, my knees pulled to my chest, shivering. "If you shoot me," I said, "everyone will know it was murder. After everything that's happened, they'll go after Roger and Nathan."

"I'm not going to shoot you," Lloyd said. He took something that rattled from his pocket—not bullets. A bottle of pills. I should have recognized the sound when I heard it. He tossed it to me and I fumbled it to the ground before I picked it up. "Take them."

It was too dark to read the label. But something told me that it wasn't a bottle of aspirin. Prescription whatever it was. "What if I don't?"

Lloyd took his phone out and held the video up again. "Something makes me think you will."

"Just wait," I begged. I was desperate for time. More time with my memories, and maybe for some hope of salvation. "My... my son. Do you know where he is? Do you know anything about him? I don't want to die not knowing. Please."

"You take those," Lloyd said, "and I'll tell you what I know. But you have to take all of them."

I nodded quickly and twisted off the cap. My heart pounding in my throat, I tilted the bottle until one of the little oval pills spilled out. Some kind of antidepressant, I thought; it looked familiar, one of the medications I had been on before I became addicted. I put it in my mouth.

"Swallow it," Lloyd said.

It took an effort of will, but I did. There was still too much panic in my body for me to do the math, but I reckoned these were probably fifty milligrams a piece. If it was meant to look like a suicide, then it would take over a thousand milligrams to kill me, I thought, but I couldn't be sure. I looked up at Lloyd as I took the second pill. "I'm taking them," I said. "Please. Tell me anything you can."

Lloyd didn't take his eyes off me. "I've been Mr. Walton's handler since he started working with my boss. When he and your husband got in too deep, I was told to give them an ultimatum. You or the kid. Normally, it kicks everyone's butt into gear. Money just magically appears. See, people who can't repay their debts are normally just not motivated enough. But in this case, well… turned out they really didn't have it to pay."

I strained my ears for any other sounds in the forest. No one would be hiking this time of night, would they? I took the third pill.

"It was Mr. Walton's idea," Lloyd said. "He cut a deal. More cash, and all debts paid. Not bad, either. That guy's got a silver tongue, you know? But, boss knew a couple who couldn't have kids of their own. Real rich family. Got tangled up with the wrong kind of people a while back, got some kind of felony tax evasion on their record. Can't adopt with stuff like that hanging over you."

"It was Roger's idea?"

Lloyd nodded. "Sure, yeah. That man's got no soul, lady. You gotta know that, right?"

I should have, it was something I should have seen a long time ago. "But Nathan…?"

"Look, don't be too hard on your husband," he said. "You don't want to take that with you where you're going. He didn't have much choice."

"Does he know where my son went?"

Lloyd shook his head. "Why would he?"

I took another pill. This one, though, I tucked behind my gums on one side before I made a show of swallowing. "And my son? Where did he end up? What's his name now?"

In the distance, gravel crunched. Wheels of some vehicle pulling into the same spot we had parked. Lloyd glanced that way, but kept his gun trained on me. We waited in the near silence. I slipped the pill out from behind my teeth and pushed it out between my lips until it tumbled down and disappeared in the brush.

"Don't make a sound," Lloyd said when I shifted slightly to cover the pill up better.

Another minute, and gravel crunched again. Whoever had stopped had kept going or turned around. I prayed quietly that they had, for some reason, decided to call the police and that they'd been able to get a signal.

"Another," Lloyd said. "Faster, now."

I took a fourth pill, and a fifth, but only swallowed one. "His name?"

Lloyd cocked his head to one side. "I could tell you anything, you know. What would it matter?"

"Then tell me anything," I said. I held up another pill and put it in my mouth. This one I slipped behind my teeth on the other side. I could pack four in there. The nurses at Northgate knew to check; patients pulled that stunt all the time. But Lloyd hadn't thought of it yet and I didn't think he would.

He watched me take another two before he spoke again. "They named him Thomas. Some kind of family name. They're good Catholics. Maybe it's for Saint Thomas, I don't know."

It wasn't the name that I'd given him, but it practically sang in my ears anyway. Thomas. My son's name was Thomas.

Whether it was true or not didn't matter. What mattered was that when Lloyd told me that name, I decided that I was not going to die that night. Certainly not without a fight.

44

I had swallowed ten pills out of the bottle, and hidden more, before Lloyd lost his patience. "Take the rest," he said, jerking the pistol at me. "All at once. No reason to drag this out."

I was already dizzy. If I did that, it would be over.

But, I saw my chance, and I took it. I upended the bottle and swallowed. Maybe another fifteen? I couldn't tell. My mouth was dry, and they didn't go down easy.

I handed him the bottle back. He checked it, gave a nod, and then sighed. "Now we wait."

For long, painful minutes we waited in the silence. Long enough for it to seem reasonable when I put a hand to my head and swayed. I tucked my knees closer to my chest.

"It'll go quick," Lloyd said. "Dizzy first, then you fall asleep. You'll be unconscious for the rest."

"Are you religious?" I asked. He'd called Thomas' new family 'good Catholics.'

"I probably shouldn't be," he said. "But, yeah."

I held a hand up to him. "I want to pray. Before... before I..."

"Can't leave any evidence on the body," he said. He didn't take my hand, but he knelt close. "You Catholic?"

The body. That's what they would call me when they found me. I shook my head. "Not really."

"Nobody is these days," he said. "Not really. Close your eyes."

When I did, he began to speak in a voice more reverent than I would have guessed. "The Lord is my shepherd, I shall not want. He makes me to lie down in green pastures. He leads me beside the still—"

I put everything that I had into surging forward with a howl of fury. My head connected with his, and we went tumbling over one another. The gun fired a deafening shot, but from a little distance to one side. The world spun around me, and for half a second we were a tangle of curses and limbs until I was free and rolling across rough ground.

Then I was up, and running blindly through the dark, my hands in front of me to give at least some warning when I ran into a tree or branch. My mind had begun to fog already. I didn't know if I'd taken enough to overdose fatally, but I had taken enough to put me out. I hadn't even picked a direction and had no idea if I was running toward the road or deeper into the woods.

"Elaine," Lloyd shouted after me. "This is a mistake. Think of your boys, Elaine."

I was thinking of them. Only of them and getting back to them. I clung to their names, chanting them in my head again and again. *Thomas. Jakob. Thomas. Jakob.*

Off to my right, I saw a flash of light. Either a hallucination, or someone turning the curve just before where the two cars were parked. I turned and ran downhill towards it with every shred of strength I could salvage from my burning legs and the deep cavity in my chest. The pills were beginning to make it harder to breathe.

It was too dark to see the ground clearly, and I missed the sudden dip as the hill dropped off into some kind of gully. The first step onto nothing turned into a jarring pain when my heel connected with ground lower than I expected, and from there it was literally downhill. I fell forward, failed to catch myself, and went into a painful tumble. Fire shot through my arm first, then my ribs. I bounced off of something and came to a stop when I clipped something massive and hard that left my ears ringing.

I couldn't hear where Lloyd was. I couldn't hear anything

between the lingering shock of the gunfire in my ears and the blood rushing there. I knew I had to keep going down, toward the road. When I tried to push myself up, my arm gave out and I instead collapsed face first into the earth. Dirt got into my mouth. I sputtered, and a wave of nausea took over me from the depth of my stomach until I thought I would retch.

All my strength was gone. Whatever I had managed to pull together was spent. My heart stuttered as it slowed, my muscles burned. I needed oxygen but couldn't get enough.

The darkness lightened. White crept in around my vision, burning away some of the shadow. For some interminably long moment I was blissfully unaware that I was on the ground. I felt light and heavy at the same time. Sounds made it through the rushing and ringing—but they weren't quite right.

Someone was laughing. A child. It was brief, and more of an echo than anything I had really heard. I knew that; it wasn't real. A waking dream, just like I remembered from before. Maybe I had taken enough to do the job.

I looked up, or tried to, and smiled. Jake was there. Healthy now, not pale or damp or sleeping. He reached for me and I tried to reach for him but I couldn't. My arms wouldn't move. He wasn't alone, I realized. There was another boy beside him. I heard a mewling cry leave my lips. "I would have come for you," I slurred. "I'm sorry, baby. I promise, I never would have stopped looking."

The two of them got up and looked at something in the

distance. Jake looked down at me. "Come on, Mom. It's time to go." He and Thomas began to walk away.

"Come back," I wheezed after them. "Stay with me. Boys. Please, come back…"

In the distance, a branch broke. A man grunted and cursed. "If you think they won't kill a kid, Elaine, you're wrong."

Jake. Thomas.

I said their names to myself until there was nothing else left in my mind.

Jake. Thomas.

It's time to go.

I rolled onto my back and bit down on my tongue to keep from crying out as I curled off the ground and then crawled up the tree I had fallen into until I felt bark biting the beds of my nails. I just had to keep going downhill and I would reach the road. I took an unsteady step and then let myself stumble down the hill.

45

I knew I had reached the road when I nearly tumbled over the metal railing. My vision was narrow, and the night was pitch black. Somewhere in that blackness, though, was the ghost of a light, down along the road, hazy and distant. I headed toward it. Every step was agony. My body was on fire, the world spun around me, and my feet were leaden so that every step jarred my injured arm and set my head throbbing harder.

Somewhere in the fog of my brain, I thought that if I could reach the car, I could get my phone. Maybe there was enough signal to make an emergency call. Or maybe I could just take it and keep running until I reached a signal. This whole area couldn't be blacked out, could it?

I fought my way to the car and, while I knew that Lloyd had to be nearby, I couldn't let myself look for him. Instead, I tugged at the door handle to open the door.

The handle didn't give. It was locked.

Despair took the rest of the wind from me. I pounded against the window with a weak arm and fist but it didn't give, it barely even made a sound. My knees gave out and I slumped against the car, one hand pressed against it to slow my descent. Gravel bit into my knees. Flashes of light that were not oncoming cars began to show at the corners of my already impaired vision.

I had tried. Whatever strength I hadn't had as a mother before, somehow, I had dug it up and worn it for at least a few minutes. Lloyd would catch up to me in a moment and then it wouldn't matter anymore, would it?

Deep in that hopelessness, I told myself that I would rather look like a murder victim. That I would take Nathan and Roger down with me if I was going to go. Someone would find me. I put a grimy finger in my mouth and pushed into the back of my throat until my stomach rebelled against the invasion and spasmed. Nothing came up. I had to try three more times before finally a slurry of bile and pills came up and spattered on the gravel.

A final act of defiance, maybe, but it gave me some satisfaction even if it wasn't going to save my life.

Footsteps crunched. I looked up and saw a big black shadow lumbering toward me.

"You dumb bitch," the shadow growled. "I was gonna make it quiet. Looks like we do this the hard way. Gonna be a long fucking night."

It loomed over me, and a huge hand grabbed a handful of my hair and jerked me forward. I fell and scraped my palms against the gravel, screaming as I was dragged across it and away from the light. Animal instinct was all that was left. I didn't make any choices, just clawed at the shadow where it held me until it let me go and my head hit the ground. It hauled me up, and something collided with my head again. I didn't care at that point. I dug for whatever I could reach with my fingers and found something soft.

The shadow screamed, dropped me, and kicked me hard in the chest. Was I laughing? I can't remember. I had a rush of vicious triumph though.

And then there were lights. Not just the white flashes at the edges of my vision, but a spectrum of colors. Someone shouted, and then the world exploded into gunfire. I curled in on myself and waited for the end.

The end didn't come. New hands uncurled me. Light shone in my eyes, and people poked and prodded at my neck, and pried my mouth open. I tried to bite the fingers that invaded my mouth, but they were too strong.

"Elaine?" someone asked. A woman. "Elaine, it's Detective Spinoza. Jesus, someone call an ambulance. Fast, goddamnit. Elaine, can you hear me? Look at me, Elaine."

My eyes were pried open. The light hurt, but there was a shape in it that I tried to focus on. It looked familiar. "Thomas?"

"No," Thomas said. It was his voice, somehow. I knew it. "Christ, is she—"

"There are pills over here," Jake shouted. "She threw them up. Could be more still in her."

"I'm okay, sweetie," I said, and reached for Thomas but he pushed my hand away.

Then, he turned me on my side, pried my mouth open, and held my head while I choked up whatever was left in my stomach, which wasn't much.

"They'll be here soon," Thomas said, close to my ear. "Just hang in there. You're okay, Elaine. We've got you."

"Thomas," I said again. "Don't forget. Thomas and Jake. Thomas… and Jake."

Then I was gone.

46

I dreamed about Jake. Or Thomas. Both, I guess. They were together, my boys, being brothers. We were in a park, and one of them fell down. The other, I don't know which, helped him up, and they came running toward me. I was happy.

Then I woke up. It took a moment for me to realize that the sky wasn't clouded over above me—it was the tiled ceiling of a hospital. I couldn't move right away. My arms and legs were too heavy. When I craned my neck to look around, a dull pain throbbed behind my eyes. There was a cast on one of my arms, and one leg was hoisted up in some kind of sling, my foot encased in plaster almost to the knee.

I tried to speak but something was in the way, and when I realized there was something in my mouth and throat I panicked; I couldn't remove it.

The door to the room opened and a plump woman in flower-printed scrubs rushed to my side. "Calm down, Mrs. Jennson, just relax," she said. "You're okay, you're at Midway Hospital, intensive care. You've been unconscious for a little while. I can get this tube out if you will just lay back and rest. Come on, now…"

Though I wasn't calm, I did lay my head back and squeeze my eyes shut as she unclipped something near my mouth and then very slowly withdrew it, muttering encouragement until it was out of me.

The coughing fit that hit me the moment it was gone felt like it was going to crack my chest open. It was ugly, but the nurse wiped my mouth for me. When I was done, I rasped at her, "My son?"

"Your little boy is okay," she said gently, and adjusted the angle of the bed so that I didn't have to strain to keep my head up. "Had his transplant two days ago, and as far as I know it's going well. Signey MacIntosh came to visit a couple of times, she said you'd want to know how he was."

"How long was I…?"

"Almost a week," she said. She came to the left side of the bed and lifted my arm to slip a blood pressure cuff over it. "I'm Tanya. I've been your nurse overnight. It's about two in the morning now. This will pinch a little, but I need to take your pressure."

She did, and it did pinch but in a distant sort of way.

"My… my husband?" I asked.

Tanya smiled. "He's been in a few times."

My eyed burned. Had Spinoza not arrested him yet? It's been a week. "Another man," I said. "Was there someone else?"

"Not so far," she said. She released the pressure and counted quietly as she watched the gauge on the cuff. "Just him and Signey. Sorry, should someone else have been here?"

"No," I said. "Can I get some water?"

The water didn't entirely eliminate the feeling of steel wool in my throat but it did help. I suspected I'd been on a drip while I was unconscious, because the coolness of the water spread through my stomach and made it just a little uneasy as if it wasn't sure whether to accept it or not. "What's on my chart?"

Tanya's smile grew taut. "Well… the leg, and the arm, both broken. A few ribs were cracked but there was no puncture. The concussion was why we kept you under."

"And an overdose," I added.

She patted my knee reassuringly. "There's a counsellor available, if you need to talk to someone."

"That's not necessary," I said. "I didn't… it wasn't an attempted anything. I was forced. Where is the detective? Spinoza or Truman?"

"I'm sorry, Mrs. Jennson," Tanya said, "all I know is that you were transferred in from Southeast in Cambridge once you were stable."

We'd been headed west, out that direction. "Why?"

She shook her head. "I'm sorry, that's all I know. I can contact someone for you, though, or if you're up to it there's a phone by the bed."

I couldn't remember the last time I had memorized a number that wasn't my own. "Is my phone here?"

It was a long shot anyway. Tanya was apologetic again. "You should rest," she said. "Dr. Powell will be in early tomorrow, and he might know more than I do."

"Tanya," I said before she left. "Unless it's a police officer, I'd rather not have any visitors."

"Your husband usually comes by about—"

"No visitors," I repeated. "Please."

She frowned but gave a nod. "If that's what you want."

I was on painkillers, and whatever they'd given me to put me out was probably still in my system. It was hard to think straight. Most of what had happened was out of reach. I remembered running. And I vaguely remembered that Spinoza had been there. How was that possible?

Linda had turned the GPS on in my phone. I took a shaky breath. If she hadn't thought of it, if I hadn't been able to take my phone into the car with me in the hope of having some record of where Thomas was…

The name caught my mind and held it. I lay my head back and let it ring in my ears. *Thomas.* My son's name was Thomas. I remembered that, clear as day, as if it had been carved into me.

I got my uninjured arm to move over a few minutes and managed to fumble the phone over the railing into one hand. I called information to get the number for the Dayton Police Department.

"This is Elaine Jennson," I said when a man from dispatch answered. "I need to get a message to Detective Amalia Spinoza or her partner. I'm awake. But I don't think I'm safe."

47

Maybe Tanya didn't take me seriously enough, or maybe she was simply away when Nathan arrived. Either way, I drifted off again and when I awoke he was there, sitting quietly in one of two chairs in the room, watching me sleep with a pillow clutched to his chest.

He put it down and stood when he saw me waking up and came to the side of the bed. "Jesus, Elaine, I've been so worried."

I flinched when he leaned in as if to kiss me.

"Get away from me."

Nathan froze, then straightened. "Look, if this is about before, I understand, but you—"

"You tried to have me killed," I hissed. "That man, that...

Lloyd, he drove me out to the woods like a goddamned dog to put me down."

"Lloyd?" Nathan shook his head. "Elaine, they found drugs in your system. I had to have you transferred here after they pumped your stomach. Are you sure you aren't just…?"

"Just what," I demanded. "Remembering things wrong? The way I remembered when Thomas died, except he didn't?"

"Thomas?"

"That's his name," I said. "It's what Lloyd told me. Thomas is the child that you sold to pay off your fucking mob debt. You and Roger."

Nathan's face went ashen pale. He stood perfectly still. His voice was hollow when he spoke. "I only wanted you to be safe."

"If you wanted that," I said, "you wouldn't have gotten into bed with them in the first place. Now get out of here, I don't want you or Roger anywhere near me."

"Elaine, if Lloyd tried to kill you then you're not—"

"I said get out!" I had nothing to throw at him, and no means to get to him, or I would have done it.

The door opened and Roger leaned in. "Everything okay in here?" He wasn't looking at me, he was looking at Nathan.

When Nathan didn't say anything, Roger entered quietly and closed the door behind him.

I mashed the nurse call button on the bed.

Roger looked at Nathan and sighed. "We don't have long, man. I know this is hard. But it's going to get worse. They're with Jake now, you should have done it while she was asleep."

"We don't have to do this, Rog," Nathan said.

"Do what?" I asked. I knew, I think. But I wanted them to say it. Either of them.

Roger ignored me and snapped his fingers when Nathan began to look at me. "It's her or Jake, Nate. Do you get that? You have to do this." He turned and picked up a pillow from the chair Nathan had been sitting on and held it out to him.

I mashed the nurse call button again and started screaming. "Someone! Anyone, someone help!"

"We've only got a few minutes," Roger said. "You do it or I will."

Nathan shook his head. "I can't, Rog. I just… I can't, I'm sorry."

Roger rolled his eyes. "This is how we got into this mess in the first place." He turned to me and held the pillow up. "I'm sorry, Elaine. I promise we'll take care of Jake, but I have to do this."

There was no regret in his face. No emotion at all. I screamed and flailed the only arm I had to swing at him, but I was drugged out of my mind still and a second later I couldn't get another breath or push enough out to make a sound. I couldn't close my hand tight enough on his coat sleeve and even if I could have, I didn't have the strength to pull his arm away.

There was muffled shouting, and then I could breathe again. I sucked in a lungful of precious air and swung at the space in front of me as my vision started to clear again, but it was empty.

Nathan had something in his hand. He dropped it and something wooden clattered to the ground. I scrambled up the incline of the bed to look around the room and saw Roger's crumpled form sprawled by the side of the bed. Nathan had hit him, apparently, hard enough to knock him out. Blood had begun to pool to one side of Roger's skull.

"I'm sorry," Nathan said, over and over again as he sat down and put his face in his hands. "I'm sorry. I never... it all just happened and kept happening and I... I just couldn't lose you. I'm so sorry, Elaine."

He sat like that for several minutes before someone finally came by the door. A nurse or an orderly; when he saw me he came in, saw Roger's prone form and Nathan in the chair in abject misery, and came to the phone to call 911 after shouting for security.

Security came quickly. Roger wasn't dead, but he was badly injured. Soon after, the police arrived. Four officers, and Detectives Spinoza and Truman.

The officers took Nathan away in handcuffs. I didn't say

anything to him, didn't meet his eyes. However sorry he was, or wanted to be, the best thing for all of us was for him to go and do it behind bars somewhere. Some part of me ached for who he was the night we met. Sweet, nerdy. A little naïve. Maybe that's why Roger liked him, too. He was easy to manipulate.

And, I suppose, so was I.

48

Jake's transplant went well, though there were a few minor complications. It took a month for me to get better, but a couple of weeks after Nathan's arrest I was transferred to Saint Monica's to recover by Jake's side.

Gertrude checked in with us just a few days before Jake was supposed to come home with me, but she hadn't come to 'make trouble.'

"I just wanted to see how you were both holding up," she said. Spinoza had contacted her on my behalf, and the CPS case had been back-burnered. Still ongoing, of course, but mostly a matter of paperwork. "I'm so sorry about everything that's happened."

"So am I," I said, standing outside Jake's door.

"What have you told him?" she asked.

That was a loaded question. "I told him that his father got involved with the wrong people, and that he would be gone for a little while."

Gert winced. "How is he taking it?"

"He's confused," I said. "I'm not sure I know what to do about it. We're both going to need a lot of therapy, I'm sure."

"You know, a lot of people think of us as the bad guys," she said, "but we do more than just remove at-risk children from homes. Family counselling is the bulk of what we actually do, day to day. I'd like for us to be involved, if you're okay with that."

"That might be good," I admitted. "I don't know how to tell him everything, or even if I should."

"He doesn't know he was adopted?"

Something tugged at my stomach. I supposed it always would now. "No, he doesn't."

"There's a right time for everything," Gertrude said as she watched him through the window. "I'm sure you'll know when that is. Right now, I'm sure it's important to focus on the future."

"Yes," I said. "That's what we plan to do."

"Open it up!" Linda crowed six months later, on Jake's birthday.

Jake eyed the box in front of him—nearly his size—with feigned dubiousness before waving Tyler over. "Help me!"

Linda and I sat back to watch the two boys tear into the wrapping paper. "I have a feeling this was a terrible idea," she said. "We're raising a couple of evil geniuses who are going to build some giant robot and take over the world."

"There are worse candidates for rulers of the world," I laughed. "So long as they wait until after their teens. I don't want to know what happens when you put moody teenagers in charge."

"Don't you?" She sipped her iced tea—the Long Island variety —and leaned forward as the boys broke into the box beneath the paper to find out what was actually inside.

Though they were much smaller, the boys pulled out a set of boxes inside the larger package and were at first curious, then elated.

"Battle bots!" Jake leapt up from where he'd been examining one of the smaller boxes.

"Look, look," Tyler shouted, and thrust one of the other boxes at Jake, who turned it over with a look of sheer wonder on his face. "We could build it and take it to the robo-fights Mr. Edmund was talking about. I bet it could win."

We'd found the parts at Mr. Edmund's recommendation, so it

was kind of cheating, and the boys weren't old enough to compete on their own but could apparently be sponsored by an adult. It would take them months to build something that would pass muster, he said. It seemed like a good way to keep the boys in check.

And, it worked immediately.

"And they're off," Linda muttered as the boys bolted through the back door and onto the deck to get to work. "I guess we know what our evenings look like for the rest of the summer."

"I'm just glad for him to have something to really capture his attention," I said.

Linda stood and held a hand out for my glass. "Another?"

"Nothing strong," I said. "Just regular every day tea, please."

She nodded and glanced at the door. "So... how are things going?"

We hadn't talked about it for a while. Linda was chomping at the bit for updates on everything but it had been difficult. For one thing, we rarely had much time alone, and I still wasn't ready to discuss the full scope of what had happened with Jake. I would put it off until he was older though he'd proven to be far more mature than I think I ever gave him credit for.

"Lloyd was sentenced a few days ago," I told her. "Attempted murder. I guess he cut a plea deal with the district attorney or something."

"They let him make a deal? That bastard." She handed me a fresh glass.

I did my best to keep a straight face when I sipped it. In a few minutes the ice would melt and water it down a bit. "It's how the system works, I guess." I shrugged. I was ambivalent myself. He'd only gotten fifteen years, with possible parole after ten. It was scary to think he'd be out again one day, but by then we'd be long gone.

"How's things coming along with Paul?" Linda asked. "I figure if you knew anything you'd tell me."

"Nothing so far," I said. "Amalia's trying to help where she can, but since it's not officially a missing person's case there's not much she can do without some kind of approval. He's found a few kids the right age named Thomas, but none of them are... my Thomas. He could be anywhere. Lloyd wouldn't tell the DA anything about it, Roger outright denies that it happened, and Nathan..."

I had to take another swallow of tea.

"You don't have to talk about it, hon," Linda said. She waved a hand at me, brushing the subject away. "I know it's been hard on you."

"You'd just think that after everything," I said quietly, "after what he did to me, and to our family, that he'd at least own up to it. But if he does, I guess it'll be more charges, more prison time. If he did, though, then they'd have to explore the fraud, and in the end, they'd take Jake away from me. So... we're just stuck."

Linda put her hand on mine. "You are not stuck, sweetie. Not anymore, not like that."

"No," I agreed. Outside, Jake and Tyler were pulling parts out of a second box and seemed to be arguing about how they went together. "No, I'm not. And right now, with it being just me and Jake, I need to be focused on the present. Right now, him and me. I want Thomas, too, desperately but... I don't know, Linda. I don't think I could choose between him and Thomas if I was offered the choice, free and clear."

"Of course you couldn't," Linda said. "You don't really know if Lloyd was telling the truth, do you? Until Paul has turned something up. I mean, he could have been blowing smoke."

"Maybe," I admitted. "There's no way for me to know. Not without opening up a can of worms I can't afford to open. Not until Jake is an adult, anyway."

Linda squeezed my hand. "I'm really sorry, hon."

"Me too," I said. "But I think right now, this is enough. It hurts, still. But I look at Jake and I think... how can it not be enough?"

The door to the back porch opened. "Mom, Mom, come see!" It was Tyler, but Jake was there with him, waving me over as well.

"Let's go see what we did," Linda groaned. "You boys better

keep that thing on the patio, don't you drive a robot into my gardenias or someone's gonna get the switch."

I followed her and watched as Jake and Tyler chattered over one another to describe how 'awesome' their robot was going to be.

Yeah. This was enough. For now.

49

The knock came almost a year later. I hadn't been expecting it, in one sense, but in another I never really stopped expecting it. We had moved. Not far, just down the street to a smaller place. A place that didn't have quite so many memories in it. After the divorce was finalized, I had needed the equity, and Jake had needed the change as well, I thought. There were still boxes here and there, and honestly, I hadn't decided if staying in the neighborhood was even a good idea. But Jake's school was here, and his friends—and my friend. My job with West End Publishing was here too.

I answered the door, assuming it was a delivery, but found Amalia—Detective Spinoza—standing there instead. She wasn't smiling—she never seemed to smile—but she at least didn't look like the bearer of bad news. "Come on in," I offered, and stepped aside to close the door behind her.

"New place looks nice," she said, nodding approvingly as she looked around. "How's Jake doing with it?"

"Good," I said. "It's not right next door to Tyler anymore, but we got them drones, God help me, so they have plenty of fun with that."

"What kids are into these days," she said. "Crazy."

"Believe me, I know," I said. "I'm happy for a visit, but…"

"Of course," she said. "I have news."

I led her to the new dining room and nudged a box away from the table so that we could both sit. "Sorry for the mess. Just getting unpacked."

"I've been in my apartment for three years," she said. "There are still a few boxes around. Don't worry about it."

"So? Is it about…?"

Amalia drew a manila envelope from her jacket, folded in half, and slid it across the table to me. "Not yet. This is about Jake."

My stomach sank. I knew it was coming, one day. I just expected more time. "Did Nathan flip?"

"Not exactly," she said. "He's at school?"

I nodded and opened the folder. Inside were adoption papers. Official adoption papers. "What is this?"

"I didn't want to alarm you before," she said. "We've been

officially-unofficially investigating. Looking for a suitable relative to Jake. Due diligence. A lot of people would lose their jobs and go to prison if it ever came out that we didn't."

"And?"

"He doesn't have any competent relatives," she said. "No one who could reasonably take custody. I got approval from two DA's, two judges and one state attorney general. No mean feat. I've told your story more times than I ever wanted to, but the recommendation is that you should officially adopt Jake. This way, there can be no problems later on."

I let out a breath I didn't realize I'd been holding. "Christ, Amalia... I mean, thank you. This is... I don't even know what to say. Thank you for all of it."

"Glad I didn't tell you?" She smiled. Just a little, and still a bit grim, but genuine.

"Since it worked out," I said, "yes."

"I'd have given you warning if it might not," she assured me.

"So, I just sign these and then... that's it?"

She shrugged one shoulder. "There's some filing, some notarization, things like that. But pretty much."

I signed. Putting the pen down felt like I was putting down a hundred-pound weight that had been hung around my neck for the past year and a half. I had to hold back tears. Amalia had become something of a friend over the last eighteen months of this—but she wasn't yet someone I cared to be a mess in front of. No more than I already was, at any rate.

"So, it's done." I said. "I can't tell you how this feels."

She nodded and took the folder back. "I'll get you copies."

But she didn't get up to leave. I looked around. "I've ah… got glasses in the cabinet, I've mostly unpacked the kitchen. We've been living on pizza for a few days. If you want something to drink…?"

She reached into her jacket and withdrew another envelope.

I watched it carefully as she put it down on the table. This one she didn't slide to me. "I've also got this. Before you open it, you need to remember your situation with Jake. We can't always make everything right. We can only try to make it right enough."

My pulse sped up as I reached for the envelope. Amalia stood to leave. "I should let you do that alone, I think."

I nodded and saw her to the door. When she'd left, I leaned against it and turned the envelope over a few times, nervous about what was inside. I wanted it badly to be what I hoped it was.

There were things, though, that once you know you can never come back from. It's a lesson we all have to learn, isn't it?

But we never do.

I opened it and read what was inside. Just a report. Three names and a town in Pennsylvania. Lloyd hadn't been lying. His name was Thomas. Thomas McNally.

END OF THE FOUND CHILD

Do you like gripping, psychological thrillers?
Discover an exclusive extract from Jo's *A Mother's Lie.*

THANK YOU!

Thank you so much for reading my book. I really hope you enjoyed this psychological thriller. If you enjoyed this book, please remember to leave a review.

You can leave a review on:

Facebook:
www.facebook.com/authorjocrow

Goodreads:
www.goodreads.com/authorjocrow

MAILING LIST

If you enjoyed my book and would like to read more of my work please sign up to my mailing list at:

www.subscribepage.com/JoCrowMailingList

Not only can I notify you of my next release, but there will be special giveaways and I may even be on the hunt for some pre- release readers to get feedback before I publish my next book!

ABOUT JO

Jo Crow gave ten years of her life to the corporate world of finance, rising to be one of the youngest VPs around. She carved writing time into her commute to the city, but never shared her stories, assuming they were too dark for any publishing house. But when a nosy publishing exec read the initial pages of her latest story over her shoulder, his albeit unsolicited advice made her think twice.

A month later, she took the leap, quit her job, and sat down for weeks with pen to paper. The words for her first manuscript just flew from her. Now she spends her days reading and writing, dreaming up new ideas for domestic noir fans, and drawing from her own experiences in the cut-throat commercial sector.

Not one to look back, Jo is all in, and can't wait for her next book to begin.

You can contact Jo at:

ıst

brown, where decomposing leaves clung to its surface like bile expressed from a liver. The jawbone was separated from the skull, its curved row of teeth pointing skyward to greet the rising sun.

Two feet away, closer to the oak tree, other bones were piled haphazardly: a pelvis, high iliac crests and subpubic angle; a femur, caked with dirt, jammed into his empty skull. Sunlight decorated the brittle bones in long, lazy strips and darkened hairline fractures till they blended with the shed behind them.

It was peaceful here, mostly. The pond no longer bubbled, its aerator decayed by time; weed-clogged flowerbeds no longer bloomed—hands that once worked the land long ago dismissed. Fog blanketed the area, as if drawn by silence. Once, a startled shriek woke the mourning doves and set them all into flight.

It was the first time in ten years the mammoth magnificence of the Blue Ridge Mountains had scrutinized these bones; the first song in a decade the mourning doves chorused to them from their high perch.

A clatter split apart the dawn; the skull toppled over as it was struck with another bone.

In a clearing, tucked safely behind the McNair estate, someone was whistling as they worked at the earth. The notes were disjointed and haphazard, like they were an afterthought. They pierced the stillness and, overhead, one of the mourning doves spooked and took flight, rustling leaves as it rose through the mist.

A shovel struck the wet ground, digging up clay and mulch, tossing it onto the growing mound to their left. The whistling stopped, mid note, and a contemplative hum took its place.

Light glinted on the silvery band in the exposed clay—the digger pocketed it—the shovel struck the ground again; this time, it clinked as it hit something solid.

Bone.

A hand dusted off decayed vegetative matter and wrested the bone from its tomb. Launching it into the air, it flew in a smooth arc, and crashed into the skull like a bowling pin, scattering the remains across the grass. With a grunt of satisfaction, the digger rose and started to refill the hole from the clay mound.

When it was filled and smoothed, and the sod was replaced over the disrupted ground, the digger lifted the shovel and strolled into the woods, one hand tucked in a pocket as they whistled a cheery tune lost to the morning fog.

For two days, the bones rested on the grass by the shed, until they were placed, carefully, into forensic evidence bags in a flurry of urgent activity: flashing police cameras, and gawking, small-town rookie officers who'd never seen their like before.

Silence blanketed the McNair estate once more, and the looming, distant mountains stood watch over a town that had seen too little so long ago, and now knew too much.

Get your copy of **A Mother's Lie** at
www.JoCrow.com

WANT MORE?

VISIT WWW.JOCROW.COM

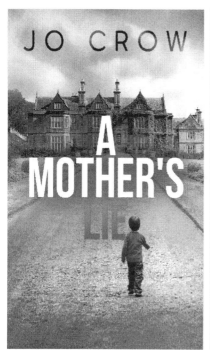

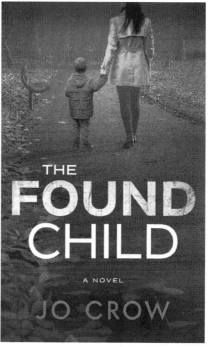

44076662R10223

Made in the USA
Middletown, DE
02 May 2019